Apart from the stereotypical images in gangsta rap videos and buppie frat flicks, there is something new and daring in how we as black men view ourselves as males and as sexual beings, and in how we see our women and our collective roles in the larger world. Both the frequency and substance of the dialogue about love, intimacy, and responsibility are increasing in our community. And it's about time!

In *After Hours*, you meet brothers who offer for your nocturnal reading enjoyment a juicy gathering of reflective stories, lusty stories, funny stories, fantastic stories—sexual adventures that will entertain and excite, inform and ignite, all written by prose stylists of the first order.

—Robert Fleming, Introduction

ROBERT FLEMING has written numerous articles for *Essence*, *Black Enterprise*, *The Source*, and *The New York Times*, among others. He is the author of *The African American Writer's Handbook* and *The Wisdom of the Elders*. His poetry, essays, and fiction have appeared in numerous periodicals and books, and his work was featured in *Brown Sugar* (available from Plume). He lives in New York City.

EDITED BY
**ROBERT
FLEMING**

after
hours

A COLLECTION OF
EROTIC WRITING
BY
BLACK MEN

A PLUME BOOK

PLUME
Published by the Penguin Group
Penguin Putnam Inc., 375 Hudson Street, New York, New York 10014, U.S.A.
Penguin Books Ltd, 80 Strand, London WC2R 0RL, England
Penguin Books Australia Ltd, Ringwood, Victoria, Australia
Penguin Books Canada Ltd, 10 Alcorn Avenue, Toronto, Ontario, Canada M4V 3B2
Penguin Books (N.Z.) Ltd, 182–190 Wairau Road, Auckland 10, New Zealand

Penguin Books Ltd, Registered Offices: Harmondsworth, Middlesex, England

First published by Plume, a member of Penguin Putnam Inc.

Ⓟ REGISTERED TRADEMARK—MARCA REGISTRADA

ISBN 0-7394-2781-4

Printed in the United States of America
Set in New Caledonia

To my brother, Anthony A. Fleming, adventurer, G-man, motorcyclist, rogue, doting father, loving husband, and man of international mystery.

CONTENTS

ACKNOWLEDGMENTS

Many thanks to my editor, Gary Brozek, for giving me the chance to do this book. We tried something new and I think we got it right. To my soul mate and muse, Donna, a first-rate word stylist in her own right, for her love, support, and inspiration that made this project easier to complete. To "our" children, Ashandra, Nichole, Dawne, and Matthew, who keep me in love with the many cycles of life. To my agent and longtime friend, Marie Brown, for helping to make this a reality. I hope this is the first of many projects we work on together. To my sidekicks, who never stray from my camp regardless of the circumstances: Cheryl Woodruff, Angela Harvey, Charles Seaton, Angela Smith, Michelle Paynter, Ethelbert Miller, Michael Harris, Anthony Fudge, and Tanya Lewis, who came through big-time for me at a real moment of crisis. And most of all to black men everywhere, who still believe there is something very erotic above love, trust, commitment, and respect.

INTRODUCTION

If there's one thing most people love, it's great sex, even in this time when our options include virtual sex, phone sex, and cybersex. Almost as good as experiencing it ourselves is good, hot, provocative erotica, stories that give us a steamy sensual lift, a natural buzz, very similar to that giddy feeling of finding a new lover. Recently, a guest on one of the popular cable TV shows was discussing why literary erotica was reaching a wider audience, exceeding the expectations of both writers and publishers alike. He said that there was only one explanation: the stories are sexy, titillating, and most of all, safe at a time when sex can be hazardous to one's health. There was plenty of anecdotal evidence, the guest added, that well-written erotica can lower inhibitions, increase libido, delay ejaculation, prolong orgasm, and deepen intimacy. While a good erotic tale may not be able to do all that and will never be a substitute for candlelight wooing or true romance, no one can deny its potent entertainment value.

There is a long history of sex and sensuality in the work of male African American writers, who have frequently used these themes to celebrate their passions, manhood, and that most human of impulses. In the past, some male writers used sex in their proud, courageous writing as another mode of protest against political, social, and cultural injustices. Along the way, that sense of defiance can be seen in the soaring prose of such writers as Jean Toomer, Langston Hughes, Richard Wright, William Gardner Smith, James Baldwin, and Chester Himes, all of whom sought to depict their own notion of sexuality and individuality. They wrote daring, challenging novels, featuring aspects of love, desire, and intimacy that defied the traditional white sexual myths and stereotypes ingrained in the popular culture after the release of D. W. Griffith's incendiary film, *Birth of a Nation* in 1915. No longer were black men going to ignore or blindly accept the lies and fantasies of others concerning their sexuality or morality.

This book also does not co-sign those tainted, denigrating images of black male sexuality; instead it seeks to provide the reader with a few hours of fantasy, escape, and fun. These stories, while erotic and arousing, provide another opportunity to view the sexuality of our men from different vantage points, often from angles and approaches not usually in our literature. Editing this book, I guess, was another way for me to help to set the record straight. As conceived, *After Hours* explores a wide range of black sexuality above and beyond the familiar obscene concepts of the oversexed black stud and predatory brute, offering a fresh glimpse at the modern African American man who is sensitive, alert, enterprising, and ready to take care of business in the arena of love, sex, and moral responsibility. Since this is not a religious primer or a New Age treatise on "The Good Black Man in Affairs of the Heart and the Flesh," these stories provide a diverse look at the brothers, fathers, and lovers among us, with a few guys who would be classified as lusty, naughty, or otherwise "politically incorrect." That is okay, however, because it is important to represent the full spectrum of black men. The characters here are fully developed and three-dimensional, and while "nice guys" have their place, they are often depicted in current literature as boring, nerdy, luckless in love, and one-dimensional. We make no judgments. With a few exceptions, there is something for almost everyone here.

And although some of the usual elements of erotica are present, every effort was made to assemble a multitude of voices, a strong collective view of the contemporary black man and his carnal appetites that most African American men and women could immediately recognize and appreciate. The goal was to find the right mix of narrative styles, talent, and vision to put together a collection that would be groundbreaking, challenging, and sensually satisfying. Whether it's unbridled lust, full-tilt erotic love, self-affirmation, or self-destructive obsession, these issues are examined in insightful, frank terms. Ultimately, the stories making the final cut were chosen for the art and style of the story told, the sexual heat of the scenes, and the universality of the themes and experience presented.

Every book starts with some kind of aesthetic guideline. Returning to that age-old argument about the differences between erotica and pornography, I sought out articles and books that discussed this issue clearly, thoroughly, and without bias. Since I worked during the early 1980s at the American offices of the French skin mag, *Oui*, as an editor writing sexual fantasies for their letter section, I gained some idea of where the line of demarcation between the two genres was. What an educational experience that was! In current books and publications, that line frequently is manipulated and blurred.

One article, a 1992 New York *Newsday* interview with Miriam DaCosta-Willis, one of the editors of the pioneering black erotic collection, *Erotique Noire*, provided me with some critical definitions and guidelines for this project. Asked about the boundary between erotica and pornography, she replied: "I see pornography as being very carnal, and I see erotica as being not only physical but also spiritual, intellectual, and cerebral. . . . Pornography objectifies the individual, whereas erotica brings two people together. You're participating in a rite of union. One is commercial, one artistic."

Employing those words and remembering some of the works from Richard Wright, James Baldwin, Cecil Brown, and Chester Himes, I plowed ahead through the stack of submissions, looking for clues to the complex, mysterious black male sexual psyche in the new millennium. While we as a community remain conservative, very moral in many ways, and deeply religious, there are stirrings of a fresh, stripped-down sensibility that runs counter to Old School chauvinistic notions of masculinity and sexuality. It's something that has not fully reared its head in the news media, films, books, and television, but its presence cannot be denied. Apart from the stereotypical images in gangsta rap videos and buppie frat flicks, there is something new and daring in how we as black men view ourselves as males and as sexual beings, and in how we see our women and our collective roles in the larger world. Both the frequency and substance of the dialogue about love, intimacy, and responsibility are increasing in our community. And it's about time!

In *After Hours*, you meet brothers who offer for your nocturnal reading enjoyment a juicy gathering of reflective stories, lusty stories, funny stories, fantastic stories—sexual adventures that will entertain and excite, inform and ignite, all written by stylists. Some are within normal limits while others sail over the top. Opening the collection is a short gem, "Cultural Relativity," by National Book Award winner and MacArthur fellow Charles Johnson, a story that tantalizes with a strong sense of anticipation—much like two teenagers on a first date, their bodies close, but afraid to give in to the magnetic pull of passion. While it may lack the overt eroticism of some other entries, it is a taut, teasing display of ideas and imagination in updating a very old tale. The next excursion into sensuality, "Twisted," by Jervey Tervalon, immediately raises the bar quite high for kinky, erotic expression and redefines the term "coupling" with a tale that explores the outer boundaries of sexual roles. In "Once Upon a Time," an excerpt from the novel *Rest for the Weary*, noted novelist and educator Arthur Flowers adds a little hoodoo flava in his modern fable of a conjureman trying to seduce a formidable female in the Crescent City. Up-and-coming novelist Brian Peterson puts a hot, quirky spin on love and desire between two horny yet cautious young black professionals in his fast-paced story, "1-800-Connect."

The thrills and moans continue with a gorgeous mystery woman and a randy Romeo amid the sandy beaches and towering palms of exotic Hawaii in Earl Sewell's "Rock Me Baby." Fans of veteran noir writer Cole Riley will not be disappointed with his latest sizzling yarn of torrid Mexican nights, bad choices, and damp sheets, "If It Makes You Happy." Kenji Jasper, author of the critically acclaimed novel *Dark*, revisits the arty boho scene in "Up," a story of an ambitious poet who wants the big time and all its sensual perks. The question of what to do when the sexual charge runs low in an otherwise solid marriage is answered in a bit of erotic trickery laced with sensory treats from the pen of Eric E. Pete, "Cayenne." Journalist-novelist Curtis Bunn contributes one of the collection's true gems with his insightful recounting of a couple's ravenous thirst for passion and time away from the children in "Home Alone," not to be confused with the dull movie with the mop-topped Culkin kid. If Prince can blend the sacred and secular, so can Tracy Grant, the author of the popular novel *Hellified*, who pulls no punches in his tale of sanctified sexual play among the holy and the fallen, "The Apostle Charles."

Laughs, loads of them, compete with the unrelenting sex romps of Brian Egleston's hilarious "Wallbanging," his chronicle of a sex-crazed American couple on tour in China bent on squeezing one more session of love into their schedule at the Great Wall, even if it gets them in trouble with Chinese authorities. Lust and humor also play a big part in the legendary John A. Williams's excerpted story, "Odell," as a quiet, well-meaning guy discovers the busty woman of his dreams is a TV junkie during a frustrating evening at home. Sexual obsession can only end badly for a buppie with a mind-numbing attraction for a pretty TV talking head in Kalamu Ya Salaam's timely "The Roses Are Beautiful, but the Thorns Are So Sharp." In "The Rumor," Alexs D. Pate uses a dash of magic realism to dispel the complaints of naysayers in a black community about the power of love and physical bliss. The trials and travails of an African American man in his late twenties seeking to lose his virginity with mixed results is the subject of horror writer Brandon Massey's "The Question." A woman celebrates the fifteenth year of an ongoing affair with her energetic lover in a public display of lust in Robert Scott Adams's "Where Strangers Meet." Clarence Major, a leading African American wordsmith and one of the early pioneers of black erotica, offers a sensational tour-de-*farce* in a sexual stream-of-consciousness hymn to oral gratification, "Anita," excerpted from his groundbreaking 1969 Olympia Press classic novel, *All-Night Visitors*. Gary Phillips, creator of the popular Ivan Monk PI series and the Martha Chainey mystery novels, contributes a very hot yet bizarre story of anything-goes sex, blackmail, and murder in a noir caper, "Wild Thang." For fans of the Monk stories, you've never seen the sleuth like this before. Closing the collection is Colin Channer's lyrical yet highly erotic meditation, "Revolution," the story of an elderly white author's surreal infatuation and ruthless pursuit of the beautiful mistress of reggae legend, Bob Marley.

Erotica, especially black erotica, can hold a mirror to the mores and morals of a people, a culture, or a generation. While reading *After Hours*, you may find yourself discovering some new personal and sexual truths between the moans and aftershocks produced by the words and images. It's all right to think, dream, and fantasize about these things. But the bottom line here is that it is better to live, love, and enjoy all that life offers. Come read and enjoy what a few gifted black men have to say about love, sex, and intimacy! Have fun!

—Robert Fleming

"The sexiest things ain't obvious, vulgar or raw. You can see in the best low-down blues ya hear. The words talk 'round a thing, hint, suggest a thing, work your head with a picture of it, then your mind does the rest. That's when things really get on simmer. That's when the music really sticks on your mind."

—John Lee Hooker

Cultural Relativity

Charles Johnson

Not long ago a college student named Felicia Brooks felt she was the most fortunate young woman in all Seattle, and possibly in the entire world, except for one small problem.

She was deeply in love with her boyfriend, an African student who was the only son of his country's president. His name was Fortunata Maafa. In the spring of 2001, they both were graduating seniors at the University of Washington. They had been dating all year long, he was *more* than she could ever have hoped for, and Felicia knew all her friends thought Fortunata was catnip. In fact, she was afraid sometimes that they might steal him from her. Most of them had given up on black men entirely. Or at least they had given up on American black men. Their mantra, which Felicia had heard a thousand times, and often chanted herself, was that "all the *good* black men were taken, and the rest were in prison, on drugs, or unemployed, or dating white women—or didn't like girls at all." What was a sistah to do? During high school and college, Felicia and her friends despaired of ever finding Mr. Right.

But then, miraculously, she met Fortunata fall quarter at the Langston Hughes Cultural Center. He looked like a young Kwame Nkrumah, he dressed as elegantly as Michael Jordan, was gorgeous the few times she saw him in his *agbada* (African robe), and he fit George Bernard Shaw's definition of a gentleman being "a man who always tries to put in a little more than he takes out." Furthermore, he was rich. He could play the *kora,* an African stringed instrument, so beautifully you'd cry. Yet, for all that, he still had a schoolboy shyness and was frequently confused by the way Americans did things, especially by pop culture, which was so sexually frank compared to his own country that it made Fortunata squirm. All of this Felicia thought was charming as well as exciting because it meant he was her very own Galatea, and she was his Pygmalion, his guide and interpreter on these shores. He dazzled her every day when he described the ancient culture of his father's kingdom in West Africa. There, in that remote world, his people were introducing the most sophisticated technology, and that was why Fortunata had studied computer engineering. But, he said, his people worked hard to avoid the damaging aspects of westernization. They were determined to revolutionize their science, but also to preserve their thousand-year-old traditions, their religion, and their folkways, even when the reason for some of these unique practices had been forgotten.

One night in June, after their final exams were over, Felicia played for him the movie *Coming to America* on the VCR in her studio apartment on Capital Hill, hoping he would enjoy it, which he did. No sooner than it was over, Fortunata slid closer to her on the sofa, and said, "I am *so* like Eddie Murphy in this funny movie. I came to America four years ago, not just for an education, but really to find a beautiful American woman to share my life. To be my Queen. Felicia, that woman is *you*, if you will have me. Because if I can't have you, then I don't want anyone. I just won't marry, ever."

Naturally, Felicia said yes.

"And," he added, "you promise not to change your mind? No matter what happens?"

She did.

From the pocket of his suit coat, Fortunata produced a ring with a flawless, four-carat diamond shaped like the Star of South Africa, for precious stones were plentiful in his country, a nation rich in natural resources. Felicia threw her arms around him. Then, without thinking, acting on what she believed was instinct, she brought her lips close to his. But before she could kiss Fortunata, he wiggled away.

"*What?*" said Felicia. "What's wrong?"

Fortunata gave her a shy, sideways look. His voice trembled. "I'm *so* sorry. We don't do that."

"What?" she said. "You don't kiss?"

She looked straight at him, he looked down. "You know I can't."

"*Why* not?!"

"Please, don't start this again." Now Fortunata seemed nervous; he began rolling the end of his tie between his fingers. "I'm not *sure* why. We just don't. The reason is lost in antiquity. Felicia, it's not that unusual. Polynesians rub noses, you know. Samoans sniff each other. And traditional Japanese and Chinese cultures did not include this strange practice called *kissing*. I suspect they felt it was *too* intimate a thing for people to do. All I know is that my father warned me never to do this thing when I came to America. We've discussed this before. Don't you remember?"

Felicia did remember, but not happily. This was the *one* thing about Fortunata that baffled and bothered her deeply. She understood that his culture was very traditional. For example, Fortunata's people insisted that sex should be postponed until a couple's wedding night. All during the past year, they'd done almost *every*thing else that lovers did. They held hands, hugged, and snuggled. But there were *no* kisses. Not even an air kiss. Or a good-night kiss when he dropped Felicia off at her apartment and returned to his dormitory. The last thing she wanted was to be culturally insensitive, or to offend Fortunata, or to have him break off their nearly perfect relationship. So on those past occasions Felicia never insisted that he kiss her. Nor did she insist on the night he summoned up the courage to propose.

After taking a deep breath, she said, sadly, "Can we rub noses then?"

"Of course," said Fortunata. "I think *that's* OK."

It is well known that when two people fall in love, their brains produce amphetamine-like substances (phenylethylamines), which are responsible for what we call "lover's high." After Fortunata left, Felicia still felt this chemically-created elixir of strong emotion; but she also felt very confused. What she felt, in fact, was half ecstasy that she was to wed the son of an African statesman and half bewilderment because rubbing noses—in her view—was no substitute for a big wet one. She was a highly intelligent woman. A woman about to graduate with a degree in anthropology. She wondered if she was being culturally inflexible. But Felicia knew all her life she had been fascinated by and respectful of the differences in cultures, how each was a self-contained and complete system that must be understood from within. She knew her Lévi-Strauss and the work of dozens of structural anthropologists. You did not have to tell her that in some Moslem countries it was insulting to cross your legs when sitting if the soles of your shoes were displayed to your host. Or that in Theravada Buddhist countries like Thailand patting a cute youngster on the top of his head was a no-no because that part of the body was looked upon as sacred. So yes, she had always taken great pains to carefully listen when Fortunata spoke of his country's history and mysterious customs.

But she *wanted* a kiss! Was that asking for so much?

In her heart, she *knew* that kissing was special, and to prove it to herself, she sat down at her computer, went to the Internet and spent the night looking at everything she could find on the subject. Just as she expected, kissing as an expression of love and affection was old. Very old. It dated back to the fifth century. And as a custom, it was even older than that! The early Christians borrowed kissing from the Romans. Clearly, it was the most *human* of practices. Everyone knew animals didn't kiss. They licked. The reason for *having* lips in the first place, Felicia decided just before daybreak, was so people could use their God-given soup coolers as the most romantic, the most erotic, and the most natural way to show they loved someone.

During the last year Felicia had introduced Fortunata to all kinds of things outside his culture—karaoke, the music of Jimi Hendrix and Kurt Cobain, the importance of Ichiro bobbleheads and why everyone needed a good-looking tattoo—and he had enjoyed *all* of it, and thanked her for enlightening him as a good Galatea would. When she finally drifted off to sleep, around 10 A.M., Felicia wondered if Fortunata had lied. That maybe people in his culture *did* kiss, but for some reason he simply didn't want to kiss *her*. But, no! She had never caught him in a lie before. It was more likely that he'd never kissed *any*one. So she was certain that if Fortunata could just experience the electric thrill of kissing *once,* and with the right woman (meaning herself), then a wonderful new cultural doorway would open for him. If she truly loved him, Felicia knew she owed him that.

As luck would have it, Fortunata dropped by unexpectedly that evening as she was fixing dinner. He was almost bursting with excitement.

"Felicia," he said, "I just spoke with my father. I told him about our engagement. We have his blessing. In my country, the wedding ceremony lasts for a week. Since my father is president, the whole country will celebrate." He paused to catch his breath. "Aren't you happy?"

To show her happiness, Felicia pressed her body against him. Before he could move, she placed her hands on both sides of his head, pulled him closer, puckered up and bestowed upon a startled Fortunata the most soulful, moist and meaningful liplock she had ever delivered in her life. She felt her heart beating faster, the temperature of her skin beneath her clothes heating up. Smiling, Felicia took a step back. The expression on Fortunata's face was unreadable. He started to speak but stopped.

And then, suddenly, he was gone.

Where Fortunata had stood, there was a full-grown, giant West African frog. It was a foot long and weighed as much as a fox terrier.

"I warned you," he said.

Felicia felt ill. She thought, *I can't handle this.* But what she said was:

"I don't suppose we can break off the engagement, can we?"

"Don't be silly," said the frog.

Twisted
(An excerpt from *All the Trouble You Need*)

Jervey Tervalon

Jordan blew off his office hours, and returned home and spent the rest of the day working on his thesis. Mostly he spent the time trying to make sense of years of notes that no longer seemed insightful or even meaningful—it was actually sort of pleasant working; *Kind of Blue* crept down weakly from a San Luis Obispo radio station, lessening the bitter boredom of reading a stack of academic journals. He forced himself through a paragraph of prose so stultifying that it had to be in some language that only idiots could or would want to read. His attention, like the jazz station, flitted in and out. He watched traffic race up and down busy Milpas, counting the cars that ran the red light. He watched the teenagers on their way to the Taco Bell as he discarded dead and useless research into the wastepaper basket. Yeah, he'd finish that thesis and then he'd submit it and get on with his life. Somebody might even find "Jazz: Influence and Fluency in Contemporary American Literature" worth reading, but he had to finish it first. He had no choice; with just a little imagination he could see the unemployment line snaking all the way to his dusty bedroom. Time to get real about finding a serious teaching gig that paid for dental care and offered all that job security he heard so much about. His mind flitted again; Daphne and tonight's dinner, what was that going to amount to? It must be getting serious, but he was probably just blowing it out of proportion; her parents probably wanted to see the kind of black man she was sleeping with. Normally, he wasn't in his room at the computer this late in the afternoon. He stretched out on the bed and shut his eyes; dinner wasn't for another couple of hours. He hoped he'd wake in time, but if he didn't, well . . .

"Wake up."

He opened his eyes to see Daphne in a flimsy dress smiling at him.

"Your hair is wet," Jordan said, sitting up.

"I was swimming at Boy's Beach."

"The nude beach?"

"Yes, it was kind of ugly. This hairy fat man, with a thing so large it looked deformed, waited at the shore for me to come out and no matter how far I swam he followed me."

"What did you do?"

"I waited till some guys came along and sprinted by him."

Usually, Jordan could hold a conversation even if he wanted to jump on Daphne's bones, but this particular battle was already lost; the thin material of her soaked dress could barely restrain her erect nipples. She stretched out next to him on the bed and immediately he lifted the damp dress and kissed the curve of her hips.

"Daphne, I uh . . ."

"Jordan, the window."

"Yeah, right."

Jordan closed the blinds and turned to see Daphne peel off the wet dress. He couldn't get out of his pants fast enough, but eager as he was he tried to slow the process down. He wanted to commit her to memory: her eyes, her legs, her breasts, her mouth. She guided him in and he worried he'd come at once, but skillfully Daphne stopped the chain reaction, slowing the motion until he could move inside her without exploding. He whispered, "I love you, I love you." He wanted her so much that if he'd died right there, it wouldn't have mattered. He held her tighter, breathing in the air she exhaled; inhaling everything about Daphne.

Afterward, they rested on his narrow bed, but Jordan's mind raced, devising ways—marriage, kidnapping, drugs—to have her again and again; he was afraid to think of living his life away from her.

She met his eyes, looking as though she would reassure him and put him at ease that she felt the same overwhelming love.

She looked away.

His heart sank.

"I should go. I need to help with dinner," she said.

He watched her wiggle into the still wet dress and leave in such haste she had to come back for her shoes. She didn't say good-bye, and even though he'd see her again shortly, it bothered him, like a window opened to an impending storm.

Jordan arrived at Daphne's on time but wondered if he should drive home to find a tie. He wore a jacket, white shirt, khakis, and penny loafers. Anybody could see he was no wild man, more like Denzel than Tupac. Her parents would see he was just an instructor . . . who happened to be freaking their daughter . . . while she was still a student in his class.

With that, he sat back down to rethink the whole thing. He was sure that this dinner would be awkward and weird, maybe even a disaster.

He arrived at that hated glass oval door and waited uncomfortably like a trapped bug for someone to answer the doorbell. Was she introducing him to her parents because she was truly serious, or in the worse scenario, for shock value?

Daphne ran down the stairs in a red sarong and with her hair pulled back and braided. Seeing her so soon after making love made him feel as though it hadn't happened. He wanted proof. Before she could say a word, he kissed her.

"I missed you," he said.

"It's been so long," she said with a laugh, and led him to the sun room behind the kitchen. Her mother stood up from the table to greet him, as did her father. He looked to be much older than the mother, with a narrow red face and sharp teeth like the Renfield character in *Dracula*.

"Glad you could make it," he said.

Jordan shook his hand. Mr. Daniels gestured for Jordan to sit. The table had a centerpiece of fruit and cheese, and next to it, two bottles of wine. Jordan imagined the old man ("More flies, Master!") begging for bugs.

"Red?" Mr. Daniels asked. "The red is very good."

Jordan nodded, wanting to laugh.

"So, you teach at the university?" he asked, in a British accent.

Jordan still wanted to laugh, and had to resort to pretending to cough for time to compose himself.

"Yes. I teach a Japanese lit class under the supervision of the provost of the college."

"You're a graduate student?" Mrs. Daniels asked.

"Yes, I am. I'm finishing my thesis."

"Daphne goes on about how much she enjoys your class," Mrs. Daniels said. Her tone was pleasant and her smile seemed genuine. Jordan relaxed a bit.

"She's a wonderful student, and about the only one who keeps up with the reading. *The Tale of Genji* was pretty tough going in places."

"I'm surprised to hear that Daphne is applying herself," Mr. Daniels said.

"Do you speak Japanese?" Mrs. Daniels asked.

Jordan shrugged. "Well, I've had four years of Japanese, but I barely can ask 'Where's the restroom?' I'm language challenged."

Mr. Daniels raised an eyebrow.

"You've lived in Santa Barbara long?" Mrs. Daniels asked, to restart the conversation.

"For almost ten years."

"So you like it here?" she asked.

"Yes, I'd like to make Santa Barbara my permanent home."

"Really?" said Daphne. I couldn't spend the rest of my life in this city . . . It's claustrophobic," she said.

He was surprised that she would disagree with him so quickly in front of her parents.

"I like it here," Jordan said. "It doesn't have to be claustrophobic."

Daphne sighed.

"You have to make your life wherever you are. I find Santa Barbara interesting and I've lived here all my life," Mrs. Daniels said.

"Maybe our daughter needs more excitement," Mr. Daniels said. "Though you would think she'd had enough at this point."

Jordan hadn't even had much of a drink or an appetizer and already the evening was on the verge of blowing up.

"So, Daphne," Mr. Daniels said jeeringly, "where would you like to live?"

"I liked New Zealand," Daphne replied.

For no good reason, Jordan said, "In New Zealand, sheep outnumber people ten to one."

"Still, even with all those sheep, Daphne managed to make a time of it there, too," Mr. Daniels said.

Mrs. Daniels obviously wanted to attempt to pacify the conversation. She patted her husband's hand and smiled apologetically at Jordan.

"You were arrested and thrown out of the country," Mr. Daniels said. Jordan glanced at Mrs. Daniels, who looked worried. Daphne eyed her father grimly. Mr. Daniels sipped at his water, ignoring her stare. Daphne picked up a teacup and gripped it so tightly that Jordan was sure she would hurl it at Mr. Daniels's head.

"My family can be difficult," Mrs. Daniels said pleasantly.

"What family isn't?" Jordan said.

"Here, here," Mr. Daniels said, and poured everyone another glass of wine.

"Len, help me with the chicken," said Mrs. Daniels. Without a word her husband stood and dutifully followed his wife into the kitchen.

"Now comes the scolding," Daphne said, smirking.

"Is everything going to be okay?" Jordan asked.

"Of course. He can be very pleasant when he's under control. He probably missed taking his Paxil."

Jordan still felt uncomfortable.

"My family has hope for me."

"Hope?" Jordan asked.

"Hope that things will work out for me, that I don't disappoint them. They treat me like I'm capable of anything—suicide, joining a cult. I used to think maybe they were right, that I couldn't hold it together, but being adopted gives me hope; that's the only reason I'm sure I won't go insane."

Jordan waited for her to go on, but she didn't. Instead, she smiled at him. He tried to contain his curiosity, but he didn't do a good job.

"Don't tell me you're surprised? I thought we talked about this," she finally said. "I'm not nearly so pink as they are."

He shrugged.

"Father was English and Mother was a mixed-race South African woman. I was adopted at four into a life of affluence and what else: cocktail parties, fund-raisers, depression, family viciousness."

"Did you ever meet your biological parents?"

"No. I used to think that I could find them, that they were out there somewhere, waiting for me. Maybe that's why I started running away."

Mr. and Mrs. Daniels returned with a roasted chicken and a plate of steamed vegetables. It didn't help Jordan find his lost appetite, but it was just as well. Hard to make a good impression when your mouth is full.

Soon as everyone was served, Mr. Daniels started in as if he were continuing a conversation: "You must know that anyone trying to understand this family has to be prepared, because we live on the verge."

"The verge of what?" Jordan asked.

"The verge of disaster," he said with a labored, straight face.

Jordan wished he were driving and not Daphne. It seemed a good idea to drop his car off and drive with her but she was barely hitting the brakes as she negotiated the hills. How much farther to her apartment? Jordan wondered, weighing if he should suggest she slow down, but thankfully he didn't have to. She turned into an oddly angled parking space, cut the engine, and burst from the car, running for her apartment up the hillside.

Jordan thought for a minute that she must have really had to relieve herself. He waited a minute, then five, before knocking, but the door was open and he found her under the covers shaking.

"Daphne?"

She didn't respond. He took a few steps toward her and she pulled the covers higher.

"Should I go?"

Finally, in a strained voice she said no.

"What is it?"

"Panic."

"You're having a panic attack?"

"It happens when I spend too much time with my family."

The covers inched down. He sat on the edge of the bed and held her still shaking hand.

"Have you been to a doctor? Can't he give you something for anxiety?"

She sighed as though she had heard this too many times.

"Of course, if I wanted it."

"You don't?"

"I have absolutely no interest in that kind of treatment. I don't want to change myself."

He started to reply but she pressed her finger against his lips.

"Let's go to sleep."

"Sure," he said, getting out of his clothes and sliding next to her, ignoring the grit of her sandy bed. She seemed out of it as they fucked, like maybe she had had too many Vicodans again. He could barely keep his dick hard; when he was about ready to give it up, she suddenly gripped his neck.

"Don't leave me," she said.

Then she came alive, her ass writhing in a new rhythm that he barely could keep up with. He didn't want to stop fucking her. He dreaded coming, and losing it, the moment. He pulled out and went down on her, sucking at her pussy like it was all that was good; hearing her low moans made him want it all. He mounted her and slipped his dick into her ass and he rode it, intoxicated with her cries of pain and pleasure. He was mad with it, then he came, and they both fell off that mountaintop. He lay there gasping, wondering how badly everything would turn out. Daphne was curled up in a fetal position, crying softly. He tried to reassure her that he would protect her, that she didn't have to be afraid of anything. He looked down at her face, at her lips, everything about her was precious to him. He held back, wanting to show her how much he loved her, how much he wanted her to share in what she made him feel. Finally he lost himself, aroused again. Daphne grasped him around the face, kissing him between half-gasped words.

"Don't hold back, I want you to give it to me. Give it all to me," she said. Like he had a choice.

Morning light: the bare white room seemed cloudy, as if he had dreamed her next to him—cold feet against his, the scent of her hair. He was almost fully awake but fought it, delaying it as long as he could. He knew once they were awake they'd part.

Boom!

Boom!

They both bolted upright to the sound of someone pounding the door. She gestured for him to be quiet

"Daphne, God damn it, Daphne! I know you're in there. I know you're home!"

Jordan's heart pounded as hard as that lunatic outside beat the door. Daphne didn't seem alarmed. She looked almost indifferent.

"Open the damn door!"

Jordan struggled into his pants; no way he was going to get shot down like a dog, in his boxers. He ran into her tiny kitchen looking for something to defend himself and Daphne with, but all he could find was a teapot and a butter knife. Hearing the chain being taken off the door, he rushed in and saw Daphne in a robe talking to a balding, powerfully built white man in an expensive suit.

"I didn't know you had company," he said pleasantly.

Daphne seemed at ease, even pleased to see this man who had been pounding at her door moments before.

"Frank Willis," he said, extending his hand, which Jordan ignored.

"What's with pounding on the door?" Jordan demanded, feeling more ridiculous by the moment, trying to look tough with a teapot in his hand.

"I'm Daphne's husband, but don't feel you should go. I'm so busy, having a working vacation as they say, that I can't spend quality time with her."

Frank nodded to Jordan and gave Daphne a warm embrace and walked out, closing the door behind him.

Jordan couldn't bring himself to look at Daphne. He dressed, ignoring her eyes as she lingered by the door, arms folded as though the man was still there. She could explain but Jordan wouldn't ask; too much mystery with her already.

"Look, I'm gonna be going."

"Jordan."

"Yeah?"

"You have every right to know what's going on."

"You think so?" he said bitterly.

She sat on the edge of the bed as he opened the door to leave. "I can explain. Give me time."

"You don't have to. Really. I'll see you around."

As he walked out of the apartment he glanced back. Her face was vacant of emotion. He knew he should have been pissed off, enraged, but something was so wrong with her. He was more mad at himself; he should have seen it coming, but still he got run down like some blind, deaf, and dumb idiot.

Once Upon a Time
(An excerpt from *Rest for the Weary*)

Arthur Flowers

I am Flowers of the Delta Clan Flowers and the line of O. Killens. This tale I tell as it was told to me. Once upon a time there was an angel. And a conjureman.

Horns, whistles, and noisemakers erupt through the thin walls of the hotel. Outside the snug cocoon of their room New Orleans parties in the New Year. She leans over him, her silvered hair a translucent curtain around their heads, her slim body searingly warm where it touches his, what happens, she says, when the dream dies.

He lays there looking up at her, hand frozen on her waist and waiting, hoping for a reprieve. The lamp behind her backlights the silvered curtain that shelters them, he puts his hand into it and gently combs it with his fingers. Dreams never die, he whispers, voice suddenly gone, what are you trying to tell me baby?

It's over, she said, you've got to leave in the morning.

There is a finality in her voice, her words, that he has not heard before. This time she is going to make it stick, he thinks. This time it's really over. In the six, seven months they've been together he has been fired six, seven good times. Half-fired even more. But always before the dream brought her back to him.

His hand slowly strokes down to her hip, aware that this might be the last time he handles her body, feels her skin against his own. The first time they've made love without watching the clock. The first time she's slept in his arms.

They had come to New Orleans for New Year's 2000. She had told him she was going down to visit her parents and he asked if he could come down for a New Year's Eve dinner with her. I'll leave right away, he said, just take you to dinner, he said. She said she would have a hotel room for when she needed a break from her parents, he could stay over if he wanted to. Stay a couple of nights if you want. I probably won't stay there with you though, she said.

She worked in the little neighborhood library at the mouth of the Park on the corner of Riverside and Person. He lived in the Park itself and alongside the river, in a little house sitting treetop tall on stilts dug deep in Delta mud. Neighborhood folk called it a tree house but it only looked that way, a tight little box of a house, old gray wood as weathered as the trees that surrounded it and barely visible in the bright months of sanctuary. The good folk of Riverside quick to point out late night lights glowing deep in the Park to folks from less blessed Memphis neighborhoods. See there, they say, where the lights are. That's where the hoodooman stay. In a house on stilts. So he can see.

He is a teller of stories and a weaver of tales, a dreamer. He met her at the library, where he likes to nest among the fruits of solitary labors. She is the reference desk librarian and it just so happens that from his favorite chair she just so happens to be in his line of sight you understand. A classic yellagal, long and lean with an unruly mane of prematurely silvered hair. They nod, exchange pleasantries, do lunch occasionally. She is a strange and fascinating woman, an iconoclastic sort within whom he detects the complex soul of an artist.

But married. A negligible little ring. Still he enjoys the occasional lunches, her iconoclastic company, the intoxicating attention of a strange and beautiful woman. They had been on nodding terms for years when lunches were inaugurated by a fortuitous encounter at the Hole in the Wall, the local jook eatery across from the library and next to the Riverside Baptist Church. Angel, she told him. Angel, he said. Hard name to carry, he said. My parents thought very highly of me, she said. She laughed then and when she laughed she threw her head off to the side in a way that went straight to his heart. He will swear later that the first time he saw her, crisp efficiency tempered by the enthusiasm of two urchins being walked through the Internet, he knew she was special. He will swear that all along he knew she was the one.

Perhaps that's why one day he blurted out, surprising himself more than he surprised her, Angel, I realize you're a married woman, I would however like to court you.

She watched him squirm with a smug and curious pleasure, intrigued as always with the power over him that she had sensed from the first time they met. (You drooled, she told him.) Rumored by the locals to be the local hoodooman. Late 40s dreadman, thick and bearded and built to take punishment, a two-headed man with a face of carved wood that showed only what he wanted it to.

He wore his face now, braced to be shot down—Highjohn I am very flattered but you know I'm a married woman and I hope you can respect that. But instead she looked at him with this stricken look. I'm sorry, he babbled, I hope I haven't upset you, I just . . . No, no, she said, you haven't upset me . . . I am a married woman though.

I know, he murmured shamefully, I just had to say it you know. I'll . . . uh, see you later. But before she turned back into the library she brushed his beard with the palm of her hand. You didn't upset me, she said.

All night long conjureman feeling the angel's brush of her palm on his beard. All night long conjureman howling at the moon.

The next morning an e-mail saying she wanted to talk. They arranged to meet at the Hole. Nervous. Eyes that fidget and flicker. The old ease gone. I can't be what you want me to be, she said. But I didn't get any sleep last night thinking about what you said. You can't . . . court me . . . like that . . . I am married you know. But we can continue to be friends. To have lunch like we have. If you're comfortable with that.

Very. Thankful even. What on earth could he have been thinking of. That evening he e-mailed an apology. She replied that it wasn't necessary. Said she wanted to finish the conversation when he got a chance.

They took to walking in the Park during her lunch breaks, voices hushed under the wooded calm. One day he told her he wanted to save the race, take the trick off the souls of blackfolk, said it with a straight face too, not that that said a lot, boy Legba Child and he do like to play. I have a plan, he said. For I have had a vision and I am adept at making real that which was not. Turning the key in the hoodoo lock. I am a conjuror you know and would one day like to be the High Hoodoo. Told her the Park was a special place. Where anything goes. Said it too was a hole in the wall. Said Brer Rabbit and his crew lived there you know. They were generally on speaking terms but there was a trick to it you understand cause the animalfolk generally wary of humanfolk. But sometimes late at night he say, I settle back you see and I close my eyes and act like I'm sleeping see, and soon enough old Brer Rabbit he come peep in the door and when he see me sleeping like that he beckon the rest of them on in and here come Brer and Sister Rabbit and Brer and Sister Fox and Brer Bear and Sister Coon and all the woodfolk and they commence to singing and dancing and celebrating. And Brer Bear he pull out he blues harp and Brer Rabbit he play he bones and Sister Coon she play she guitar bigger than she and Brer and Sister Fox they do like to dance and before you know it they a kicking up they heels and letting the good times roll and sometimes I get in the spirit see and I forget myself see and I open my eyes and the music stop and they all hide away and they stay hid till I close my eyes again.

In spite of such flights of apparent fancy, or perhaps because of them, she found herself showing him some of her most precious gems, dreams she had long carried in her most secret places. Showed him a story she once wrote, young and starry-eyed, about a goddess of the night, a nightblack goddess born of stars, storm, and thunder. Kinda corny huh, she said, I've never shown it to anybody, she said, nobody. And he found himself listening, listening with all his power while she told him about a wildweed childhood wandering the story tale streets of New Orleans when she should have been in school. About her old school New Orleans family, funny ways and all, and the second master's she almost has, the doctorate she wants if she can find the time somehow someway. About archeology classes over at the University of Memphis, the summer dig on the Harriet Tubman

Home in Auburn, New York. An extraordinary woman, she said, Delta sun leaping off the river and glittering in her eyes. Most people only know of her slavery time and Civil War exploits. But she was a warrior without end. In her last years, herself weary, she built a home for the elderly. For homeless ex-slaves. She never quit struggling. Struggled until the day she died. People just don't know her like I do. Love her like I do. She speaks to me.

The first time he kissed her was in the Park. Spring probably, pollen so thick you could taste it. They were standing high on the bluff and she was standing entirely too close. She turned to say something, their eyes met and flickered away bruised. Before he realizes it, he is leaning in to kiss her. He caught himself. May I kiss you, he said. She nodded most imperceptibly. Then he kissed her and his world lurched spun shouted while he savored her lips, her tongue, the very fact that he was kissing her, kissing Angel, his Angel. He opens his eyes to look at her face up against his, puts his hand lightly on her neck to feel the warmth of her skin, the blood pulsing under his finger. She drew back suddenly and pushed at his chest. No, she said, I shouldn't. He stepped back and she dropped her head into her hands. Something moved in me, in my body, she said, years later and still trying to understand, and I knew this was a dangerous thing we were doing, I knew it then. He stood there frozen, sorry, he mumbled, he never ever wanted to cause her any grief, not ever. I just want to be good for you. Good to you. He backed up a step, to the edge of the bluff. It's not your fault, she said, I shouldn't have said yes. I need to get back. Sure, he said. They crossed the bridge over the expressway that separated the Park from the city without speaking, much too aware that they had crossed a line and of the fact that even now they were holding hands.

There was, she told him one day, a colony of ex-slaves founded here while they were fleeing the Civil War and Reconstruction. I found mention of it in the records of a congressional inquiry after the riots of 1866. The true record is still buried here and I will dig it out one day. They too found sanctuary here. A story I will tell. Harriet would approve.

The second time was better than the first. This time he held her in his arms. This time she let him. But it was the first time they made love that the earth moved shifted changed forever. Making out, got carried away and found a deep and easy peace that wrapped their souls in a little warm blanket.

Then she fired him. I was going to tell you it was over, she said, pulling away and sitting on the edge of the bed, body still sleek with sweat. He heard the opening but he was too hurt to take it. Sure, he said, no problem. She would be back he thought and when she came back, she better have a better attitude. He was still cool when he watched her drive off. Then he got to thinking. What if she didn't. Come back. He always played command games and generally won. But could he take that chance with this one? Would he? What if she didn't. Come back.

That evening, conjureman walking the neighborhood like he do, village witchdoctor keeping his finger on the pulse, making sure the patterns are unbroken, the harmonies clean. His invisible thing, I see but am not seen. Of course some folk see him, others just feel the passing breeze. Hoodooman walking. But this time he is distracted by the very same things that generally please him. Families sitting comfortable on wraparound porches, greeting folk and watching the day fall. Couples walking, holding hands. Light glowing through windows as the sky darkens. This time the conjureman retreat into the leafy darkness of the Park. How did it ever get to this? Damn near 50 and living in the Park. A kid playing games.

Conjureman sitting on a driftwood throne and handling he roots in he hand. He is afraid. Fighting an impulse to withdraw, slip back to where he was, comfortable enough and answerable to nobody. When they were just flirting it was one thing but now that they have been intimate it is entirely another. Now it is real. Already he can feel significance lingering about the edges. Already he knows that she is not something he can hit quit and move on and de conjureman don't like nothing happening to him he don't control. De conjureman he live in little worlds of his own making and he does not care for distraction. But this one has touched my options and disrupted all my plans. She is Fa to me.

He feels it but can he trust it? Surely just the overwrought passion of new love. The trees are greener after all, the air fresher and his dreams once again bright and shiny things. No, it is the power talking to him. The power to which he has learned to listen. There is nothing I would not do to be with her. Nothing I would not do to keep her happy. To win her I would change the world.

He called. Cleared his throat and asked her to lunch. Said he wanted to talk. If that's alright with you. Okay, she said.

In the Park and on the bluff again, across from the jagged tree line of Arkansas. I tried to be cool, he said, when you said what you said yesterday. I should have fallen on my knees and begged you to reconsider.

I wrote you, she said, wrote you a letter. I don't want to break it up.

I am such a bohemian, he told her. That's not necessarily a bad thing, she said. You have no idea, he said.

If I do go with you, what kind of life would we live?

He will hoodoo her, bind her to him with a web of love magic. He commenced to spinning dreams. I will immortalize you, he told her, I will immortalize my love for you. I will tell stories of you and my love for you that will be a beacon light unto the generations. With all my heart and all my power I will serve you. I will fill your life with magic.

And he felt the power stir within.

The letter was there when he got home. She really cared for him, it said. She cared for him and she cared for her husband and she was confused, she said, two men she cared for in her life, two fires, one for her husband and a growing one for you. Not contacting him would be hard, she said. I do love you, she said. And he was glad he hadn't made her work at it, glad he had come to her first.

She canceled New Orleans twice. Twice she relented. The day he was supposed to leave he didn't answer the phone for fear she would tell him not to come. Didn't know what to expect until she met him in the lobby of the hotel with a warm smile. A classic French Quarter hotel, small and intimate, old world and slightly decadent, a little elevator pushing them together, forcing a hug, a quick stolen peck.

An equally classic room, with thick brocaded walls and lace-covered window doors. They were just above the old-world rooftops of the Quarter and a rainy drizzly day shrouded the crenellated roofs surrounding them. They sat on a wrought iron balcony drinking champagne with bread, fruits, and cheeses and only occasionally came inside to make candlelight love on the big brass bed.

God this is good. The way life ought to be. Sleeping together for the first time. Spooned up behind her. God I want you, he said. So does my husband, she said, he wants me too. Well, what do you want, he said. She turned and looked at him then, snuggled into his chest. I want you, she said, so soft he more felt it than heard it, my warrior, she said. And corny though it be, his heart swelled and his power glowed hot like a burning sun. And when he came in her it was like he was claiming her. That's what he told himself, convinced himself. Claiming her. Murmured in her ear as she was coming on him and he in her, Do you want me to be faithful to you baby, do you.

Oh yess, she moaned, oh yes baby.

But it was walking the little streets of the Quarter, weaving through the festive New Year's crowds of tourists and natives in beads, sequins, and feathers, that he is happiest, holding her hand, being a couple. He wants to walk down the street holding her hand like this forever. That lunchtime loving just don't get it. I'm going to drop all my women, he told her, all my negotiations. I'm going to tell them all that I'm in love with you. I can't ask you to do that, she said. After all I am married. I just ask that you be careful, that's all I can ask. I know baby, he said, entwining his fingers in hers, that's why I asked you when I did.

If I come with you, you won't always love me like this.

There is nothing I would not do to keep you happy. Nothing I would not be. I will astound and delight you with the quality of my devotion to you. With the quality of my service. The pelts I will lay at your feet.

Oh he got mack. She don't question that. His stability maybe but not his sincerity, he believes each and every word. They wandered into Congo Square. The milling New Year's Eve crowds were left behind in the Quarter proper and here it was quiet, somber, and fitting, huge trees draped over it like dignified sentinels. The enslaved used to come here to do their dances, she told him, their ancient dances. There is a lot of history here. They sat beneath a sprawling elder and it was a comfortable moment. Until she said, If I do leave my husband, it doesn't mean that I will get married again.

He ignored the heart beating in his chest and asked, why not?

Why would I, she said, fingering beads she has accumulated. Been there, done that.

He blinks. Pulls a silver mask off his head. Tries to absorb what she is saying without panicking. Maintaining absolute cool is critical in moments like this. He knows she resents her husband. Sees marriage as a trap. An inescapable trap. I don't read books written by men, she once told him. She rarely speaks about her marriage to him but de conjureman always listening for hints of what it is that has driven her to him. Dude don't work goes a long way. Call himself consulting but he don't hustle. Whenever it comes up she goes rigid with anger. So does Highjohn. How could any man treat her like that. Not appreciate what he got. Try to keep her dependent and submissive. He didn't even want her to know how to drive. She had to wait until he left the country to go sneak and learn how to drive. Even now he prefers to drop her off and pick her up. With a car she paid for. But Highjohn, he realize though that he is not much better. A matter of degree. Always been the boss. Assume any woman he with will adjust herself to him. His work. His way. At least he pay his way. What kinda man don't pay his way. What kinda woman take it. Just thinking about it piss him off. How could anybody abuse an angel. He takes a deep breath. Check yourself. He been thinking optimal scenario: Angel leaves husband, marries him, they live happy ever after. But no. Leaving husband is just the first step. He will be dancing forever. Growing forever. Her husband has become jaded. He's forgotten the steps and no longer hears the music. She is emotionally starved and de conjureman he open she heart with massive doses of unconditional affection. De conjureman he resolve swear vows conjures. If I do get her I will court her for the rest of my days. I will grow as necessary to love her properly and well.

Shalabongo.

They spent the night wrapped up in the moment and he was spooned up tight behind her, bodies fitted in all particulars, when he told her that I am jealous of him.

In a twenty-year marriage, she said, distant in the dark, there is not a lot of sex left.

Well that's good, he thinks, but not what he's jealous of. I'm jealous, he says, of him snuggling up with you before you go to bed. Of every laugh. Every moment. Of him wiping your brow when you are fevered. Of that burn on your arm you told me you got taking apple pie out of the oven. I'm jealous of you sitting down to breakfast every morning with him before you both rush out to your jobs.

I'm the only one rushing out, she said bitterly, her body suddenly stiff against his and no longer fitted. Well, he said, is your husband going to ever get a job or are you going to keep supporting him?

No, he's not, she says after a long and brutal moment. You spoke about it, he asks? Yes we did, she said, I'm going to keep working. That's okay with you, he asks? No, it's not, she said. He gently palms her stiff back, fingers tracing the knobs of her spine like a blind man finding his way. When I'm away from him I resent it, she said, but when I'm with him I don't. You aren't a gardener, she said, but it's like two plants and over the years their roots are twisted up together and one is suffering but if you try to break up the roots you might destroy them both.

You deserve more than that, he finally got out. You should be treated better than that. Fucking pimp.

She shifted in the dark and her body no longer touched his. My husband is a good man, she said coldly. And you don't know him. You don't know what it is about him that keeps me with him. In his own way my husband is good to me.

If he was that good to you, he thinks, you wouldn't be here with me. But he says, I'm sorry. I knew what I was doing when I said it. I know you did, she said, and turned the bedside lamp on, I know you did. That's when she leaned over him. Asked him what happens when the dream dies. Told him he had to leave.

Oh he was cool. Oscar Brown ain't got nothing on the kid. I was cool. Stone cold cool. Since I have known her I have been braced to be fired.

Okay baby, he said, New Year's rising deep crescendo around them, I will officially quit chasing you. This time I will. He turns away from her. Strokes the forearm next to his face. Watches the hairs on her arm flicker under his airbrush touch. Can you, she said, can you quit?

When he got back to Memphis he disappeared into the leafy sanctuary of the Park and walked the river bluff, a kiss once blessed, olive drab towel wrapped around his neck and collecting driftwood altars in an old army duffel bag.

A letter. Postmarked New Orleans. He sat on the top of the rickety steps that ran up the side of his tree house. There is a hurricane building in the Gulf and Memphis is braced for the fringe. It is the quiet before a Delta storm and nothing moves, the earth holds its breath and the trees are still and waiting. Conjureman handling he high johnny conquer roots and sitting still as a mountain's heart. He put he roots down and he open he letter. She thinks they should just be friends. Says she doesn't think he's ready for a real commitment. Real life. Real world. Says he treats love like it's a fantasy. Says she is not a real woman to him. Says he has control issues. Too fond of head games. And finally she says, I am committed to somebody else and am unable to give you the love and attention you need. Can you, she says, can you quit?

So be it. At least I am free of this ongoing anxiety, he told himself. At least I can be a man again, he told himself. The old Highjohn that I know and love. Tired of feeling like a beggar, a fucking supplicant. I don't need her, he told himself. I am free of her spell.

Then the Delta wind come moaning and around him trees bow low and sing homage. Windsong whistling in great gusts through the trees shift he roots ever so faintly and lift he dreads in a whipping halo. Branches brush against the walls of his aerie in arboreal symphony, the sky open wide and the rains they come. Stormbringer raise I man head to the cooling spray.

Conjureman can't help but be amused. Thought he would bring so much magic down into her life that she would never consider leaving him and instead brought the magic down into his own. Called himself hoodooing and got hoodooed.

He handle he roots, he begin he story. One that will make the world as he wants it to be. One in which he dreams come true and he soul be saved. One that would be rest for the weary.

Odell
(An excerpt from *Mothersill and the Foxes*)

John A. Williams

Odell Mothersill was flying home, speeding through Washington Square Park, the first dried leaves of autumn, carried on a slightly chilling wind, swirling and scraping on the walk beneath his feet. The arch was lighted and the streetlights up Fifth Avenue gleamed in the dark. Down here it was quiet, the pace more civilized, even, as now, promising excitement. His stomach was filled with spaghetti, and his head buzzed nicely with wine. He touched Shirley's elbow and she turned and smiled at him, nudged him with one of her ample hips.

Shirley, matching him stride for stride, although he was the taller, smiled again at his obvious eagerness. It pleased her to think that he'd been waiting for these two weeks.

He'd come into the bar in the afternoon with that older fellow she often saw there, and she was sure they'd come to see her. Shirley accepted the fact that when she was on duty, the patrons were far more numerous than when she wasn't.

Now Mothersill smiled as they moved quickly past the empty fountain. Gibson had taken him to the Emperor's Bar after the conference. Like most adoption agency conferences, it had been long and dry, with half the white people there scared to death because they were in Harlem. But, since the Catholics had great inroads to the black population, weaning people away from the Methodists and Baptists—and the people had been eager to break away from these fundamental religious ties—there had come under the jurisdiction of the Church more and more black orphans requiring homes. So it was fitting that the conference took place uptown. Old Man Gibson, long a figurehead in the city's adoption programs, took Mothersill to the Emperor, his tongue clacking in his mouth, so badly did he claim the need for a drink. "And besides," he'd said, "they got this fabulous bartender, got the biggest tits in the world. Name's Shirley. And, Odell, I tell you I've done some of everything there is for a man to do, but I haven't been able to get next to Shirley."

They drank their first martinis like they were water, and then Mothersill studied the bar and Shirley. The bar was at least fifty feet long and could accommodate as many men leaning on it and another fifty behind them. There were a hundred pairs of eyes on Shirley, who walked proudly from one patron to the other, moving with a grace and sexuality that Mothersill felt grinding in his genitals after the third drink. Normally gin was not his drink, but the Catholics had driven him to desperation; he was glad he worked for a nondenominational adoption agency.

Mothersill and Shirley walked out of the park and hurried between the old dark garages and factories that were almost indistinguishable from the New York University apartments and office buildings. He slipped his hand into Shirley's and they increased their pace, neither noticing how heavily they were starting to breathe.

Shirley liked the feel of his hand. His taking hers was a gesture she associated with him, like the shyness that came through at the bar that day; or like his smile, which wavered somewhere between the streetwise grimace she was so used to and a schoolboy's nervousness. One got tired of being hit on by anyone who'd bought a couple of drinks. Just because she worked in a bar didn't mean that she did not want to be treated with consideration. Odell was a stranger in the bar that afternoon; she'd spotted it in a minute. A man of some other cut than she was used to. She smiled again, thinking how often she'd wiped the bar before him, leaning way over so he could peruse her breasts. That way, she could look at him and study his expression. Joy. Not that hard, measuring quality of some of the glances—most of the glances she got. A young, exuberant kind of joy. She had said, "Yes, lover," when he'd asked if he could take her to dinner, "Yes, lover," to his popped-eyed astonishment. But she had been sure that he wouldn't call, that she'd been talking to his martinis and they'd been talking to him.

A half block from his apartment building, Mothersill slowed; he had it made now. Earlier he'd plucked Shirley down from the upper floors of Esplanade Gardens and eased her past the big guards who paced the lobby, their great buttocks jangling guns, keys, and flashlights, and A-trained her downtown. He'd promised to show her something of the Village and had told her that of course she could wear her toreador pants and spiked silver heels. She'd been a hit, even in the Village. Now they were heading home and a heavy, warm erection began in Mothersill's pants. But he knew she wasn't one of those women you grabbed from behind while they stared at your bookshelves. Oh, no. With Shirley, you would not do anything until she was ready for you to.

Ahhhhh, he thought when they were in his apartment and he was helping her off with her poncho, the tiddies on this woman!

"It's nice," Shirley said, looking around. "Is that color TV?"

"No," Mothersill said.

"Shit."

Mothersill glanced quickly at her. "Sit down."

"Turn on TV?"

He hesitated for a moment. How could he refuse? Could he lie and say it was broken? But if she found it wasn't she might leave. He was suddenly filled with hatred for the object, which, until they walked into the room, had been inanimate, without life, a collection of glass, plastic, and cheap metal. "Go ahead," he said, miffed. Mothersill was also puzzled. Only moments ago Shirley seemed to have nothing on her mind save being alone with him. But now she was crouching before the set, when ordinarily there'd be small talk about the record player, the couch, the carpet; that was the way it was with other dates. (For as shy as Mothersill appeared to be, he was sublimely unaware of it.) The talk would move from one thing to the next, easily as Romans spoke of stuffed grapes, battle, and nubile Nubian slaves.

For Shirley, TV was companion and comfort—and also a mechanism of defense. She lived alone on 120th Street, just off Lenox; that is, she was constantly living alone and enjoying it. She was free to see whom she wished, but at the end of the afternoon shift at the bar and the grabbing, clutching eyes, the softly dropped suggestions, she enjoyed being alone with her TV set. Even when she was away from it the voices kept her company. TV allowed her to enter a world outside her own. Sometimes at the bar she found herself talking like one of the characters in a morning serial.

The set was a defense now because it was approaching *that* time. To be sure she had looked forward to making love with Mothersill; there was something, she thought, so young, different, and unstreet-like about him. She did not know that they were the same age, but she did feel that working among men, and having known many of them in many places, including bedrooms, she was wiser about them than most women. But now it had come down to the same thing. The hand-holding was over; the sweet talk, Mothersill's bashful smile, would vanish. It was bedtime and she wished to hold onto her illusions of TV love and romance.

In the kitchen, Mothersill fixed Shirley a strong drink and listened to the sounds coming from the set. TV, he sniffed. Here in Odell Mothersill's crib and she wants to look at TV. But her smile was so bright when he gave her her drink that he was encouraged to place her head in his lap.

Shirley fluttered her lashes at him when she felt his penis hardening along the softness of her neck, and Mothersill, also aware of it and pleased that she did not move away, thought a sigh of relief. All was going to be fine, and he raised her face to kiss him.

Shirley tossed up a tongue like a piece of warmed-over chitlin; her attention remained on the set. Mothersill cupped one of her famous, large breasts, trying to make her turn away from the TV. She made a sound and he chose to accept it as one indicating that, if he mined deeply enough, he'd find some passion; he rejected its being a sound of annoyance, which was precisely what Shirley was trying to convey. Mothersill slid his hands beneath her blouse. Wow! These is some tiddies, he thought. He ran his hands around her buttocks, which were encapsulated in a panty girdle, and then back to her breasts. Only then did he become aware that the program she was watching was ending.

Resignedly, Shirley leaned forward, starting to undo her blouse. Might as well get it over with, since it was going to be the same old thing, only with a Greenwich Village setting. "You want to get with it, right?" she asked, sounding as if she was asking a patron to repeat his order at the bar.

Mothersill nodded dumbly.

Shirley undid the blouse, the snaps on her bra. The shoes, stockings, panty girdle panties, and there it was solid, plentiful. She smiled at him as he rushed out of his own clothes. Shirley thought it was cute.

"Oooo," she said when she reached out and stroked his penis. Sure can't tell much about these quiet ones, all that still water running deep. Mothersill ran his fingers over her broad, sloping shoulders, kissed the breasts which, although large, were firm and shaped, and ran his hands up between her legs and felt her tremble. They first knelt and then lay down on the rug, commercials on the set ending in the background. They kissed, felt, moaned until Shirley, feeling once again a curiosity about this thin, angular man, pulled him to her. Just before he entered, a new program began and Shirley rolled away from him. "Hey! I forgot. *Cheyenne* is on. That's my man, Odell. I don't miss *Cheyenne*." And she didn't. Every week she watched the tall, dark-haired cowboy who spoke as though his tongue was located in his throat. He was big and strong, but there was about him, too, a quality of gentleness she loved in one so capable of breaking people in two. Shirley patted Mothersill on the cheek, her eyes on the set, while Mothersill, astounded, held his melting penis captive by the scruff of its circumcised neck.

For forty-five minutes, he watched and listened as Shirley cried: "Kick his ass, Cheyenne! Whomp! Aw, do it, Cheyenne!" She paused between exclamations to smile at Mothersill. He, however, was willing his limp penis to rise, but the flesh was weak, mortified and unable to sustain his imagery. Finally it sulked between his thighs as if seeking a hiding place.

When the show was finally over, Shirley turned off the set and lay down on the rug, drained. "Now," she said, waiting, holding up her arms, anticipating his warmth and slimness, him in her.

But Mothersill remained motionless. He wished for the most massive of erections, so he could beat her to death with it, send her into the street on her knees. How was it that she could go from about to making love to *Cheyenne* and back to wanting to make love again without a change of pace? No niceties. No feel for mood, atmosphere. Just rip off some here, a little here, bam-bam. Now, he thought, his penis dangling impotently between his trim thighs, his rage short-circuiting his desire.

Shirley turned and looked at him, saw his cold eyes and knew instantly, if not frighteningly, that this was not the boy-man she had taken him to be. This awareness made her beat a fast retreat into a kind of barroom toughness. "Whatsa matter, you can't get it up?" she said as nastily as she could. This tone had shriveled up many a man.

Coldly, Mothersill said, "Get offa my rug. Put your clothes on and get out. You and your goddamn Cheyenne."

Shirley met such denunciations quickly and vigorously. She jumped to her feet and began pulling on her clothes. "That's cool, faggot. You can't get it up, I might as well leave."

With a sinking feeling, for he felt himself rising lazily, Mothersill watched her smooth brown muscles flowing and jerking under her skin as she dressed; his mouth dried instantly when he understood that he was not going to kiss or suckle her breasts; she had rejected him, his gift to her. His pleasure would have been drawn from giving her pleasure. Old cracker antebellum term—pleasuring. But Shirley was shouting at him:

"All you cats living down here is faggots anyway!"

He recoiled, and almost watched his own words emerge and hang in the air: "Cheyenne is a faggot." He saw that she was stung now; the implications inherent in digging faggots was too much. But, momentarily mesmerized, examining the meaning of his words as intently as he, and noticing for the first time an ominous tone, heavily larded with contempt, Shirley fought back: "No he ain't no faggot, he's a man."

Mothersill backed up and looked at her. This was silly, he realized. Didn't she, too, realize how silly it was, arguing about—Now he shouted, "What're you talkin' about, woman? *Somebody made him up and took his picture.*"

"—you're just jealous!" she stormed, watching him narrowly; his words carried an unfamiliar import, and she didn't want to hear any more. Quietly, with the air of finality she had used with drunks a thousand times over the bar, she said, "I'm ready. You takin' me to a cab?"

Bitterly, but just as quietly, Mothersill asked, "Baby, does Cheyenne have wings?"

He watched her stamp to the door, snatch it open, and pull it closed behind her with all her strength. *Blam-lamm!* The paintings on the walls bounced and flapped.

With a mixture of rage and sadness, Mothersill thought, Aw, she'd make a rotten mother anyway. Then, damn, Shirley, this isn't the way it's supposed to be.

1-800-CONNECT

Brian Peterson

It was creeping up on 10:30. I knew this because my eyes were getting heavier, my body begging to go horizontal. Same thing happens most weeknights around this time. That 6 A.M. wake-up call catches up to me, as I guess it should. I hooked up my caffeine fix, French vanilla instant, kick-starting my second wind. There was still work to be done before I could call it a night. Always was in Mr. Carter's world.

Good thing was I'd already run through my lesson plans for the rest of the week, while Allen Ivy and his Philly crew were running through the Celtics earlier in the evening. Shut down Big Green's whole operation. I remember when Bird and the boys used to have the East on lock. Back when Dr. J was finger-rolling, Magic was no-look-passing, Isaiah was knocking down pull-up jumpers, and Moms was fussing at me about doing my homework in front of the TV. I always told her it wasn't a thing, my brain could handle both. My mostly A's backed up my claim. Fourth quarter was the only part I really watched anyway, when the game was on the line. Ain't nothing changed, 'cept the Celts' winning ways.

As I thumbed through a stack of eleventh graders' World History essays, catching bits and pieces of whatever the ten o'clock news deemed noteworthy that day, the cordless lit up on the end table. A pleasant-sounding recorded messenger told me that I had a collect call. And an all-too-familiar voice inserted the name "Naomi Campbell."

Of course I accepted the charges. Wouldn't you?

"Naomi! Been a long time, girlfriend. What's crack-a-lacking?"

"Um, excuse me. Supermodels neither crack nor lack," she sounded out, prim and proper.

"Oh, my bad," I replied with as much seriousness as I could muster. "I didn't know it was like that. Well, what's been going on? How's Mr. Diddy treating you?"

"Mr. *Who*?"

"Diddy. You know, P. Diddy. Got the keys to your city. Bad Boy for life. Heard on the radio that you and him were an item now that J-Lo done hopped the broom."

"Well, you shouldn't believe everything you hear on the radio. If he and I were making the rounds, why would I be calling you?"

"Good point, playa. But even better, if you were really Naomi Campbell, why would you be dialing my broke ass collect? Shouldn't you have the million-minute titanium plan?"

We both broke into laughter, signaling the end of our role-play. For now . . .

"How's the conference going?" I asked "Naomi," better known as Satchelle, my girlfriend of two and a half years and roommate of seven months. She was named after Satchel Paige, probably the greatest man to slang fire over homeplate, Negro League or otherwise. Her Pops was a Negro league historian. We had a whole lot to talk about at her family reunion this past summer.

"The conference is about as boring as it could possibly be," she replied, clearly not pleased. "My highlight today was the smoked salmon at the luncheon."

"That bad, huh?"

"Let's put it like this . . . after sitting through those morning sessions, hoping for a single shred of useful info, I could have gotten half a tuna hoagie and some stale chips, and that would have been my highlight. But I present tomorrow, then I'm outta here. Job done, thank the Lord. How was your day?"

"Well, in Econ, Juwan figured that forty acres and a mule would now equate to a 6-apartment condo and an Escalade, and he's got a crew of homeys ready to launch a campaign to get what's overdue. Then in the afternoon, Miss Angelette put her entire class out again, so I had an extra fifteen homeless students for half of sixth period."

"I think she's doing this on purpose. She's jealous because she knows they like you better."

"I think you're right. But you know what? None of her kids gave me any problems. They sat right there on the floor and took notes."

" 'Cuz they know Mr. Carter don't play that," she laughed.

"Ya damn skippy. My room, my rules," I boasted, like I've been known to do sometimes. "Oh, but let me tell you the line of the day. Jonelle announced that she's not happy with her mock portfolio. She wants her group to buy stock in hair weaves."

"Hair weaves?"

"Hey, I told them to invest in what they consume. And God knows that child is dropping some bills to keep her mane tightened up, so I can see why she'd be looking for a return on the investment, other than Friday night movie dates. But for some reason we had a little problem finding weaves on the ticker."

"Give it some time. I'm sure they'll go public soon," she laughed.

"The world will always need synthetic hair," I laughed back.

"Miss me, Marcus?"

"Maybe," I replied, staring at the other end of the living room sofa, where she'd be right now if she was in town, legs wrapped around mine, reading through a pile of photocopies for one of her grad school classes.

"Maybe?"

"You know I do, girl."

"Tell me why you miss me," she said in that innocently sensual voice that always stirred my imagination. Especially over the phone.

I thought back to how it used to be. Before I met her. The games I played with other women. The games they ran back on me. The searching, but not knowing what I was looking for. Not being ready to see it even if it was looking at me. The insecurities. The unreturned phone calls. The hanging on for no good reason. All the bullshit that didn't need to be.

I was taking a break when I met Satchelle. At least, that's what I called it. Actually wasn't looking when I bumped into her at First Fridays, a monthly social mixer for the "young, urban professionals" in town. Both of our first times going back there in a long minute. Both of us not sure why we came. Feeling a little out of place, but happy to have struck up a decent enough convo with each other. Feeling each other out, searching for clues but careful not to open up too much, too soon. It was hard, though, for me anyway. The way her breezy summer dress flowed and dipped, clinging to her curves, and how the humid evening air on the terrace gave her brown skin that glistening, postsex glow. Those things first caught my eye. Damn, how I wanted to touch her. But each time she spoke, each time she laughed, each time I knew she wanted to look at me longer, but broke away with a smile—those things caught my heart and made me want to *know* her.

There were so many reasons why I missed her. She made me feel sane again. Added a balance that I hadn't recognized was missing but subconsciously knew I'd been longing. She talked and she listened. I'd dated others who could only do one of the two. Some couldn't handle either. But sometimes Satchelle was so good that she didn't have to say a word. Her look would tell it all. Calm. Caring. Compassionate. It made me focus in on everything we had, everything that was really there, and not what I fooled myself into seeing with women before her. For the first time, the picture looked right. Felt right. Was right.

"As corny as this sounds," I said to her, and to myself, "you've made my house into a home. So it hasn't felt like home without you here these past few days."

She paused for a second. I could feel her smile lighting up on the other end.

"You want some, don't you?" she asked.

"Now you know I don't just say nice stuff when I want some. I'm a gentleman."

"But you do want some, don't you?" she said with a little more spice.

"Well . . . you know . . ." I replied, smiling.

"Been thinking about me, huh?"

"Daily. Hourly. Completely. You?"

"Why do you think I called?"

"Speaking of which, what's up with your cell? What made you call collect?"

"The cellie's charging in the corner. The cord wouldn't make it to the bed so I had to use the room phone."

"Oh, you're in the bed. About to go to sleep, are we?"

"No, not just yet," she replied, her voice slipping in a sliver of sensual mystery.

"Reading?" I asked, baby-stepping into the intrigue.

"Nope."

"Journal?"

"Did that earlier."

"So . . . why are you still up?"

"Because I was thinking about you. I needed to hear your voice. Needed to feel you. Needed to connect."

Her last three words were breathed, not spoken. Dipped in a yearning passion, sprinkled with cinnamon desires. Made the whole living room warmer while my insides tingled with anticipation.

"Do you feel me?" I asked, anxious to continue this tango. To feel more of her heat.

"I hear you, but I don't feel you."

"Well, how can we change that?"

"I want you to tell me a story."

"What kind of story?"

"A good story," she purred.

"Where should I begin?"

"I've already begun, dear. Sitting here all alone in this hotel room does things to a girl. Especially when she's missing her man back home. So I need you to help me finish what I've started."

"Oh, it's like that?"

"It's like that and then some," she said, sealed with a soft moan.

I imagined her stretched out on the hotel room bed, queen-sized, only the bedside lamp and her libido turned on. Her hair pulled back, her peach satin negligee inched up her smooth, perfectly thick thighs. Her fingers moist, standing in for mine, doing the things mine have done to her over and over. Her legs parting on their own, two fingertips stroking faster, disappearing into her wetness.

My own hand reached down and stroked the growing hardness that poked through my sweatpants. Rubbed my tip through the cotton, thinking about how much I missed her body heat, her kisses, her love. My head sank back into the sofa cushions, eyes closed. Only seeing her in my thoughts.

"Are you still on the bed?" I asked.

"Yes."

"No you're not."

"Where am I?"

"You're right here in the living room, on the sofa, next to me. You're in my old Gap button-down. The one you wear around the apartment all the time."

"You like me in your shirt, don't you?"

"I do. The way you leave the top buttons undone so your bra peeks out. You know I like that. I'm easing to your side of the sofa and slipping off your reading glasses. Now I'm kissing your cheek, your lips, your forehead, your neck. Slowly. Not missing a spot in between. Undoing a button. Then another. Then another. Rubbing your shoulders. Slipping the shirt down your back. Tracing a trail with my fingers. Taking my time."

"Then what?"

"You've got your black bra on. The sheer one. Your nipples are poking through, getting harder, thinking about what I'm going to do to them."

"You see them?"

"I see them. I'm tasting them through your bra. Teasing them. Now I've undone the clasp and am sliding the straps off your shoulders. I'm massaging your breasts. Barely grazing them with my fingertips. Then cupping them, rubbing them. Stroking your nipples between my thumb and fingertip. Feeling them rising."

"I love the way your hands feel, the way you touch every part of me. Even though my breasts are too small."

"They're not too small. They're perfect. Why do you think I spend so much time there?"

"You do give them an awful lot of attention. They appreciate the love," she giggled.

"I hope you're ready for more 'cuz I'm about to give it to you. I'm licking your nipples now. Circling my tongue around them, over and over and over again. Slow then fast. Fast then slow. Wrapping my lips around them. Do you feel me?"

"I feel you," she moaned.

"Are you touching them?"

"Yes," she whispered. "Yes . . ."

"My fingers are moving down your body. I'm kissing your stomach. Your thighs. Stroking the back of your legs. Kissing your knees . . . your ankles . . . your feet. Watching you squirm. Listening to your body call for me."

"Oooooooh . . . Like this?" she whispered, dizzying my emotions with her midnight music.

"Just like that," I said, reaching into my sweats, stroking faster. "Now I'm moving back up, fingers tracing up your legs. Sliding off your panties. Feeling how warm you are. Kissing your thighs. Licking. Teasing. Touching you there. Right along the edges. Then sliding slowly inside. Watching your face smile with that delightful tension as you feel me. Touching your wetness. Feeling you ride against my fingers, wanting me. Needing me."

"Now what?" she begged, patience giving way to the frenzy of our impromptu liaison.

"You know what's next. You want it, don't you?"

"Yes . . . you know I want it . . ."

"I'm giving it to you. Tasting you. Licking you exactly where I know you like it. That special spot. Are you touching it?"

"Yes . . . yes . . ." she said, her breaths getting heavier. Words more difficult to finish.

"Pull me to you," I commanded. "Wrap your hands around my head. You know I love when you do that. I want to know I'm making you feel good."

"You are . . . God, it feels good . . . so, so good."

"My tongue is moving faster. Darting around your spot. Flicking over it over and over again. Making you grab onto me. Your fingers digging into the back of my neck. Wanting me even more."

"Marcus . . . ," she whispered. "Give it to me. Give it all to me."

"You want all of me?" I asked, wanting to feel the yearning in her voice.

"Right now, baby. Right now," she pleaded.

"I'm leaning overtop of you. Looking down at your beautiful brown body. Kissing your lips. You're touching me with both your hands. Rubbing me. Stroking me. Getting me ready."

"Do you feel me, baby? Do you feel me touching you?"

"I do. Your hands feel so good wrapped around me, guiding me inside of you. I'm pressed against you now. My tip moistened by your love. Your fingertips press into my back as I enter you. I'm going slowly. Easing inside of your walls. Watching you watch me. Feeling you feel me as I get deeper. Then your eyes close. You lean back, curving your body into me. Taking me even deeper. Your legs wrap around mine. Pulling me into you each time I push. You feel so warm around me. Makes me never want to leave. Makes me want to be with you like this forever and a day. You feel that?"

"I felt it the first time you were inside of me, Marcus. And every time since. I feel it every morning when we wake up together. And every time you tell me you love me."

"I do . . . you know that don't you?"

"I do . . . Oh, how I do . . ."

Together, we had left the places that we were. Left our isolation and whatever had been on our minds earlier in the day. We connected in this other space and time where our words and the passions that formed them became a living, soulful lust, the deepest desire being to please each other and to know that the other was being pleased. We touched each other through each other's thoughts.

We spoke to each other with each other's love. We soaked each other with each other's happiness. We were apart, but more together than even we could understand.

Touching myself as we caressed each other with sensual words, I was taken back to my first time, when I didn't know what I was doing. Damn sure didn't know why either, embarrassed as hell, feeling guilty and afraid of going blind. But I did it anyway. I wanted to know what it was like to be with a woman. Why they made movies and wrote stories about it. Why all of my friends talked about it or wanted to listen to someone else who knew more preach on the topic. But at fourteen, I didn't have a woman. I'd only ever been on first base about a half-dozen times, spinning bottles in friends' basements. Youthful impatience made me want to know more.

I'd felt it rise before plenty of times, during R-rated clips of nudity on cable, or when I stared too hard at the older girls in the neighborhood, their summer tank tops filling out on their own, no longer needing Kleenex. I knew in that rise was where it started and ended. So I took matters into my own hand.

That night in the bed I slipped off my PJ bottoms. I'd never slept nude before. Never had a reason to. I took my fourteen-year-old dick in my hand, stroking slowly. Rubbed its tip against my sheets. Thought about Tameka from down the block in her tight Jordaches. Lost myself in the heat of my Jody Watley crush back then. I daydreamed about things I only had slight clues of, creating my own fantasy world of cheerleaders, slow-grinding, and long, nasty tongue kisses. My hand moved faster, with a mind of its own. I felt this thing building up inside. This thing that I'd never felt before. This thing that I couldn't stop. That I didn't want to stop.

Then . . .

Satchelle cried out that she was coming. That was all I needed to hear to push me over the edge. My breath stopped, my body clenched, and I listened through the phone to her sweet sounds being sung from so far away but touching me so closely.

We both lay there in silence afterwards, catching our breath. Returning back to earth. Our post-coital moment, lighting a virtual cigarette. We giggled about our little episode as I took the cordless to the bathroom to scoop up a towel. She joked about needing a cold shower and an earlier flight back home to me. Then we wished each other a good night and hung up our phones. I went into our bedroom, climbed into our bed, and set the alarm for an hour earlier than usual. Those student essays would get looked at tomorrow, instead of my morning paper. I stretched out in the space where she'd be if she were here, again thinking back to before. How far I'd come. How good we were. How we made each other feel tonight.

Back in my early teens, I knew I'd had a wet dream or two before. I remembered feeling something happening in the middle of the night, waking up the next morning and stuffing my PJ's in the bottom of the hamper. But those dreams were just my subconscious leading me through unscripted fantasies that I couldn't recall. That night, the night I did it myself, I was in control. It was so much different than before. Like the difference between fucking and making love. The difference between saying you love someone and devoting yourself to them. The difference between Satchelle and all the rest.

Rock Me Baby

Earl Sewell

It was late in the evening and I stood at the edge of the pier wearing a loose-fitting pair of drawstring baby blue slacks, with my hands stuffed deep inside of my pockets. I was twirling a piece of lint between my thumb and fingers while I gazed out at the horizon on the Pacific Ocean. I closed my eyes and took a deep breath. I could smell the threat of a rain shower in the air. I'd been in Hawaii for about six weeks, mixing business with vacation while redecorating my cottage on the island of Maui. I was supposed to fly back to San Diego the day before but I got side-tracked and dropped everything for a woman I'd met a month ago.

Being side-tracked by a woman was not like me. I'd made a promise to myself long ago that I'd never allow a lady to manipulate me, trigger irrational reactions, or influence my thinking in a way that I didn't enjoy. My logic was a safety net I'd set up out of fear of losing command over my emotions. Promises are all the same, however; someone will always force you to break them. Angela must have placed some kind of Polynesian Voodoo Root on my behind because I thought about her constantly, damn near to the point of obsession.

A sudden breeze whisked past me from behind, bringing with it the soft melody of Angela's voice calling my name. I turned around to face her as she strolled toward me. She was carrying a lei and wearing a white V-neck sleeveless sundress with a yellow flower print pattern. She had a flat, oval face with blemish-free sugar-brown skin, distinguished eyebrows, and engaging eyes.

"Aloha, my love." I loved the tone of her voice and her sensual way with words. I bowed my head as she placed the lei around my neck. She gradually unbuttoned the top three buttons on my shirt, rubbed my chest and twisted my nipples until they became hard like tiny pebbles. I was fond of the attention that she gave me; most ladies I'd dated over the years were stiff when it came to public displays of affection. I removed her hand, wanting to kiss her fingers, but she insisted on having things her way. She twirled her index finger around the tip of my tongue. A naughty girl's grin spread across her lips, and a playful twinkle formed in her eyes. She removed her finger from my mouth and tapped the tip of my nose. She had me exactly where she wanted me, in unfamiliar territory. Angela turned around and headed back down the pier twitching her round and voluptuous behind, which placed me in a trance.

I followed her down the pier to where she'd left her luggage. We were driving my boat from Honolulu to Maui. We had been spending a lot of time snorkeling, exploring the rain forests on the islands, and talking about our childhoods. After I returned the boat, I was going to fly home to San Diego and get back to my nine-to-five, or at least that was the plan. Angela's bags were heavy as hell. When I asked what she had in them, she just winked her eye at me and climbed aboard. There was so much mystery about her and I was not accustomed to dating mystery women. Yet I found myself trusting her like I'd never trusted anyone before. It was something about the confident way she carried herself. It was as if she had no doubt that everything was going to go the way she planned it.

We shoved off toward the island of Molokai, which was the "hot" island for tourists seeking fun before Maui got popular. Once we were a good distance from the shore, she told me to slow the boat down because there was no need to rush. I disagreed with her because the clouds above had turned from fluffy white to threatening shades of gray and black. It was certainly going to rain and rain hard.

"Be a little daring, my love," she suggested. "It's only water." She blew me a kiss and then ducked down and went belowdecks.

I sat down at the stern and continued on. When she returned, she set a duffle bag down beside me.

"What's in the bag?" I asked.

"There you go asking questions again, my love." She took a step closer, reached over me, and removed the key from the ignition.

"Twist the seat around and turn your back toward me. I have a game that I'd like to play." That was one of the things that turned me on about her. She always had little games that she wanted to play, naughty games, and being a freak at heart I was all for it.

"Close your eyes, my love, and keep them closed while I prepare you for an adventure," she said, and a twinge of excitement rushed through me as I shut my eyes. *An adventure*, I thought to myself, *how much freakier could we get*? I heard a loud clamping sound as she placed handcuffs on my ankles and locked them to the steel seat post beneath me.

"Whoa! What are you doing? And where in the hell did you get shackles?" I snapped at her, because being locked up was not what I had in mind. On top of that, I wouldn't be in any position to stop anything that she would do.

"Trust, my love. You must trust me." She leaned toward my ear. "You have to learn how to release your control over your emotions and enjoy all of the delights that pleasure offers." She traced the lines of my ear with the tip of her tongue. Before I knew it, I became liquid, like an ice cube left on a hot stove. Angela was such a cunning fox; while I was basking in the glow of pleasure, she cleverly reached into her bag, swung my arms behind my back, and handcuffed my wrists. The sound of the rapidly clicking handcuffs brought my ass back from la la land.

"Wait a minute, I'm not comfortable with this. You've got to set me free." I began attempting to jerk myself loose. She slapped me on the jaw with the palm of her hand and it stung. She rotated the tips of her fingers in a circular motion, massaging away the sting. She kneeled down and met my gaze with eyes filled with mischief.

"Be a good boy, my love, and do everything that I say." She rubbed her cheek against my own. "Or you will walk the plank." She placed her hand on Hannibal and gave him a good squeeze. He got so damn hard that he threatened to bust through the fabric of my pants.

"I see that Hannibal understands my intentions. Sometimes the little head is much smarter than the big head." She knew just what to say and how to phrase it. Angela was turning my ass out and I knew it. She reached into her duffle bag, pulled out a coral-colored silk scarf, and covered my eyes with it. She leaned forward, nibbled on my earlobe, and spoke with an aggressive tone.

"Pirates have taken over your ship. The captain of the boarding ship is a woman named Cleopatra and she's a real pistol. She has been sailing all over the Pacific Ocean in search of a mighty cock called Hannibal. Rumor has it that you're the man who can lead her to him. But she's also heard that you're the type of man who doesn't like to let go of anything, especially information. So she's going to torture you until you submit and give her what she wants."

"Oh, yeah," I responded with a mannish tone. "Tell her that I'm not giving up without a fight."

"Good. She will be pleased to hear that." She got another silk scarf and used it as a gag for my mouth. I laughed, hardly believing that I was actually playing along with this game of hers. I was all for some freaky shit but this was an entirely different level of kinky. She told me to brace myself because Cleopatra was near, and then there was silence. After a moment, I heard the faint sensual sounds of Angela moaning. *What in the hell was she doing?* I wondered to myself.

Suddenly the wind began picking up from the west. I could feel the boat being rocked hard and tossed about. I could hear the faint grumble of thunder off in the distance. From what I could tell, a nasty thunderstorm was headed our way and moving fast. Angela and I would have to play this game another day. I muttered her name as best as I could but I got no response. *Shit!* I thought to myself as I began to panic, I didn't want to be struck by lightning. *Where in the hell did she go?*

At the moment when I was between terror and desperation, she puckered her lips and blew a breath of warm air on the side of my neck. I quivered.

"My fingers have been playing with Cleopatra. She told me that she enjoyed observing you while I made her hot. She wants to make you her sex slave," she whispered as her moist fingertips traced my lips. I maneuvered the tip of my tongue around the gag to scoop up and taste her sweet nectar. I felt her fingernails scrape across my chest and then down my belly. My skin was so sensitive to her touch that a queer sensation shot through the length of my body, which caused me to start panting heavily. I kept swiveling my head from right to left, attempting to figure out where she was going to strike next.

"I'm going to take great pleasure in breaking you in."

Suddenly I heard the sound of fabric being sliced. I could feel her cutting upward toward my neck. She yanked swiftly, cutting the last piece of material that held my shirt together. She placed the stiff and razor-sharp blade against my skin.

What in the hell was she doing with a damn knife? I asked myself. I was about to demand that she set me free because I didn't want to play her little game anymore, but then she placed her warm, moist lips on my neck and began kissing me. I felt safe as I exhaled, and tossed my neck back and let my eyes roll up in my head. I'd never experienced the thrill of being turned on and on the edge of fear at the same time. I needed to touch and caress her but it was impossible.

"You naughty boy. You can't get free. You're not in control of anything. I am." She said, "What I've got in store for you is so wicked that I get wet just thinking about it." *Damn! She's got a hot way with words*, I told myself. The wind began to howl and whistle. I could tell that the waves were getting larger because the motion of the boat became more violent. I heard the growl of thunder followed by the hissing sound of the rain splashing against the ocean. I thought for sure that Angela would end the game but she didn't.

The rain began falling fast and furious and although I was getting soaked, the rain felt gloriously warm, like a hot shower. I felt the blade tugging at the cuffs of my pants. She cut me out of them. Then she cut me out of my underwear. The rainwater bursting against my bare skin was highly erotic. She removed my gag and blindfold.

"I've been waiting for this," she said as a flash of lightning streaked across the night sky like a crack in a windshield. The lightning startled me because the threat of being struck by it was very real.

"Baby, we may have to continue this down below. Water conducts electricity and . . ." I didn't like being trussed up when that light show was going on outside.

"A bolt of lightning is nowhere near as hot as I am right now. Besides, you only live once and Cleopatra is tingling with a wild passion that you must satisfy." Angela cut me off midsentence, then removed her sundress, tossing it to the side. She didn't have a thing on under it. I watched with tingling anticipation as she stretched her arms out wide, allowing her brown skin to become slick with rainwater. I began to blink rapidly and shake my head because water was running down my forehead, into my eyes. Lightning flashed again and the crack of thunder that followed vibrated everything on board. The entire moment was surreal like a twisted dream but I was fired up by the risk of it all. Angela sat on my lap and allowed Hannibal and Cleopatra to merge.

"I want it rough!" she demanded as she kissed me forcefully and nibbled at my bottom lip. Her brown breasts were inviting.

"Put one in my mouth," I said, "and let me lick the water off of it."

She lifted her breast, holding it gently in one hand, and placed it on my lips. It turned me on, just flicking my tongue around her erect nipple, and slurping up nature's water off of her glistening skin. She tossed her head back, sighed deep in her throat, and thrust her hips against my body fast and hard. She dug her nails deep in my skin, looked me directly in the eyes, and told me that I was hitting her spot. Her gasps rose in pitch and I felt Cleopatra bathing Hannibal with her nectar. She continued her vigorous thrusting, causing her moans to become more frequent, intense, and dramatic. I wanted to touch, embrace, and caress her but it was impossible. My only option was to let myself go and enjoy the sensations that pleasure offered. My wet skin, the saturated warmth of her love tunnel, the soothing sound of rain splashing on top of the water, the feeling of being restrained, the rocking of the boat, the roar of the thunder, and the danger of being struck by lightning. Everything that I was experiencing was on a level I'd never achieved before.

We grinded into one another, pushing our desire to its limits, until finally an orgasm of magnificent magnitude began whirling around inside of me like a raging twister. It began consuming my entire body. I clinched a piece of flesh on her neck with my teeth. My orgasm released itself in a loud, jerky, and gratifying manner, which left me breathless, depleted, and dizzy. She placed my head against her chest while she continued churning her hips in a slow circular motion. It seemed she was far from being finished.

"Oooo baby, you had an awful lot of it stored up. I feel every drop of you." Angela said it with a purr, in a satisfied tone.

"I've never experienced a release that intense before in my life," I confessed.

The storm blew over just as quickly as it had come and a thick fog developed in its wake, making it difficult to see. Angela ducked down below deck to cut up some fresh fruit.

Where had I met this hellcat? Oh yes, I remembered. I met Angela at a stoplight in South Kihei. I was riding my gold and silver Suzuki Hayabusa motorcycle when she pulled up right next to me on the exact same motorcycle. The only difference was she had on a skintight Lycra riding outfit that matched the motorcycle. When our eyes met, she gave me a seductive grin, which was full of mischief. She pulled back the throttle on the motorcycle a few times, warning me that she could deal with anything I might pull. I just chuckled to myself because she didn't know whom she was toying with. When the light turned green, she pulled the throttle back hard, forcing the front wheel to leap upward in the air. She rode wheelie for about a hundred yards to the next stoplight.

I leisurely pulled up next to her, fascinated by her display of showmanship.

"Are you afraid to ride, really ride that bike, cowboy?" She looked at me, grinning as if she'd called my bluff. To her, I existed on the straitlaced side of society. My typical day was filled with coffee, meetings, and high doses of stress. As the chief operations officer of my corporation, I had no other choice. My motorcycle provided me with an outlet by altering my mood, and making me feel as if I were a badass with a fearless disposition. A rebel, an outlaw.

I smirked at her, then pulled back hard on my throttle, revving my bike up.

"Have you ever pushed the limit, and done the 160 mph that this bike can do?" I asked, more than willing to put her little attitude in check. She flicked her wrist, making her motorcycle roar, accepting the challenge.

"Are you single?" she asked.

I quickly answered yes as I pulled back the throttle a few times, causing the motor to growl with a rhythm.

Minutes later, we were speeding by the sugarcane fields with the next stoplight a good fifteen miles up the road; the only thing in front of us was open road and opportunity, so the setting was perfect for a careless contest of speed and skill.

"Do you know where the coffeehouse is up the road?"

I answered yes.

"The last one there buys the coffee," she smiled, and then winked at me.

I released my tongue and allowed it to moisten my lips. She'd ignited a fire deep within me and suddenly I was willing to take any risk. The light turned green and we both shot off to the sound of tires squealing against the pavement. Before I knew it, I was cutting 90 mph and she was right beside me, zooming along without fear. Out of the corner of my eye, I saw her fold over, resting her chest flat against the gas tank of the bike, and punch a passing gear.

I wasn't about to take that so I crouched down in the same fashion, feeling the machine vibrating against me, and opened that throttle up as wide as it would go. I quickly jumped from 90 to 130 mph and I was not about to slow down. I was moving so fast that the road came together from the sides and formed a point. The wind whistled past my ears, tugged at my hair, and pulled at my clothes. I'd begun to pass Angela and I wasn't about to surrender. At the rate of speed I was traveling, I was confident that she'd back down. However, as I shot up beside her, she held her position, going full throttle. She had nerves of steel and was totally unafraid of high speed. I glanced down at my speedometer; we were both traveling at 160 mph. I'd met a woman who had the guts to do anything, no matter how daring or dangerous. At that moment, I wanted to know everything about her.

When we pulled into the coffeehouse parking lot she turned off her motorcycle and removed her goggles. "God! That was intense," she said with a delicious charge in her voice, then began removing her riding gloves with her teeth, one finger at a time.

Her sassy style turned me on, excited me, and at that instant, I felt something deep within myself come alive. I suddenly felt energized by her very presence. I could tell immediately that she preferred to live on the edge, where outrageous acts were not uncommon.

Still, Angela was way too damn secretive and untamed. The only thing that I really knew about her was that she had once toured with a theater group as a tango dancer. She had a newspaper clipping framed and hanging on a wall in her apartment. The headline read, "Tango, an Irresistible Temptation." There was a photograph of Angela wearing a gorgeous evening dress with a generous split on the side. She had her back arched backward at a bizarre angle and her leg locked around the hip of a man with slick black hair and a keen profile, wearing a black tuxedo. The article went on at length about Angela's stage presence and uncanny ability to cast a spell over an audience and leave them totally captivated.

When I asked about it, she became very evasive. It was obvious that subject brought forth unpleasant memories. She offered me a few scraps of information, mere tidbits, but nothing that was worthwhile.

Shortly after my first visit to her apartment, Angela moved from Maui to Honolulu. That was a while ago.

Now, Angela surfaced from belowdecks with slices of fruit on a paper plate and glasses of wine. We made our way to the rear of the boat to sit down on the bench seat. I sat and she straddled me, placing her weight on my lap.

"Have you ever made love outside in a thick fog like this?" she asked, taking a sip of chardonnay.

"No, I can't say that I have. Have you?"

She released a girlish laugh. "No, but I've got a remedy for that," she said as her fingers placed a slice of pineapple in my mouth.

"You're such an untamed wildcat," I said while caressing her derriere. It was soft yet firm, delectably shaped, like a ripe plum.

The next day, we finally made it back to my summer home in South Kihei on the island of Maui. I went into my den and called my office in San Diego to let them know that I wouldn't be back for a few more days. When I returned, Angela was relaxing on the sofa, skimming a trade publication that featured an article on me. She glanced at me seriously as she read a few lines from the story.

"Forty-five-year-old Deon Humphrey is one of the wealthiest men in the computer graphics industry," she read aloud. "The young go-getter, who started his company fifteen years ago, states that his success is due to long hours, dedication, and a burning desire to succeed."

I smiled and took a mock bow.

Angela paused and nodded her head. "So you're an all work and no play kind of man."

Let Angela draw her own conclusion. I smiled. "I know when to play." I walked over to the phone. "I want us to go out to Bubba Gump's over in Lahaina and have dinner. You could tell me all about your career as a dancer while I satisfy my hunger for some jumbo shrimp."

Angela cringed. "I have to fly back to Honolulu."

"What do you mean? We just got here. I just told my staff that I wouldn't be back for a few more days so that I could spend time with you."

"Don't worry, my love," she responded with an innocent voice. "You'll see me again."

"Don't give me that crap!" I became irritated. "Why is it that one minute you're all over me and the next you don't have time for me?"

"Don't be angry." She attempted to caress my face but I jerked away. "I have important matters to attend to," she said, sighing.

"Come on, Angela, you're breaking my heart here." I was so upset because I had not planned on being alone. "When will I see you again?" I asked, changing my approach, fearing that I'd overplayed my hand.

"I'm not sure. I'll call you."

"What?"

"Shhhhh, don't raise your voice, my love. In time I will tell you everything that you want to know." She wrapped her arms around me, embracing me tightly.

What kind of woman was this? I sat there, sulking.

Looking deep into my eyes, she spoke in a manner that I'd never heard before. It was as if she were afraid to tell me the truth. "I like the way you treat me. You're not arrogant or abusive, and that's comforting to me. I'm just a little unsure about some things right now, and I need time to think. Now please, I need you to drive me to the airport. It's important that I get back as soon as possible."

Flights between the two islands only took twenty minutes, and the planes, usually turboprops, left regularly. After her plane took off, I boarded the next flight back to Honolulu. I couldn't stop myself; I couldn't function knowing that she had a secret that she couldn't share with me. I'd become obsessed with finding out what the mystery was. I needed to know why she was so cloak-and-dagger. I'd never been the type of man to hunt down a woman, a stalker, but since Angela had waltzed into my life, I'd found myself doing a multitude of things that I'd never considered in the past.

When I landed in Honolulu, I realized that my decision to fly there had been an irrational and emotional one. I had no idea where to look for her, so I decided to take a cab over to Waikiki Beach and sit under a table with a beach umbrella to think while I watched the sunset and ogled tourists. I thought maybe she was living a double life or was on the run from something or someone. I just had no clue. All I did know was that she was the most exciting, contagious, and irresistible woman I'd ever met.

Before I realized it, the sun had set and the nightlife in Honolulu had come alive. Just as I was about to head out to the street and hail a cab, someone extended a hand out to me.

"Do you want my arm to fall off?" I glanced up and saw Angela looking down at me.

"Is that tired Billy Dee Williams line supposed to work on me?" I asked with a bit of sarcasm in my voice.

"Come with me," she said, "I'll explain everything once we get there."

Angela rode me on the back of her motorcycle, which was a real switch for me. I was used to someone holding on to my waist with their cheek pressed against my back. Not vice versa. We stopped at a small, unmarked brick building. She opened the door, threw a switch and the lights came on. It appeared to be an old warehouse, which was undergoing construction to be turned into a theater. I followed Angela down the aisle and we went behind the stage, where there was a huge dance studio with polished wooden floors, dance bars, and floor-to-ceiling mirrors. She grabbed an envelope and a chair from the corner of the room and scooted the chair to the center of the floor. She told me to have a seat and open the envelope.

There were photos in the envelope. The first photo was of Angela wearing a face mask that covered her eyes, dressed in a stunning red beaded bikini costume that left very little to the imagination, with an exquisite headdress made with large red feathers. The second photo made my eyes buck because I'd never seen anything quite like it. It was another photograph of Angela. She had her torso twisted toward the camera with her arms stretched out wide like the wings of an airplane. She was wearing a Native American Indian feather headdress with a feather covering each breast and one covering Cleopatra. The rest of her body was painted with brilliant shades of yellow, green, blue, and red. She had on red high-heeled shoes that laced up around her ankles. She looked like some type of exotic female warrior. I sat there speechless, with my mouth gaping open at her beauty.

"You look like a cat has got your tongue," she chuckled, then walked over to the dance bar and rested her foot on it. She began stretching.

"Where were these photos taken? Mardi Gras?" I finally asked.

"Oh no, honey. Mardi Gras is much too tame for me. Those were taken during the parade of samba schools in Rio de Janeiro. I go to Carnival every year and dance for days at a time." I kept staring at the photo, thinking that I was way out of my league.

Angela changed the subject. "You surprised me tonight. I saw you through the bank window where I was standing. I didn't think that you were the type to follow a woman."

"Trust me," I said. "This is not the norm for me." I placed the photos back inside the envelope. A lascivious smile formed on my lips as I made a mental note to take time out and experience all of the wonders of Rio de Janeiro.

"It's a relief to hear that." She paused for a moment, took off her shoes, and placed her other foot on the bar. "I'm thirty-nine years old and I've been dancing since the age of six." Angela began offering more useful information about herself. "My family is from an island called American Samoa. I am a proud Polynesian woman who has dedicated most of her life to studying the performing arts of my culture and others'. I have a Ph.D. in theater and I've traveled to Asia, Spain, South America, and the U.S. mainland, absorbing all that I could. I know how to tango, salsa, samba, tap-dance, jazz dance, and hula dance. And if you catch me on a good day, I'll break it down for you like a sister in a hip-hop video."

"Well, move over Debbie Allen," I said with a smile.

"That's right!" Angela continued with a haughty tone. "I traveled around the mainland for several years with a theater company but I left the stage because of an obsessive and physically abusive husband. He was the man you saw with me in the newspaper clipping. We've been divorced now for five years. I used most of my life's savings to buy this building along with two friends of mine, Maria and Sonya, who are from Mexico and Spain. We are all dedicated to bringing our knowledge of other cultures here to Hawaii to share and to teach."

"So this was your big secret. Why didn't you tell me?"

"When I met you, I had no idea who you were. I was just out being a Betty-Bad-Ass and having fun that day. When you revealed to me that you were an affluent man, I instantly wanted to ask you for some monetary assistance to complete the construction, but I didn't want you to think that money was the reason I'm interested in you. I like you for the person that you are, and I just refused to place a black eye on our relationship. It was important for me to get back today because I needed to make a payment on the mortgage. I've fallen behind on it trying to complete the construction work. But I've found another way to raise the money needed to complete the theater."

"And what way is that?" I asked, curious as to what her solution was.

"Well, I'm going to start stripping at a gentlemen's club."

"What?" I said, surprised at the zaniness of her solution.

"Shit, Deon, I'm serious. Strippers can make as much as a grand a night. I've got the talent, the costumes, and the moves. Besides, my body does not embarrass me. Gravity hasn't got me yet. While in Chicago, I fell in love with blues music because it can be so suggestive and the perfect kind of music for my strip routine. Would you like to see what I've been working on?"

"Yes," I said with complete awe. She went over to a small closet and changed clothes. When she returned, she wore a trench coat and a black fedora-style hat with the brim curled down over one eye. She popped a CD in her boom box. A slow, sassy tune started playing that I instantly recognized. It was a very evocative blues song called "Rock Me Baby," being sung by Ike and Tina Turner.

"Rock me ba-bay! Rock me all night long!" Tina's voice was gritty, sexy, seductive, and provocative all at the same time.

Angela walked toward me with a swing in her hips that was mesmerizing. I crossed my legs at the ankles and leaned forward, completely intrigued by this woman. When she got to me, she placed one foot on Hannibal and massaged him with her toes. I glanced down at my lap as she wiggled her toes up my belly, to my chest, and finally into my mouth. I kissed her toes and she cooed. The girl most certainly had skills. She stepped back and untied the knot in the strap of her trench coat. She pulled the strap from around her waist, dangled it out to the side with the tips of her fingers, and finally let it drop to the floor. She turned her back to me, lifted the coat off of her shoulders and let it shimmy down her back. She removed one arm from the sleeve and flung the coat around her body in a dramatic fashion, as if she were a matador expecting the charge of a bull. She then dropped the coat. Angela had put on a black, skintight skirt with the zipper on her behind and a hemline that stopped at her ankles. She unzipped the skirt while she churned her hips hard and grainy like Tina's voice. She wiggled around some more, pulling the dress down until it finally fell to the floor. She had on a garter belt, a lace thong, thigh-high stockings, and a heart-shaped ass that I wanted to nibble on. She bent over at the waist, ran the palms of her hands down the backs of her legs to her ankles and shimmied her behind. She twisted around and flashed her eyes at me from under the hat. She moved toward me with a purpose in her step and a steamy glow in her eyes. She sat down in front of me Indian-style, making sure that I saw Cleopatra. She leaned back on her elbows, raised her long legs high in the air, and made the letter V.

"I want you to rock me—like my back ain't got no bones." Tina continued bellowing out the lyrics. Angela bent her legs at the knees and rotated them in a circular motion to the beat of the music, making sure that I was completely caught up in the spell that she was casting. She straddled me in the chair with her back turned toward me. She flexed her butt cheeks and made them bounce up and down like a man can make his chest muscles bounce up and down.

"Roll me dad-dy—like you roll a wagon wheel." The lyrics turned raunchy, and Angela added emphasis by rotating her behind on Hannibal, who was at full attention. She gracefully removed herself from my lap and unclasped her bra, teasing me by gradually exposing herself bit by bit until she finally removed it completely. She had tassels around her nipples and she made them twirl around like the blades of a fan. She placed her thumbs under the fabric of her thong and swayed from side to side, pulling downward, with her eyes locked on me the entire time. Once her underwear hit the floor, I sprang to my feet and embraced her.

"Did you like my little performance?" Angela asked, knowing damn well she had me all fired up.

"Don't worry about the money for the construction work, baby. That type of dancing is private and reserved for my eyes only," I said, since I was certain she wasn't after me for financial gain.

"Is that a fact?" she answered with a smile in her voice.

"Yes it is," I answered, then I motioned for her to have a seat. "You're not the only one who knows how to strip, and perform a lap dance. Brace yourself for an adventure."

"Oh shit!" Angela said as she plopped herself down in the chair and crossed her legs. I quickly flipped through her collection of music and found a song that I hadn't heard in a long time. It was "Kiss" by Prince. I pressed play on the boom box then stood in front of her and rocked my hips in a sexual manner.

"How am I doing, baby?" I asked as I clinched my tongue between my teeth.

"Aw shit now! I see that you know a few freaky Prince moves." I winked at her and began singing along.

"You don't have to be rich, to be my girl, you have to be cool to rule my world." Angela licked her lips. I laughed and began tapping my ass with the palm of my hand. She made me feel like a revitalized man, a bold man, a sexy and dangerous man. I loved the way I was feeling. I stared transfixed at her while I ran the palms of my hands down my thighs and back up on the inside of my thighs. I turned my back to her and shimmied my behind to the fast plucking of the guitar. That move seemed to excite her because I noticed a horny glint in her eyes.

Angela was the woman for me and I had known it from the first time that we met. She was smart, ambitious, and sexually sophisticated. There was no way that I was about to let a woman that fascinating walk out of my life. I wanted to live on the wild side of life with her. I wanted her. I needed her. I wanted to make her happy and I was going to see to it that I did just that.

If It Makes You Happy

Cole Riley

You're not so damn tough and probably not so bright either, big man."

The woman looked directly at him when she said it. Her voice. It was the voice of a color: deep, dark red. Fiery, suggestive, and full of passionate promises. Her voice, rich-toned and throaty, was the first thing he noticed about her and the thing he would always remember about her. Her voice of sexy, crimson hymns.

He knew the moment his eyes saw the woman that trouble would soon be on his doorstep. She was handcuffed, metal confining her wrists behind her back, silhouetted against a high white wall. The guys from Hopewell Corrections Center were trying to figure out how she had managed to escape from her cell for three days before a traffic cop spotted her coming out of a fast-food joint. She never told how she did it. Now she was being admitted to Newton psychiatric facility for observation. Her behavior was deemed erratic at the time of her capture. He couldn't see it. She seemed calm and serene as she stood in custody. But it was what happened in the elevator going up to Processing that twisted his mind out of joint and started his obsession with her. With guards flanking her, she stood in front of him, her hands behind her, touching and caressing his genitals. Stroking him until his legs were almost buckling by the time the ancient elevator reached the seventh floor. She was something else, not your usual brand of woman.

"Don't forget me," she whispered to him as they led her away down the dimly lit corridor to the front desk.

And he didn't forget her. He was totally fixated on her. Being a guard at the facility meant he often saw her on the grounds, in the hall, or in the cafeteria. There were always people around her, usually men, laughing and talking loudly, so he had no access to this woman who was slowly driving him mad. He watched her eat, how her mouth with its large soft lips worked, how her long tongue flicked at its corners. He watched her walk, the smooth rolling of her wide hips, the inviting space between her thighs as she moved seductively among the other inmates. Once, coming up the stairs before him, she stopped, backed into him, and did a quick bending twist of her ass into his crotch. Oh, he was hooked. Totally and completely. Yet another black man bamboozled by lust and a hard dick.

"Don't forget me, sweetheart," she whispered to him again. An orderly, carrying a tray of meds, interrupted their chance meeting, standing watch until the couple exited the stairwell and went their separate ways. No fraternizing between staff and patients.

He never asked anyone her name. He wanted to hear it first spoken from her very own lips. In that dark red voice. The day before he tossed his life away because of lust, a vivid imagination, and a stiff libido was the first time they really talked. They squeezed into a supply room among shelves laden with towels, gowns, rubber gloves, and canisters of liquid soap. The woman was pressed close to him, too close for comfort, and notions of taking her right there flooded his mind. With her young, gorgeous, Lena Horne–looking self. The post–Cotton Club Lena, in full bloom. But everything had to be right. Exactly like he pictured it over and over every night as he lay in bed and touched himself. Her and her dark red voice.

"I see you watching me, every day, all day," she said, her eyes locked on his. "You don't have to say what you want. I know what you want because I want it too. But everything comes with a price. Nothing is for free, not in this world."

"I hear that," he replied, thrusting one hand into a pocket to subdue his growing excitement. "What is your name?"

"You know it. Don't play dumb. I hate an ignorant man." She stepped back some.

"I really don't know it. I didn't ask. I wanted to hear it from you."

That made her smile, the full soft lips parting like lush rose petals. "Amina. What's yours, Mister Man?"

"Terrance Stokes. My friends call me Terry. What is it you want? What is the price?" He moved back within kissing range, so close to her that she could feel the heat of his flesh through his cheap uniform.

"I want out," she hissed at him, the colored heat sparking in her words. "You get me out and you can have me anyway you want. Nothing is too kinky, too freaky. Anything you want but you must get me out first. Once I'm back in the world, baby, I'm yours to do with as you please. How does that sound?"

"Hey, I'm no fool," he said, afraid to admit to himself that he was even weighing such an offer. "How do I know you'll keep your end of the bargain? How? I'm risking everything here. My life will be fucked as soon as I break you out. It'll be over."

Amina laughed softly, the sound of it much like the tinkling of piano keys. She reached down, unzipped her hospital-issued pants, and inserted her fingers into herself. That got her squirming a bit and she coated her digits with her juice, laughed again, and brought them to his lips. Tart yet sweet, like the taste of an exotic fruit from a tropical island untamed.

She knew how to close a deal, playing on his dissatisfaction with his job and life, putting a spotlight on the collection of failures and disappointments that had hounded him from the very day he graduated from high school. He was a loser. But this would change things. It was a chance to tell the whole world to kiss his black ass. The entire planet, all the doubters and badmouthers. Now he was calling the shots in his life for once. Everybody would know his name, if only for a hot moment. His fifteen minutes of fame, coming right up.

Busting her out was not that hard. All it took was a few Benjamins for the guys at the main gate, some more for the crew on the supply truck, several lies and even more for the cat with the small plane to take them to the Texas border. The pilot, with his tiny Cessna eggbeater that shook and fluttered with every breeze, was spooky with his endless talk of the ancient Aztecs and their knack for human sacrifices. He didn't want to hear that mess. Just get them to the border. When it was all done, he was tapped out, very little green in his reserves. Spent some more bucks on a little cheap Tex-Mex grub and a rundown 1949 black Mercury Club Coupe. Slipped the Mexican guards a fistful of Yankee dollars, insuring that they were not stopped at the border nor were their suitcases opened and searched.

"When do I get a chance to collect?" he asked while they walked in an open market among the stalls, buying sombreros and sandals in a God-forsaken unnamed Mexican village. "When do I get my night? I've done my part."

"Be patient." She laughed, showing very few teeth. "I gave you my word."

They crossed the street to where the car was parked, in this area where gringos were rarely seen, especially black ones. He concluded that Amina was a beautiful pit bull with a mouthwatering body and vacant eyes, more *Hustler* than *Penthouse* and *Playboy*. The town was essentially dead, except for the burst of activity at the market. Walking together, they entered the battered hotel, its awning hanging by a couple of bolts, and went up to the desk where the somber man took their money and gave them a key.

"I'm beat, wore out," Amina mumbled. "I need some sleep. A few winks and I'll be as good as new. Then you'll get your surprise, big man."

She shed her clothes quickly and quietly, allowing him his first real look at her shapely brown body. It didn't seem to matter to her that he watched her so intently. The heat was stifling. He wondered if this was normal, if it was because of the diminished ozone layer or the abundance of satellites in the atmosphere. What was he doing with this crazy woman? He knew some things about her, much of her troubled history, her dark fugue states, her loose grasp of reality. Her criminal file was sealed, so much of the information he really needed to know was lost to him. Getting off the plane, she'd hinted she was a murderer, but didn't elaborate on that bombshell. Before she went to sleep, she told him she'd forgotten to bring her Thorazine when he broke her out of the state hospital back in St. Louis.

He laid on the bed beside her as she slept, their bodies clinging together with a sensual dampness, close in spoon fashion. Through the window, he could see an old man wearing a frayed sombrero leading a swaybacked mule packed with baskets of fruit slowly across the square. His red-lidded eyes followed the man's wobbly steps, one by one, until he disappeared from view. Amina stirred in slumber, mumbled under her breath, then flopped her curvy brown leg over his. Gently, he took her tiny hand in his big one and kissed it, noticing the diagonal lacerations along both wrists, deep and multiple. Tributes to her madness. He felt a strange compulsion to lick her wounds, softly and lovingly, but he moved closer instead to kiss her full on the lips. Suddenly she opened her hypnotic eyes, the stare in them still vacant and unforgiving, and did nothing while he tenderly planted kisses on her heart-shaped face.

"I think you're frightened of me," she said. "You know I killed somebody."

"But you explained that. You said it was an accident. You said he came at you wrong and you had to cap him. Shoot him before he raped you."

She worried her eyes with the heels of her hands. "Yeah, right, forced vaginal entry. He wanted to pop the coochie. I told you that but I left out some things."

"What did you leave out, Amina?" He couldn't afford to let her off the hook.

"Nothing I want to get into right now," she replied flatly.

Quietly, they laid on their sides, naked and sweating from the unnatural heat, pressing their fronts against one another full length. A total body hug. This was driving him over the edge, the nearness of her and her deep red voice, the touch of her soft bronze skin. Occasionally she kissed him, near the ear and on the neck, swift and popping kisses much like a boxer's jab. He couldn't stand it. But then nothing had gone exactly as he'd planned it. The thought that he couldn't go back to his old stale life lurked in the back of his mind, and then there was what she'd said: *But I left some things out*. What the hell did that mean?

To be honest, he didn't want to think about whatever she had not told him. But that was not cool either. What you didn't know could kill you. This was their third day together.

Finally, with some coaxing, she started talking, first about her family, about herself and her hospitalizations, and once she began, there was no stopping her. Her past suicide attempts. Both wrists, pills, overdoses. A dive off a four-story balcony, a fall broken by a landing on some bushes. Her walking in front of a car on the turn-pike. The things she heard and saw in her head. Paranoid, schizo-phrenic, slightly delusional, with psychotic thoughts. But none of that mattered. She was a beautiful black woman who had survived, was still standing despite everything, and maybe all she needed was some guy who loved her. Really loved her.

"What are we going to do if you get sick again?" he asked after the reality of her condition hit home. "We're on the run and there ain't a doctor or hospital for miles. Who knows what kind of care you can get down here?"

"What are you saying?" she asked, gazing up at the ceiling.

He watched her hungrily, naked, stretched out on the dingy white sheets. Her breasts and nipples seemed swollen, ripe for seduction, her long neck, her slightly rounded stomach, the triangle of short black curly hair between her damp thighs. While she chatted away, he scooted down so he could put his lips on the dark aureoles of her breasts. Even from there, he could smell the exotic scent of her sex. One of his big hands could barely conceal what this delicious vision of her was doing to him, his flesh hardening and throbbing, wanting to be inside her, if just for a moment.

"You know . . . with all this pressure and shit . . . anything can happen," he sputtered. "Hey, you haven't been out of lock-down that long and you're not back to your real self yet. And we don't have any pills to cool you out if something happens. I don't know what other junk you got in your bag."

She glared at him, her face morphing from a mask of concern to one of growing indifference. He'd touched a nerve, fingered an old emotional wound, and she was pissed off. She got up in his face and jabbed a finger into his chest.

"Don't come at me like that," she snarled. "I thought you were on my side. That's why I left with you. Don't disappoint me. I've been through really bad shit. I'm due for some good times and real happiness. And if I can't find it with you, then I'll go elsewhere."

Then I'll go elsewhere. That's what his wife had done years ago. He'd been here before. Like that time when this honey, a coworker from the facility, drunk at an office party, called his house and left a jive message on his answering machine. It's yours if you want it, Terry. And his wife intercepted it, almost cost him his marriage then and there. She made him pay dearly for that one, went elsewhere, and for a time they both ventured outside their marriage with other lovers. New carnal thrills. She only came back to him when one of her Romeos went berserk and whipped her ass. He took her back for a time, until the whole mess started up all over again. Now he was here, waiting to collect, waiting to get the reward of a very special night. It'd better be worth it.

"Are we still cool?" she asked. "I need to know."

He was still somewhere in his head, mulling over old terrain. He'd heard her question but didn't answer right away.

"Hey Terry, are we still tight or what?" she asked with teeth in her words. "You're taking too long to answer. Don't scare me, man. Don't get shaky on me now, not when I need you most."

"No problem, sweetheart," he replied halfheartedly. "It's all good. I'm in this to the limit, to the end. You and me."

Close to tears, she leaned back on the bed. "Don't fuck this up. I'm counting on you."

That short explosion of talk had certainly altered the mood in the room, settled something between them, and now he looked at her, really looked at her. Amina. Without the fog and haze of their situation blocking his view, he saw she was possibly one of the finest women he'd ever met, a real fox. Bronze, curly black hair, classic looks, a puffed mouth that guys would love to kiss, and the leggy body of a model with full, natural breasts. No silicone, not like his insecure ex-wife.

It was time to collect. Through the window, he could see the full golden moon rising in the dark blue of the Mexican sky, an Aztec night with infinite possibilities. Her hand on his rod broke him out of his thoughts and it sprang back to life, lengthening. He scooted back to her again, landing quick feather kisses at the soft base of her neck, up on her eyelids, and then down around her nipples. Slipping one nipple at a time into his mouth, he worked on them with consummate skill, all the while stroking her between the legs, teasing her clit with his thumb. She seemed to relax, submitting to her body's urges, her eyes rolling back in her head, ecstatic, as he trailed his tongue along the smooth flesh of her inner thigh, sending a long surge of heat up into her stomach. When he traced his tongue in soft motion along the soft, meaty folds of her sex, she wiggled underneath him, her hips lifting off the bed. He parted her restless legs even more with his rough hands, his nose pressed against that precious slit, his mouth relentless against it. Her moans increased in volume as he slipped expertly deeper down into the wet, fragrant cleft between her legs, the pink snake in his mouth exploring the sensitive nerves just inside her box, rotating and caressing her into new levels of desire, until she grabbed his head and held him hard and fast there. After her moist body trembled a second and third time, she broke off his oral assault on her and told him it was her turn to please.

Slowly, she moved over him on all fours, her butt high in the air, stopping only when her face was mere inches from his dick. She gripped it at the base, squeezing the engorged flesh until it became this monstrous thing of a deep violet hue with thick veins crisscrossing its shaft. Giggling to herself, she took him into her mouth, sucking and humming, head bobbing, bathing it with hot breath on her tantalizing downstroke. His legs quivered and bounced on the bed from the waves of pleasure rushing through his entire body. Her hands cupping his ass, she drove him deep into her throat, as if she was determined to swallow him whole.

"Easy baby, easy," he mumbled, feeling himself close to the brink. "Stand up, follow me. I don't want to get my knees scraped up."

She followed his lead and got up, with him watching her every sultry move. It was as if they were young lovers, unable to keep their hands off each other; their first night of passion together. He cleared off the top of a wobbly wooden table against the far wall, knocking everything in haste onto the floor. Neither of them spoke. He motioned for her to come, kneel over the chair onto the table, with her smooth, unblemished brown ass turned toward him. When he rasped for her to show it to him before he entered her softness, she did as he asked. Ravishing thug-ass thoughts. Of taking her long and strong. Passively, she showed it to him longer, her glistening pinkness. He moved in behind her, breathing in short bursts, entering her gently, grinding against her with purpose, each hand gripping a finely formed butt cheek. Each plunge was rapture. He accelerated his rhythm, picked up the pace as she arched up to meet his thrusts, her hands powerfully grasping the table.

"Tell me you love me," she said in that deep red voice. "Tell me, Terry."

He didn't want to appear soft, a wimp, so he said nothing. He kept busy, rolling his hips, feeling himself pulse inside her. She reared back, opened her legs wider, letting him slip even farther into her, into her sweetness, making a hissing sound much as an agitated cat would do. She wanted him. He gasped, gripped her shoulders now as he urgently pumped into the back of her womb. At the same time, he felt her change her tempo, rocking her plump ass against him in faster, wilder circles. They banged harder into one another, lunges, and this was crazy love. Maddening, animal passion like he'd never experienced before. He felt her dripping, wet on him to the base, tightening around him. She vibrated again and again like an unruly tuning fork, as though she sensed every throbbing inch of him inside her, her fingers moving slow and intense on the swollen nub where the center of her pleasure lived.

"Say it, please," she pleaded. "Tell me you love me."

He finally conceded and said the magic words while she rode him as if she couldn't get enough. It had been a long time for the both of them and never like this. His dick filled her again and again, to the hilt, withdrew and then went back inside to the point of her muffled shout. His thrusts became faster and harder still as they rushed toward climax, their moans in harmony as they soared together, their sexes matching thrust for thrust. Soon she was peaking once more in an intense burst of pleasure, overcome so strongly with the power of a clitoral explosion coupled with his continued pounding, coming so hard that she lost her senses for a moment. Her eyes went wild, crazed. When the raging storm of desire finally subsided, she stared at him like she wanted to kill him. Her eyes burned into him, dark and brooding. Eventually, her mood passed and she eased into his arms, lying still, mouth to mouth. It was evident that something had snapped inside her. *But I left some things out.* That was the last thought he had before sleep seduced him.

A few hours later, they got a bite to eat, beef tacos, beans, and yellow rice, chased with three chilled bottles of Corona beer. She wanted to walk around town after the meal, although the sun was still strong and very few people were out. He relented and let her have her way. On the outskirts of town, they rented horses from a wizened old man who thought they were gringos, albeit *los Negroes Americanos*, brought in to repair the roof of the ancient cathedral there. They rode out into the flatlands several miles away, following a dusty trail that ran south along the river. She laughed when his horse, a brown stallion, whinnied loudly from thirst and stopped to drink the grimy water. He stayed atop the animal, clutching the reins tightly, feeling its warmth and bulk beneath him. She dismounted and walked in front of her horse, near the ragged sagebrush and cactus. For him, it was good hearing her laugh.

Eventually, they tied up the horses, took off their clothes, and waded out into the river. The water went up to their necks, briefly cooling them. She swam closer to him, smiling, and put her arms around his neck. Her weight made him slip and he went under, the water going into his nose and mouth before he could resurface. They laughed and kissed after he got his breath back. He watched her swim out into the middle of the river with short, powerful strokes, the water shimmering as it rolled off her back and neck. Twice she dived under the surface of the water, with her exposed sex pointed up toward the heavens. He swam out to meet her, and they played like kids, swimming side by side, floating on their backs and splashing water on each other.

When the frolicking was over, they swam back to shore, where she took a blanket from her animal and brought it out to the riverbank. They sprawled on the blanket, ate the last of the dry tacos, shared the remaining warm beer, and cleaned sand from their toes. She kissed him and closed her eyes, holding an arm over her face to shield it from the blazing sun. He laid there silent beside her, enjoying her company.

After a time, she moved close to him, touching his face. "Baby, I left some things out."

"Huh, what?"

She said nothing else. Her full, soft mouth covered his own and her tongue slid easily between his lips. Maybe his leaving everything behind was not so bad. His ex-wife was never this hot or spontaneous. Everything was planned, thought out to dullness, according to schedule.

"The man I killed was my husband." Her voice was drab, lifeless. "He deserved to die. He wouldn't give me a divorce. I was in love with another man and he knew it. He made my life hell. I only turned to someone else because he was such a mean bastard. My young lover left me too, walked out, after I killed my husband for him. Something went haywire in my head. The doctors said I had a complete psychotic break, totally nuts. Lost my mind completely. Do you hate me now? Do you still love me?"

"Yes, I still love you," he stammered. But he had some doubts and fears.

"Does this change anything with us?"

"Not really." He examined her face carefully for obvious signs of madness and found none.

"I really am nuts, you know," she said, taking his hand to suck on his fingers until he pulled away. He could feel his sap rise along with his dread of her.

Later, they made love all night, going at it in every variation possible, until they collapsed exhausted in the juice-soaked sheets, totally sated. He slept the sleep of the dead, as the saying goes. When he awoke, Amina was gone, all of her belongings as well. Most of his remaining money was gone from his wallet. She had left him chump change, a few dollars. Panicked, he raced down to the street to see if everything was gone, and yes, his precious black 1949 Mercury Club Coupe had been stolen too. His woman with the deep red voice. Damn her!

While he stood bare-chested in his shorts in the spot where his car had been parked, a very pretty Mexican woman with dark features carrying a basket of white plastic skulls approached him, holding something. An envelope. She stood and watched him open it.

The letter consisted of four sentences, hurriedly scribbled in childish handwriting. His hand trembled with anger as he read its painful black-widow message:

> *I still left some things out. I am crazy and you could get hurt. I really like you. There have been others, before you, like you. This is the best way, for both of us.*

He stood there dumbfounded, completely confused, like he had been slapped three or four times in the face with a blackjack. Or knifed in the heart. A real fool. Threw everything away for one night of pleasure, his entire life. Across the square, he saw three people in skeleton outfits marching in a group toward the empty market. A truck full of mariachi musicians, fully dressed in their stage costumes with guitars, pulled up and the men jumped off and walked into the hotel. One of them held a large skull in his hand. Tomorrow was the start of the two-day Mexican Day of the Dead festival, the celebration of Death and its many wonders—how appropriate for him right now.

And maybe he was crying a bit because the cute Mexican woman patted him softly on the shoulder and said: *"Mujeres, ellas dan mucha lata."* Which loosely means: "Women can sometimes be a pain in the neck." Possibly true, if you don't know where and how to pick them. But not in this case. Amina knew who she was and what she was about. He was the one who didn't know anything about himself. She did him a favor, walking away before she took his life too, and added his scalp to the others. A real blessing, her gift of his life after that night of miracles. In his hands was this new start, this fresh possibility, Amina's gift. All he would do now was wash up, eat, and take another accounting of his few assets, and then there was time to think about tomorrow and the day after that.

Up

Kenji Jasper

The emptiest rooms are the ones that are fully furnished, the ones with the thousand-dollar sofa, the state-of-the-art sound system, and the perfect view overlooking the City. Those rooms are the ones you pay for with chippings from your soul. And the surrounding walls are always splattered with identical paintings of the heaviest cross you have to bear.

That emptiness is where I live. And I feel like I'm stuck up here forever, because I forgot what was important in the midst of things that were just the opposite. Ambition can be love's assassin. And its bullets are always lethal.

Above everything else, I believed in my words. They were the purest form of my truth, whenever the ink stained them onto pages. Then my mind absorbed them and they became a performance, an experience on the dimly lit stage at The Spot, for all to see. With each of those performances I owned the crowd, mind, body, and spirit. But my baby and I owned each other. And I told myself that that was more important.

"Say it," she whispered in her breathy, raspy voice. The moist flesh of her calves rubbed against my shoulders as I went in and out of her. She leaned back on her hands against the basin and I sucked that one spot on her neck that always tasted like sugar. The rest of her was like coconut cream, rich and smooth as she tightened around me, begging me to burrow deeper into her, her face barely visible in the dim candlelight. But I could never go as far as I truly wanted to.

I always wanted to disappear into her womb altogether, the one place in the world where I imagined that I could always be safe.

"I love you," I said, just before she gave me what I needed to come, our hushed voices bouncing off of the porcelain-tiled walls around us.

"I love you too, baby," she said. I let her down and she hugged me tightly. A shiver ran through the both of us. "You ready?" she asked.

It had been our ritual for over a year. And everyone at The Spot knew it. I hit the stage. Then she hit the stage. And then we met in one of the two unisex restrooms and hit each other off. Then the DJ would come in and the crowd would forget all about the words and let rhythm creep across the dance floor.

All the regulars knew about us. With one there was always the other. They even said that we were starting to look alike. And every Wednesday night, when we finished in there, we'd leave without a word to anyone, go home, and do it again, and again, until we had to head to our day jobs not long after dawn the next morning.

I'd found her for the first time when I first found The Spot. The DJ had brought in "No No No" and you could see scattered brown hands holding their lighters in the air, the swaying torches of a mob moved to musical action. I was at the bar, sipping on a shot of Appleton as if it were the last in the world, feeling as if I'd made a mistake in coming there, to The Spot, and furthermore to the City.

My first poem had only drawn scattered applause. I need a standing ovation, whoops and cheers to make me feel complete. And with that I was there drowning dreams headfirst in my tiny little drink.

"Taking your time with that one I see?" she asked from behind the bar. I couldn't believe I hadn't noticed her: perfect teeth, blond locks twisting and curling everywhere, and two soft honey-colored globes her baby tee could barely contain. I wanted to say something clever but at the time I didn't think I had it in me.

"It wasn't that bad," she said. Her wide eyes were a sparkling brown as she smiled at me.

"What?"

"The poem," she replied. "The thing you're sitting here looking so pitiful about."

"What makes you think that?" I asked.

"What else would you be here for? You been nursin' that one shot for like a half-hour." She gave me another grin. I tried to do the same but my sadness wouldn't allow it. I had come there to conquer and felt like I was going to be run out at the first opportune moment.

"You never get it your first time up there," she said. "I know I didn't. But that's not what it's about. What's it's about is what you feel."

She went on to tell me that she was from the north side of the City, that she'd been writing since she was eleven and worked as a waitress at a C-grade diner on the West Side on the lunch shift. She told me the place was so dingy and greasy that she nightly drowned herself in a hot tub of peppermint and olive oil just to feel clean. I framed that image, her naked breasts floating atop a lake of soapy water. And with that, I started to want her.

We talked all night, and at closing time I walked her down to the train. We were traveling in opposite directions but I waited to see her vanish from my sight before I left. When I got home I wrote a poem called "Empty," two whole pages about the vacant space in my heart I wanted her to fill as I watched her train speed down the platform toward the unknown expanses of downtown. I told her I loved her six weeks later to the day. And a year after that nothing had changed. She was what got me through my days of delivering packages and asking for signatures. But there was something inside of me that wasn't happy. The words wanted more space to flow, a bigger audience to impact. Something inside of me was about to burst at the seams. And the night came when it all began to tear open.

2.

I could still feel the sweat trickling down my back as my wet palms rubbed against the slickness of the bar's marble top. My baby and I had just finished our most recent lavatory episode, and I headed for the bar to get back a little of what I'd just given. And Priscilla, the Panamanian girl from the Bronx that Billy, The Spot's manager, shared a bed with, gave me an ice-cold bottle of water without a thought or a charge. Then I started on my way back to my baby, who was getting her bag from the other side of the room so we could leave.

"You could be doing better than this," a voice said from over my shoulder. I turned around expecting to see the woman talking to someone else. But she was looking right at me and my bald dark brown dome. She was a chocolate woman in blue that I should have noticed.

God had sculpted her legs into powerful tools. Her light brown hair was permed and hung down to her shoulders, making her stand out in a room full of puffed-out afros and locks. She was a sore thumb on manicured hands. And I had almost looked right past her.

"What did you say?" I asked for clarification.

"You were the best person up there tonight," she replied, just before taking a sip from her glass of zinfandel. "And I listened to *everybody*." Pride eased a smile onto my grill.

"Well thanks," I said. "You don't look like you come in here too much."

"Never been here in my life," she said. "But somebody told me that I should come check *you* out." She looked me up and down like I was something she wanted to buy.

"Who?" I asked, trying to play as if I didn't see what she was doing. She was baiting me for something, something I might not be able to resist.

"I just heard some people talking. But what I want to know now is where you want to go with your work. Music? Books? Acting?"

I didn't care which. I just knew that I wanted up and out of The Spot, and my pain-in-the-ass job too. I'd come to the City to make it, to blow up as the spoken word artist of the new millennium. And the closest I'd gotten was this one little nobody Wednesday night venue with its little relatively nobody sponsor. This woman was humming my tune.

"Wherever I can take it," I said. "I mean, I love it here but I hope I can get a bigger audience."

"I *know* you can," she replied. "And I want to do that for you." I turned and scanned the crowd for my baby. She was across the room, looking at me but trying to make it look like she was talking to her girl Charlene by the wall. She wasn't used to other felines sniffing around her milk.

"So what you sellin'?" I asked.

"Nothin'," she replied innocently as she threw up her hands for a moment. "I just think I can help you. I've got a few contacts. And I've been looking for the right kind of poet to put in the right kind of places." She glanced over at my girl and their eyes met. "But I see that something else has priority right now. Here's my card. Call me if you wanna talk about it." The card said that she was Andrea Joseph of Power Management.

"Alright," I said, as a million thoughts bounced through my head at once. "I'll do that." I left Andrea at the bar and crossed the dance floor to reclaim my heart. But for the first time in a year I felt an excitement deep inside of me that didn't have anything to do with my girl. That shouldn't have bothered me. But for some reason it did.

"Who was that woman you were talking to?" my baby asked me back in our home. The scent of sandalwood hung in the air and our candles were burning into a flat mess of wax over by the window.

"Oh, some manager," I said. "Said that she could blow me up. Told me to give her a call."

"Well, are you?" she asked. There was something in her tone that I didn't like, a kind of worry that I hadn't heard before.

"I don't know," I said, trying to keep from admitting that the woman had been on my mind since I'd met her. "It ain't like there ain't been other ones. Everybody says they can blow you up."

"I don't like her," she said. "I ain't ever said a word to her and I get a bad feelin' about her."

"Come here," I said, beckoning her from our futon to sit on my lap in the recliner across the room. She hesitated for a moment and then came over and lighted on the designated spot with a smile. She leaned in and I kissed her deeply. She seemed immediately reassured.

"We both sick of workin', ain't we?" I asked. She nodded in the affirmative. "You never know, she just might get us away from these damn day jobs. Shit, I'm twenty-four. I ain't tryin' to be bikin' around with packages any longer than I got to."

"I know, sweetie," she replied. "But I still don't like her."

I mentioned Andrea in my journal that night. The little book I wrote in only talked about things that came from the depths of my being, places where I allowed no one, not even my baby. I was in trouble.

I sat there, in the dim corner of our efficiency, looking at the journal page and wondering how many more times I could pen a verse for those same thirty people. How much longer could I limit myself to life in a glass of water when there was a whole ocean out there for me to swim through? I looked at the clock. Then I went over to the nightstand, only a few inches from where my woman was sleeping, and picked up the business card. It was one-fifteen in the morning. But something told me that it wasn't too late to call.

"So how long have you two been together?" Andrea asked me as she added detergent to her load at the all-night laundromat across the street from her high-rise apartment building, on the very expensive north side of the City. She'd been born up there, and at twenty-seven, had a master's degree and managed all kinds of acts. Spoken word was a pet project and she wanted me to be her guinea pig.

"About a year," I said, as my jaws worked diligently at the block of Bubble Yum between my teeth. "Maybe a little more."

"And you're happy?" she asked, as she cut her eyes in my direction. The fluorescent lighting overhead was blinding. A baby T-shirt and gray Swarthmore gym shorts clung to her frame. I could see every curve. Her nipples poked through the thin cotton material. Her tail was flatter than I would have wanted.

"I didn't know happy until I met her," I replied.

"Interesting," she said. There was mischief in the tone of her voice. I felt like I needed to be cautious.

"Well, anyway, like I said, I think I can give you a big leg up if you let me manage you."

"What kind of a leg up are you talkin' about?"

"There's a slam in Chicago in two weeks. First prize is ten thousand dollars and a five-minute spot on *The Tonight Show*." My eyes lit up like something out of an arcade game.

"Ten grand for a poetry slam?"

"That's the big time, baby. And I know the people puttin' it together. I'd just want 10 percent if you won. You don't owe me a damn thing if you don't. And it's like that wherever I take you, whatever *we* do."

When I told my lady about the offer I happened to leave out the time and place of the meeting, and what Andrea was wearing. I didn't want her to worry. I didn't want her to feel insecure. I didn't want her to think that I was packing a bag to spend the weekend with some temptress who was trying to take me away from her. I told myself that I was just trying to get ahead, trying to live up to my potential so the both of us could have a better life.

"This bag is gon' be heavier when I come back," I said to her with a smile. She was sitting on the edge of the bed with nothing on but her bra and a pair of cream drawstring pajama bottoms. Her skin glistened from the heat in the un–air-conditioned apartment.

"Why?" she asked without a clue.

" 'Cause it's gonna be an extra nine grand in it."

She flashed me a grin that I knew she didn't feel.

"What's wrong?" I asked her.

"I just got a bad feelin'."

"Bad feelin' about what?" I asked.

"That you gonna get stuck up there."

"Up where?"

"Where you're going," she replied. She didn't say another word after that. Instead she got up and went over to the record player. The Dells hit the air. She was sending me a message, begging me to stay in her corner.

3.

The slightly elevated stage at Club Conundrum made me feel like I was standing in a concert arena. There were people everywhere, a million hands snapping and clapping at the end of each set of words, lines, and phrases. The judges were stone-faced, their number cards the only expression of their feelings and emotions. So when I took my mark in the dim light of gelled lights and scattered candles, I knew that I had to kill it. I didn't want to go back to that tiny little Spot empty-handed. But over the course of the weekend there had been something growing inside of me like a fetus, something that didn't want me to go back to a place like The Spot at all.

When the first word hit the air, I knew I had them. On the second they were hooked. By the third line they were twitching for the next fix. And when I finished, sixteen lines later, they exploded like a tantric orgasm, a hundred people with head rushes channeling their excitement back at me, their artist, and soon to be Conundrum Slam Champion.

I shook and hugged and slapped and caressed the sea of bodies that congratulated me from the stage all the way to the street. Outside it was 2 A.M. and it lightly occurred to me that I hadn't called my baby since I'd left. But I told myself that there was time. I had other things to do. Andrea had said that we needed to talk back at her hotel room, that we should get some champagne and celebrate. And I felt like I needed to drink. I needed to talk to someone who knew me before I became the champ. Or maybe I needed more than talking.

It all happened so fast. Everything blurred as I began to lick the dark spot of a birthmark in the small of her back. As I entered, I felt like I was acting in a world of pure chaos. Voices screamed that I was wrong, that it didn't make sense. But Andrea was dripping wet, her fluids smearing against me. And I tasted them, just before I slammed into her from behind. I went in and out until the voices stopped, until the dead silence told me that what I was doing was right. And when I came, I felt nothing, only the fluffy comfort of those goose down hotel pillows, the ones that are always softer than the ones you have at home.

❖   ❖   ❖

"So what do we do about this?" I asked her, as I stood naked and guilty, looking out of the suite window at the skyline of a city I didn't know anything about.

"About what?" she asked calmly, her voice lightly muffled by the pillow she was resting on.

"I have a woman," I said.

"That's your problem," she said. "I only manage *you*. There's another slam in Seattle in three weeks. You're hot right now. *We* need to capitalize on that."

I didn't know what kind of an answer that was. But I took it as the only one that she had to give me. A few minutes later she was snoring, deep into the kind of sleep I wouldn't have for months.

"Told you my bag was gonna be heavy," I said with a smile as I came through my front door. I didn't hear her response. She was sitting in the living room recliner, her back to me.

"You didn't call," her voice said. I started toward her chair. But then I stopped myself. My facade wasn't going to work, and I needed the distance to get my thoughts together. "You call me twice a day when you're here. And I haven't heard a word from you since you walked outta here on Friday."

"It was crazy there, baby. I wasn't really near—" I wasn't a good liar.

"You woulda found one if you wanted to use it. I just don't think you wanted to," she said plainly. I walked over to the chair. I wanted to look her in her eyes. I wanted to see if she really knew. I wanted to see if she loved me enough to tell me what I'd done, so that I didn't have to do it. She'd added a T-shirt to the pajama bottoms I'd left her in.

"Did you win?" she asked solemnly.

"Yeah," I replied quietly. "Told you I would."

"Good," she said. "I'm glad that one of us did."

Those were the last words we shared for the rest of that Monday, our mutual day off from the daily grind. Tuesday came and I was still nine grand richer, but still at work, delivering packages. My baby barely crossed my mind that day. I was thinking about the future, about Seattle, about doing whatever it took to stay hot. I was in the real game now. I'd made it outside of the City, which had once been the be all and end all for a suburban boy like me.

And during the hustle and bustle of my day job, which I knew would fade away sooner or later, I came to the painful but important conclusion that staying hot was what I really cared about. The home my baby and I had built might have just been a place for me to live in, and grow, and outgrow like plastic training wheels. But then Wednesday came, the all-important day for my return to The Spot, and what I'd forgotten hit me like a brick upon arrival.

They all knew. When I came in, there was a strange vibe in the place. It hung in the air with the smells of body oils and incense. Familiar faces looked at me like I was a fool for even bringing my face across that threshold. I had wounded their queen, and had thus forfeited my own throne. I took two steps toward Billy and "the list" and he immediately moved his head from left to right.

"Already closed," he said plainly. My watch said 7 P.M. and I knew the list didn't even open for another fifteen minutes. I scanned the room for my ex-baby but she wasn't there. Both restroom doors were closed. No one asked me what poem I was reading that night. No one congratulated me on my win. I started looking around for the rail they might ride me out on. But I didn't wait for it to come. For me, the new Conundrum champion, The Spot instantly became a stain, a splatter of blood from the heart I'd shattered, spilled all over my new princely robes.

So I went back up to live in Andrea's high rise, until the next date, and the next city. I started building the kind of life for myself that was filled to the brim with challenges, rewards, accolades. But no matter what I do, it's still empty. The nights with Andrea always end the same way, with her snoring and me staring out the window, looking for a way out of my grand but empty tower. Maybe one day I'll get to fall, down, to the place where I left my heart long ago.

Where Strangers Meet

Robert Scott Adams

There is something erotic about just the thought of meeting some unknown person for the first time and getting so turned on that you are completely willing to risk compromising your traditional ideas of acquaintance, courtship, and ethics in order to just go ahead and get taboo love. On the other hand, lots of married or otherwise hooked-up couples who think they need a little spice in the relationship have flirted with the idea of risking it all regardless of the consequences.

With that in mind let's see what our couple here did during a recent outing where they put their relationship on the line for pleasure. Carlotta and Miguel were in the last forty-eight hours of another one of their now-infamous rendezvous, spending the last five days in our nation's capital, days that had been filled with their usual orgy of food, fun, and glorious sex.

Washington D.C. was their favorite American place to meet, especially in the fall. Springtime was nice, summer was usually unbearable, but there was something special about autumn in D.C. that seemed to elicit their most amorous of feelings. Maybe it was the slow, almost delayed reaction of the impending change in color of the leaves, coupled with the season's inconsistent temperatures. In October, you might have a seventy-degree day that plunged into a thirty-degree night, followed by a few days of fifty-degree highs and lows. Maybe it was the way even the Potomac River seemed to quiet its usually deep under tides. It appeared to delicately adjust its sluggish currents as it prepared to settle down for the impending winter's nap. The air smelled different. Even the usual frenzied pace of a typical northeastern city began its customary decline. The daily rushed pace of politics and business of the District almost compelled you to slow down enough for your senses to reawaken during this kind of lull, especially for your eyes to take a look at the enormity of everything from the phallic imposition of the Washington Monument to the grand statue of Lincoln, the Great Emancipator. Each of these massive structures boasted its own special design statement, artificially framed by trees. Countless trees that took their own sweet time as they changed from green to various hues of rust, gold, and red.

For whatever reason, both Carlotta and Miguel loved it. They reveled in the joys and pleasures of the autumn. They often stood transfixed during their walks around the city, taking in its sights while the seasons shifted from one to the other. On this day, the midmorning sun did its best to stake its claim in the dull gray sky. The overcast veil of low, dark clouds that had threatened rain for the past two days denied El Sol his desired entrance. For now, he was forced to submit to the whims of the evolving season.

Although the morning air carried a crisp breeze, Carlotta, being from the West Coast, refused to let it dampen her spirits as she stood barefoot on the balcony of their hotel room overlooking the perpetually snarled traffic, amazed at how it never seemed to lighten up regardless of the time of day. Besides being barefoot on the fake turf that covered the floor of the balcony, she wore only the thin, sheer nightgown she had slept in the previous night. Nothing mattered to her now. She had just gotten out of bed fresh from a night and morning of fierce, passionate sex; the fall air felt good against her satin-smooth skin. She could still feel him inside her, probing, deep. Her short, black spaghetti-strapped nightgown barely covered her knees. His smell was still on her, on her flesh, on her fingers. The taste of him was yet in her mouth, on her tongue.

Standing there, she looked down at her body and the lust-perfumed gown. Its low-scooped front had a difficult time trying to restrain her full, round, chocolate-colored breasts. Her nipples were always exceptionally sensitive, always either aroused and pointed or on their way to being so. The cool, subtle breeze teased them the way Miguel's tongue had done just a few scant hours before. She was easily aroused, especially when she thought of how intensely she and Miguel made love.

As she began to recall how good it felt to be ravished by her lover, Miguel appeared from behind her and slowly slid his large, soft hands around her waist, causing a low moan to come from deep down in her throat. He pulled her back, away from the balcony, so her behind was firmly pressed against his groin. Miguel wore only loose-fitting sweatpants. He could feel himself harden when Carlotta started to grind her ass against him, rotating her splendid cheeks against his crotch, provoking his lower torso to respond in kind. He moved his left hand slowly up her body, feeling the fabric, plotting the course upward, moving into a more seductive position. God, he wanted her again. He could never get enough of her.

"This is what I need to do," he whispered in her ear.

"Yes," she responded, feeling an erotic tightness between her thighs.

As his left hand changed direction, from vertical to horizontal, he caressed her skin softly, surrounding her waist, while his right hand impatiently moved to her head, tilting it to the side so he could brush his lips softly against the sensitive base of her neck.

"Oh shit, baby." That was all he could decipher from her basically unintelligible gasps. He knew how to work it, how to tease her into a smoldering frenzy.

His skilled, obedient tongue gently moved to the nape of her neck and her short, cropped hair. Each of his hands cupped a breast, engulfing them, taunting them into an exquisite hardness. Playing with Carlotta's body was always an adventure. It was the thrill of trying to see just how turned on he could get her. Miguel was dramatic. Carlotta was just as cerebral as she was carnal, always ready for his kisses and caresses.

In fact as far as she was concerned, it was one and the same. She wanted to hear Miguel's voice, his moans, his filthy talk, as he did things to her. It pushed her to do things she only fantasized about but would never do if she really considered them. In the bedroom, he had the ability to get her to exceed her moral limits, to try sexual experiments seen only in the pornos, mainly because she loved him so much.

Consequently Miguel would question her, admonish her, and dictate to her while trying to whip her into an erotic frenzy with his mouth and fingers. She didn't care. She only wanted to please him, to fulfill his needs as he wished to do with her. She never left him wanting or unsatisfied.

"Damn, these titties are so soft," he cooed, nestling his mouth still at the base of her neck. "You taste like I need to eat you up. Don't you know how much I love you?"

Carlotta couldn't respond. She heard herself say "yes," but in reality no sound came from her mouth. Her body was burning up from his touch. Nothing made sense when she felt like this. Every inch of her on fire. Her hands reached back, gripped his hips as he continued grinding against her. She slammed her hot ass into him, almost pushing him backward into the glass door that led onto the balcony. Once turned on, Carlotta, unlike most women, had no set rhythm for her sex dance. She just moved in tune with the small electrical shocks and tremors that coursed through her body, responding to the sensation of the moment.

"Can't you see that I can't help myself?" he questioned her as he stepped up his lusty assault on her breasts, bringing each one carefully to his lips. "I have to do this. You leave me no choice."

His voice was almost pleading, virtually apologizing to her as the passion between them kept building. It had always been his fantasy to see how much pleasure she could bear. What was her limit? How would her face look after her sixth, seventh orgasm? Would she be able to bear it?

At one point, they retreated back to the bedroom, where Carlotta quickly sat on the edge of the bed, pulling Miguel to her as she hurriedly undid the rope on his pants. As his trousers dropped to the floor, she took him into her mouth, slurping and groaning as she sucked and licked his hard dick. When he began to thrust into her mouth with more intensity, she grabbed his hands, pulled them to her head, and forced him to shove it down her throat until she made little gagging sounds. He'd learned by now that he wasn't hurting her when this happened. She had to have all of him as deep in her mouth as she could take it. Rough, frenzied, almost bestial. This was her ritual, her part of the sacred love act, her way of giving back just a bit of the pleasure he gave her.

Finally, after what seemed like hours, Miguel let go of Carlotta's head as he surrendered his passion into her mouth, buckling at the knees. It seemed like the more he came, the harder she sucked and swallowed. She wouldn't let him collapse. And despite his pleas to "please baby, baby, baby, you gotta slow down, you're going to kill me, please, slow, slow . . ." she ignored him, her mouth working hard on him as she also approached orgasm.

It was over. The middle of the day had quickly turned into early afternoon, and they rested and slept. When they finally awakened, they were hungry. The weather was still in autumn overcast mode and the television, which had been on all the time, was issuing a dangerous storm warning for that evening. They agreed it was time to get out of the hotel, before, as Carlotta put it: "We fuck ourselves to death."

Energized by their nap, they walked for blocks, enjoying the moist fall air. They eventually found a restaurant, a chain restaurant full of happy-hour patrons and oversized alcoholic drinks.

"So, what do you want to do later?" he asked as they drank from an apple martini so large a family of five could have gotten drunk consuming it.

"I don't care," she replied. Then she stopped for a second, tilted her head as if she were listening to a faint, distant voice. "Remember that club we went to the other night to see that jazz band? You said they have dancing upstairs, right? Well, what do you think about that meeting at the club where we can act like we're meeting for the first time? Would you like to try that tonight? Might be fun."

Miguel laughed. "Do you think you can handle it after all this liquor?" he asked, poking fun at Carlotta. Even though she loved to hang out with Miguel, and party time was anytime they were together, she had her limits and sometimes she reached them without knowing.

As she prepared to answer, Carlotta reached across the table to grasp Miguel's hand. "Oh, I can hang," she responded impishly. "Can you?"

"Aww, shit now. You know I can hang. If you're down, you know I am."

"What time do you want to go? It's, oh, six-thirty now," she said, looking at her watch. "By the time we get back to the hotel, take a shower, get dressed, and . . . wait, how is this going to work? Do I go around the same time as you do, or do you come later, or the other way around?"

"We'll do it the way we always said," countered Miguel. "You go. I'll get there about, oh, an hour or so later and we'll go from there." It was set.

They headed back to the hotel, where Carlotta showered, did her make-up, and prepared to get dressed. Miguel always applied lotion to her back after her showers or baths, continually having to remind himself not to get excited by touching her. He also had to decide which little black dress she was to wear.

As she got dressed, Miguel marveled at her body. She wasn't supermodel slim. She was a fine, better-than-well-preserved forty-year-old woman with full hips, a fine ass, long legs, and full, firm D-cup breasts. Her body weight fluctuated, causing her dress size to hover between a twelve and fourteen. This trip she wore the short, clinging size twelve . . . showing lots of leg and even more cleavage. The legs were the thing, however. She finished dressing by having him buckle the ankle straps of her black, open-toed pumps, and stepped back for him to take a look. She did a quick turn to show him all of her. Again he was amazed how good she looked and how he was immediately turned on just by looking at her.

"Well, I'm going to go over there," she said, doing a little twist that always drove him wild.

The club, The Cheetah, was a black dance spot on the waterfront on the southwest side of the District. It was known for its great DJ's and its hot combination of hip-hop, R&B, Caribbean, and African music. As one woman friend of Carlotta's once said, "You go there to party, not to stand and look."

"Well, baby," she said, giving him a quick kiss. "I'm out. See you in, what, an hour or so?"

"Yeah," Miguel said approvingly. "Remember," he cautioned, "in the words of Kevin Kline in *A Fish Called Wanda, don't* touch his dick!"

"The only dick I'm touching is yours," she joked.

Before she left, she looked at herself one more time. "Y'know, I was thinking about wearing the pearls you bought me. What do you think?"

"Naw," he replied. "Wear the fake ones. I got a surprise for you."

She left. Miguel sat there and watched TV, killing time. I'll give her an hour, he thought.

Meanwhile, Carlotta arrived at the club. As she exited the cab, she noticed a group of three well-dressed black men, tall and muscular, standing outside the club. It appeared as if they were debating when they should go in. As she passed them, she nodded to acknowledge the tallest one, about Miguel's height, dark with his head shaved just like Miguel.

He mentioned to his boys, winking, "Shit, that's it. If they got more like her in there, I'm in."

And with that, he and his boys followed Carlotta inside the club. The music was hot. The black and Hispanic crowd lovely, all ghetto fabulous. There was an intense sexiness in the air, a sense of uninhibited lust. Still, it wasn't necessarily a pick-up, meat market kind of place. But if you did find the right person, well you'd have no problems getting everything worked out.

Carlotta went to the bar. Now, keep in mind, there were women in this place young enough to be her daughter. But she was by no means the only woman her age in the place. She was the finest specimen in her category, but she was loyal and faithful to Miguel. Well, as faithful as a woman who was already married could actually be. They had a relationship that had endured some fifteen years, in contrast to her tiresome marriage, which was in its seventeenth year.

In that time, Carlotta had given Miguel cause to be jealous on only a very few occasions. And by her own admission, she was so in love with him. She only had eyes, hands, lips, and pussy for him.

But she was fine. She knew it. She loved to dance. And like all women, she liked to be admired. Her only weakness, other than her mad passion for Miguel, was that she craved attention. So when one of the tall, shaven-headed, dark brothers came up to her and offered to pay for her drink, she let him. When the same brother asked her to dance, she got up and hit the floor.

Carlotta danced like she walked, like she made love—smooth like liquid mercury. Rolling her ample hips to the sultry beats of the reggae, Latin, and R&B mix being slammed by the DJ, she began to get turned on. Not only was she getting turned on, she allowed her dance partner to do things to her on the dance floor usually reserved for Miguel. He touched her places, forbidden places, secret places. She felt the wetness between her legs spreading. She danced closer to her partner, touching him now, pressing against him in a way that said she wanted him. They got closer as the music encouraged everyone to throw caution to the wind and let their partners know how they felt.

As they became more suggestive and sexual, Carlotta found herself sandwiched between her initial partner and his boy. She was feeling good from the music, the attention, and the power she was wielding as she commanded her body to respond to her partners. Her first partner, the darkest, tallest one, was behind her with his hands around her waist, as Miguel's had been earlier that day on the balcony. He was gyrating against her butt as she held her arms in the air, waving them like she just didn't care. She wondered if he knew she wasn't wearing any underwear.

The other guy, a little shorter than her partner, was mimicking her hands-in-the-air style as he positioned himself between her legs. It was a dance floor orgy of Biblical, Babylonian proportions. It was freestyle sex, but fully clothed. She grinded and pushed against both men until she felt their excitement, front and back. That alone set her head spinning.

The hour passed quickly and Miguel got out of the cab in front of the club. He was dressed as Carlotta liked him, all black. Similarly, as he exited the cab, he was observed by two women who were trying to decide if they should enter.

"That's a full-size meal right there, chica," one of them, a short, caramel-colored, Hispanic-looking woman with huge hindquarters poured into an animal-print dress, moaned as Miguel walked past her.

"Oh, girl," she said, watching his walk. "Let's get up there so I can get me some of that!"

Men are strange. They are jealous and in reality don't want no-body messin' with their women. Miguel was no different. He was raised in a house full of women, having been reared by his mother, grand-mother, and aunt. His father was around but he worked all the time. A good provider but little else. He was married to his moms for fifty years, so most of Miguel's thinking was from a female perspective. He was raised to understand that, as his grandmother would say, "Baby, you got to just allow people to be who they are. Most of the time ain't nobody tryin' to do things to hurt you . . . like make you jealous or anything. They just do what they do. So some things you just can't take personally."

Even with that in mind, it took all of Miguel's resolve not to rush the dance floor, pick his woman up caveman-style, and take her home. He adopted the cool demeanor of a man who, at least on the outside, was completely confident. He assumed the role of the fan-tasy lover, according to their plan. He was in the joint, he saw some-one he wanted, thus he was willing to wait until he had his chance. Carlotta was still doing her thing and hadn't looked up to notice Miguel. When she did, she didn't stop or modify her behavior. She simply smiled, and turned her back to him so he could get a glance at what was going on front and rear. Two men, two dicks.

Finally, Carlotta was down to one guy. It was the third one of the group who had spied her when she arrived an hour or so earlier. If she was attracted to any of them, this guy was not the one. He moved her the least. Oh yeah, he was tall. But he was a little lighter than she

liked them. He was bald also, and while he danced with her, he kept
rubbing his hands around his head like he was a genie and his head
was a crystal ball.

Either that or he thought he was Prince. Or DMX. Miguel got a
kick out of this. As he drank his martini, he smiled to himself. Carlotta was visibly humored by him also, and she smiled back at Miguel
and lowered her head, apparently to avoid laughing out loud.

Not to be outdone, Miguel collared the Latin bombshell who had
spied him earlier and made his way to the dance floor. Although it
was early in the evening, the dance floor had already reached tribal
proportions, with everyone acting out their primal roles. Everybody
was shaking their thing in a calculated prelude to an all-out knocking-
boots session. Miguel and his partner were going at it with a ven-
geance. She had backed that thang up on him, and he was truly
waxing that ass!

He looked to see if Carlotta was watching, and she was. She
smiled and exited the floor as the music went from reggae to a slow
jam.

That was his chance.

To the dismay of his partner, Miguel headed straight for the bar,
where he ordered two drinks. One for himself and one for Carlotta.
As he approached her, he noticed her talking to one of the men she
had been dancing with. As he got closer, his ego was stroked as Carlotta politely turned away from the guy and smiled at Miguel, her
body language signaling that she was ready for a change of suitor.

"Hi there. I'm Miguel. It looked as if you might need something
to cool down that fire you started out there." It was not a terribly
strong opening line but it worked more often than not.

She smiled the smile that always let Miguel know who she was
and what he meant to her. As she would put it: "My man."

"Thanks," she replied, staring deep into his brown eyes. "I'm Carlotta."

They made small talk. As they did, it was obvious to all the men
and women who had designs on either of them that they were out of

luck this night. And if they didn't realize it initially, they certainly did when Miguel reached into his pocket, pulled out the string of pearls he'd purchased for Carlotta, and replaced the faux ones on her neck with the real ones.

After that, they hit the dance floor and danced. Unlike the last dances both of them had done with other people, this one took on a pre-mating ritual type of vibe. When they couldn't take it anymore and their four or five drinks had taken full effect, they left the club to the dismay and wonderment of hopefuls who had thought they had a chance with either of them.

Miguel and Carlotta emerged into the cool night air. It was way past midnight and the wind was picking up. The hotel was within walking distance, and although they were quite intoxicated, they decided to forego the cab and walk back. It was just nice to be together.

They walked up the hill toward the hotel with the freeway on their right. Because their minds were still entranced by the antics on the dance floor, the sounds of the passing cars only served as background noise. They laughed and joked about the night's proceedings. At a small concrete observation point that separated the sidewalk from the grassy knoll of the freeway, passion seemed to overtake them and Miguel grabbed Carlotta, pulled her to him, and began kissing her passionately.

Carlotta was always turned on immensely by Miguel's kisses; his skill with his tongue was legendary, and as he held her close with his left hand, his right hand journeyed down to that spot between her thighs which by this point was already dripping wet. There they were, leaning against the concrete portion of the observation area, making out like teenagers. It got hotter and hotter. Miguel then spun Carlotta around, pulled her dress up, exposing her bare bottom, rubbed her vagina some more to insure its wetness, and took his rock-hard member and entered her right there on the streets of Washington D.C.

As they made love right there, the cars roared by the entangled lovers, who were totally oblivious to anything but their passion. Carlotta was approaching orgasm. Before she could reach her peak, she turned around, pulled Miguel out of her, dropped to her knees and began to suck and lick him. It became even more intense.

While Carlotta quickened her pace, clutching him with both hands as her head bobbed and weaved into his crotch, the wind began to howl and rain poured from the night sky. Undaunted, she rose from the ground and led Miguel to some steps that descended from the sidewalk to the edge of the expressway. These steps were apparently used for the grass cutters to get down to the side of the highway to mow the grass.

There, with the rain falling in torrents, she sat on the steps, put him back in her mouth, and sucked him to completion. She felt him flow into her mouth, gripped him harder, and worked on the head of his dick until he pressed her face into him and almost toppled backward.

Miguel let out an orgasmic roar, sagging against her. Totally spent.

"Damn, baby, damn," he mumbled. "I can't believe you sometimes."

With their clothes soaking wet, they calmly yet quickly walked back to the hotel. Wet, but satisfied and still turned on, they entered the elevator and continued their lustful escapade until they arrived at the floor of their hotel room, where they rushed to get into the room, took off their soaking wet clothes, and continued until long into the night.

The Roses Are Beautiful, but the Thorns Are So Sharp

Kalamu Ya Salaam

Theodore didn't know why he wanted to kiss her private lips. Didn't know why the sharp energy of her smell made the large muscles on the inside of his thigh twitch. Didn't smell like sex. Didn't even smell human. Undomesticated, wild, maybe a pine-needle bed where a deer had rested. A fragrance borne by the wind from whence only the wind knew where. Didn't know why, but he liked the memory of his slow kiss-rub-lick-suck of the cleaved dark of her. And he liked that she liked it.

Theodore sucked the caramel-colored coke through a straw, drawing out gurgling sounds as the last of the liquid, mixed with air, cascaded upward through the crushed ice. He took the cup, tore the plastic top off with the straw still in it, and threw it into the litter receptacle; swirled the cup, tilted it upward, shaking shards of ice into his mouth, sucked on the ice, and thought of her moan. Her. He nodded hello to a coworker on his way back to his desk from his ten-minute break. Her. Her moan.

I close my eyes. I am crazy. I open my eyes. I am crazy. Her. Her moan. I do my work and when I finish working, every time, I am crazy. Obsession. Her. Her face, her smell, her touch. I try to fight my need for every day to be night. I battle my urge to be with her, to see her. I tape the evening news, using the timer on my VCR, and later look at her over and over. Beauty itself. Her eyes. I know the qualities, the details the TV camera never sees, never recognizes. Sometimes I watch with the sound turned down. I read her body language. The subtle motion of her jaw as she speaks. Count how many times I see her tongue on screen, the tongue that could bring me so much joy. How often they show her hands. Remember the feel of her nails across the curve of my neck. The rhythm of her satin voice reciting my three syllables: "The-o-dore," except she enunciates it: "Thee-I-*adore*." I listen to her voice, "That's the news. This is Ann Turner. See you tomorrow." I think, see you tonight, baby, tonight.

The bronze points of her breasts cut a curvature into his consciousness. Why continue, Theodore thought as he went on with his day. A man shouldn't be consumed by desire. This would get him nowhere, this controlling lust, this blinding fixation. His imagination fed him visions of the inside of her thigh, soft and alluring, in a flash as quick as the picture of a darkened room momentarily lit by a sudden bolt of lightning.

Obsession. He drank in her features, her loveliness, even when only sitting in front of his computer. A blank screen except for the tantalizing image of her dark, mesmerizing face. Drank and drank and was never quenched.

One day he refused to call her. The whole day. He concentrated on not calling her. Her. He tried but his refusal made him sick, sick like an addict staying away from the needle or a rummy neglecting his romance with the bottle. It caused him pain and suffering but he stood his ground and kept away from the telephone.

I can do this. She doesn't own my fingers. My feet are my feet. I have a good job. I wear a suit and tie. I drive a sports car—all fast, red, and sleek. Here is my off-ramp. I like the feel of taking a curve at my own speed, leaning into it. It's like when I ease into her. I'm gripping the wheel firmly but lightly, like I do her breasts. I brake a little, back off the clutch, let the engine slow a bit, and hit the accelerator slightly at the top of the curve, pushing through the small herds of cars on the highway. Through the steering wheel, I can feel the car's power surging and responding to my every expert move. Like Ann. Her.

     ✿   ✿   ✿

"The roses are very nice," Ann says, something glacial in her voice. I watch her face. I'm speechless. I've bought corsages for proms. I've bought flowers for Mother's Day. I've even given my aunt a plant for her anniversary. This is the first time, the very first time I've bought roses for a lover. I'm not especially romantic. And she says they are only "very nice."

"But I cannot accept them," she continues, her rejection hidden in a pleasant tone. She is an expert with words and tone. She makes her living with them.

I'm stunned. I start asking myself some questions, maybe questions I should be asking you. What about when you kissed me? What about that great dinner we cooked together in your kitchen, trading culinary tips, and ate quietly in the afterglow of our passionate evening? I fed you dessert. A fruit salad from my fork, then the grapes from my hand and that last strawberry we shared lip to lip as I kissed you deeply. I kissed you with the succulent, deep red meat poised between my teeth, letting it fall into your mouth as you sucked my lips. You slipped your fingers into the bowl, then inserted them, one by one, into my mouth. I sucked the juice off your smooth brown skin, cleaned each finger with a gentle sweep of my tongue.

And the night we spent drinking in the French Quarter, waiting around, waiting for the sun to awaken, delirious and crazy with love. Sensually delicious in each other's eyes. The first time. The second time. That Saturday evening in the thunderstorm with all the lights out and a very good bottle of inexpensive wine. Us. With the comforter on the carpeted floor, the sound of the rain against the panes accompanying our rhythms of love. The third, fourth.

Damn it, last Monday, two days ago. "My legs are wide open," you said. I almost cried in your arms I felt so happy. There was no denying what we felt. Now, I pick you up from work just about every day, every day you allow me to. Sometimes we even shop for groceries together. Or clothes. That linen jacket, the pink one. For you. The surprise manicure and facial treatment certificate. The health spa, six-month membership.

"My legs are wide open," you said. That's more than nice.

*   *   *

Her face changed in expression and hue. He knew what she was saying but was unable to understand the words.

"I said, I can't accept them," she said. "No, don't come in. Please."

Obsession. Rejection. A love denied. Then I forced myself past the three-quarters-opened door. I didn't mean to knock her down when I pushed my way inside. But she fell. And then something happened. Looking down at her, I saw the shock on her face. You see, it doesn't feel good getting pushed around, I thought to myself. Now you know how I feel sometimes from the way you treat me, I continued thinking as I silently observed her. The beginning of a smirk unconsciously edged its way onto my face. It was as if I rose above myself and was outside of my body, watching myself standing there. I could see everything. I knew everything. I knew she was surprised by how hard I shoved the door. Even so, I could see she wasn't hurt, sprawled there on the floor. Embarrassed but not hurt. After I left, I knew I had slammed the door behind me. I knew she didn't think I had it in me, this anger, this rage. All for her. I could tell by the way she looked up at me.

As she fell backward, slammed into the wall, and toppled onto the floor, he closed the door quickly. And then, as though she'd misunderstood him the first time, he held out the roses to her again. She had one knee up slightly. Her straight, woolen, beige skirt with the deep slit in the front had ridden up high on her shapely legs, falling away at the knees.

Anger and fear overpowered her perfume. She didn't smell pleasant anymore.

The red, red roses swung in front of her face. Nothing.

I'm more than nice, he thought, weighing his next move.

The phone rang. They both turned toward its sound.

She covered her face with both hands, then lowered one to the floor, pushing herself up, to stand. He stepped forward, blocking her path. She stopped, her eyes searching his face for his intent. He knew she could not reach the phone in time. He wouldn't let her. Let her damn machine answer the intruding call. Four rings and the noisy interruption ceased.

After the phone quieted, he bent slightly, almost level to her face, and pushed the roses at her again. She batted them away. She didn't want to be distracted by them. She wanted no part of them or of him. That was obvious.

Her hand moved slowly, keeping them away from her. Why was he insisting? Why were the flowers thrust at her like a gun? What did he want from her? What?

He'd unbuttoned his trousers. They slid down to his feet. He stepped out of them. He remembered what she'd said just two days ago: My legs are wide open. He remembered her perfect body, her closed eyes, her smell, her breath in his ear, as he lifted her legs and moved deeper into her. Into her hot, wet center. Her flat belly against his. Their desire had grown in intensity until they clung so tightly to each other, an aching tenderness between them. What right did she have to defile that act of love? Why was she doing this to him? Could a woman love a man one minute and toss him aside like trash the next? She told him that she loved him, loved it. The goodness of his dick hadn't changed since that moment. She wanted it then. She gave it up then. Now was then. In his mind. He eased off his Jockey shorts. He still wore his shirt and tie. And jacket. And the roses were still in his hand.

"What, Theodore?" She almost screamed the words at him.

That was her only response, what? He didn't understand.

He was standing there with his penis erect, swollen with lust, and finally he shed his jacket, laying it on the floor near his trousers. He knelt slowly, placing the flowers beside them. He pushed her skirt up and she closed her eyes. Her flesh was cool beneath the nylon of the panty hose. Then she moved, only slightly, at the softness of his caress on her thigh. Her head shook from side to side, no, not like this. She covered his large hand with one of hers, a momentary halt.

She tried reasoning with an unreasonable man. "Are you going to use something? I'm ovulating now."

He ignored her. She knew he would do this. She felt his anger. He began pulling at her panty hose.

"I'm not going to let you do this," she said in a flat voice. Emotionless but firm.

She started to struggle silently, surprising him with her strength as she tussled with him. The thrust of her arms rocked him backward. He admired that she didn't hit like a girl. He didn't want to rape her, force her to do something against her will. He just wanted it all to be like before, to be like it was two days ago. Her and him. Now she was on one knee. He pushed her once. Not as hard as he could. She sprawled backward. Her shoe slipped and her legs flew from under her. As she lay disheveled on the floor, trying to decide whether to kick him or to run, he pushed the roses aside and knelt before her, like a parishioner at prayer. There was a sadness, a bitter sorrow in his eyes. He looked between her legs, which were awkwardly gapped open. What he saw there nestled between her silky thighs was the reddest rose. That was the thing that had driven him crazy, made him act like a fool. Made him do something he said he would never do. He only wanted things to be like they were, just two days ago. When she said she loved him. The reddest rose. The soft petals of her vagina flower. The thorns of her refusal to receive him into her body.

Suddenly, she pushed him harder than he'd pushed her. He fell back on the flowers. The thorns bit deeply into the palm of his left hand. There was blood.

He picked up the flowers and threw them at her. Hurled them into her face. Hard. A thorn cut her cheek. She felt a faint sting. When her hand came down from her jaw, a long, bloody smear had creased the middle of her palm. A crimson lifeline burned into her palm.

He expected her to cry. He felt like crying; how could everything go so wrong so fast? But she made no sound. Did not even whimper. She only stared at him with an undisguised hatred, utter disdain. The force of her stare stunned him. It hit him harder than any punch that she could have thrown. He stood up. She bolted up without hesitation, mad and defiant. She balled up her fist, standing boldly upright, silently daring him to touch her again. He backed off silently, re-trieved his clothing, and dressed. Every time he glanced at her, she was still glaring at him, unblinking rage. Her blouse rose and fell as she took deep, soundless breaths. He turned and walked briskly out the door, slamming it behind him. Still furious, she stepped over the flowers and quickly locked the door.

2.

They were sitting at the movie theater. He cheered when the hero smacked the actress portraying his wife. Ann froze, instinctively knowing for sure that Theodore Roosevelt Stevens III was wrong for her. All of the little signs she'd ignored were suddenly obvious. She'd ignored them because she was tired of searching for someone to share her life with and had settled for someone with whom she could have a little fun. After applauding the hero's response to his wife's cinematic betrayal with brief applause, he turned to look at Ann. Actually, he was celebrating the hero's refusal to be suckered rather than applauding the slap. But that was not how it was interpreted by Ann. He admired anyone with the insight to know when a game was being played, especially one played by the female species. His right hand pawed the air, seeking Ann's hand to hold again, but her arms were folded.

"What's wrong?" he asked.

"What's right?" Her reply was terse.

"What do you mean?"

He caught the tone, the cutting nature of it, the coldness. Theodore knew this was fire that he could not walk through with his bare feet. He had to do something to calm her down.

"What?" he asked innocently.

She bit her bottom lip to keep from talking. She was preparing herself to do battle, not a battle of her own choosing, but one that she would wage without giving any quarter.

Leaving the theater, she was still on simmer. "Let's go for a drink. We need to talk."

"Sure. Where?" He couldn't figure out what he had done to piss her off.

"Anywhere." Clipping tones. Her claws were still showing.

Anywhere was close, but the drive there was long.

"What's up?" he asked.

"This is the last . . . I mean . . . I don't think . . ." She swung her head quickly to look away. They were waiting at a stoplight, right before the turn onto Causeway Blvd. He glanced at her during the pause at the light. Her unblinking, angry eyes were focused on him. She read him the news, at least that's how it felt to him; all of her emotion was released through unforced, well modulated tones. Like a newscaster, like the TV anchor she was.

"I thought about your question to live together and the answer is no," she said smoothly. "And I think we need to break this off. It's not working for me."

The light was green. Theodore said nothing, and kept driving. He circled onto the expressway, still silent. She was waiting for his reply. He'd heard her. Suddenly he pulled over to the side of the road, emergency lights flashing. He turned off the tape deck, flipped the key, and the engine stopped. She had not stopped looking at him the entire time. This was Tuesday. Nothing will be settled this night.

Two days later, he will bring roses and apologize.

Everybody thinks it's easy to be me. To be the epitome of charm, style, and poise on the weekday evening news. A face recognized. Gwendolyn Ann Turner. Actually, Gwendolyn Ann Turner is the real me, and most of the world, or most of the city, only knows me as the voice: "This is Ann Turner, your evening anchor, sharing today's news of New Orleans with you." Most of them only know so small a part of my real self and yet they think they know me.

I was so fat as a child, so "Gwenie." Overweight, intelligent, gifted with a lean, hard mind. Maybe too hard. Through college, I was always "the brain," never the beauty. When my birthright beauty began to emerge, it was hard to see how beautiful the flower would become since only the bud was just appearing. I had to run in P.E. and found

myself liking the solitude and challenge of the long runs, figuring out
how to run without wearing myself out, how to swing my arms, how to
use my body. I pushed myself and enjoyed that. The more I ran, the
more my physical side came out, and that was because I relished the
meditative side of running. I also enjoyed the physical challenges because I soon found that beauty was within my reach, becoming "fine"
and "thin" and all that implied. But the thorn on the flower was that
becoming attractive made being me more difficult and demanding. I
split into two people. Still, it was so easy to be pretty, to be wined and
dined because my body shape was appealing and pleasing to the male
eye. I loved the attention and everything that came with it.

The thought stopped her: "I hated being fat and I'll never be fat
again." She stopped at the roadside and put her hands atop her head,
getting her breath back. Her legs were ablaze with pain but that was
the usual for a long run. She was used to the aching muscles at this
point. She looked at the dawning sky and summoned strength for the
remainder of the run. She was beginning to resent the deference given
to her for all the wrong reasons. Well, not so much for "wrong reasons," but for the Ann Turner reasons and none of the Gwendolyn Ann
Turner reasons. Everything favored the glamour girl, the celebrity.

Supposedly I have everything. But that is not true. Here I am,
twenty-eight years old, sexually active, and so far away from any serious relationship that it doesn't hurt anymore. I'm never alone unless
I want to be. I've never met anyone that made me feel as if I wanted
to spend any real quality time with him. Being so popular a media
personality makes being alone as a private person that much harder.
You no longer belong to yourself; you belong to the public.

If I hate being beautiful, why do I run every day, stick to my diet,
groom myself immaculately? Wear the latest styles. Pedicures. Man-
icures. Facials. Ann runs every day and Gwen waits. Waits for what?

Gwen waits in a desk drawer, in a diary, in five completed stories,
seventy-nine poems, thirty-four unfinished sketches and outlines for

stories. On her drawing pad, there were monthly self-portraits, all etched with soft lead pencil while looking into the dressing table mirror. This ritual started in college. During the first week of every month, Gwen sketched Ann, and afterward Ann would stare at the drawing, looking for Gwen. Gwendolyn went to college certain that writing was her destiny but circumstances sidetracked her. The path from Gwen to Ann started not from her own volition but rather due to her physical presence and personality.

As the new Gwen blossomed, Gwen hated the attention even though some small part of her loved it, fed off of it, and grew more confident, stronger by the week. That was how she eased into broadcasting. When she took the mandatory broadcasting courses, it was immediately obvious how effective she was behind the mike. Her instructors steered her that way: "The camera loves you. Your voice soothes and exudes sincerity. I know you want to write but I think it's apparent your future is in announcing."

Meanwhile, Gwen the writer patiently waited for release. Now, years later, with a professional broadcasting career firmly established, she knew that writing was not possible as a career option, not to mention economically unfeasible.

Even Gwen, who rarely spoke, told her: "Ann, you do television because it's easy for you. There is no challenge for you to stay in shape. Reading news copy is so easy. We always liked to read. Ann, you like to read and I must read. That is one of the only ways we can coexist. At other times, you know I'm shoved into the background."

These two people in me: Gwen and Ann. Gwen wants to be a writer, a deep thinker, and Ann, well, Ann pays all the bills and acquires all the frills. Or something. What does Ann want? Ann is not a want, Ann is a thing, a procurer. Ann's ultimate job really ought to be to create a space for Gwen.

She begins walking, builds up to a trot in a few seconds, and then is running again.

3.

Theodore turned his head, tremendously pleased with himself. Happy about his manliness, his sexiness and skill as a lover. What good fortune! He was fucking Ann Turner and loving every minute of it. Everything was in order. At his office, his commissions were bounding upward. When clients saw him, they were impressed by his smooth, articulate, fastidious image, his intelligence, business savvy, and youth. He was quite the man! These days he was always impressive, so impressive that clients flocked to him the way those chickens used to do at his grandmother's farm in the summers when he was a boy. He'd go there for a few weeks, waking early, getting dressed, running into the yard with a cup of feed, throwing the kernels on the ground and calling to the birds in his young baritone.

Because he was looking at himself in the mirror, he watched the stream of urine leaving his body, heard its splash, but in his head the beauty of her big round booty moved beneath the skilled caresses of his hands; because of all of that, he neither saw the seriousness of her eyes nor heard the coolness of her voice.

"What?"

"I realize this might sound a bit strange to you but I've got a thing about hygiene," she said slowly, as if talking to a small child. "When you use the toilet, please sit."

"What?"

"Put the seat down and sit. Urinate sitting down. When you stand, your urine splashes and it's unhygienic."

Much head as she gives, she's worried about a little urine on the toilet seat. She swallows. She loves it. She licks me clean. And she's worried about me standing up pissing. I'm standing here naked, holding myself. I'm about to shake the last drops away and then she says this shit. What's up with her? How can I shake it if I'm sitting down? Damn, she's a trip.

✿   ✿   ✿

I watch him, typical male. Disgusting. I'm sorry but that is one of my pet peeves. I hate a dirty, unhygienic bathroom. He can't understand that. I knew he wouldn't.

Theodore didn't understand what her griping was about. Ann turned back into the shower, almost regretting that she had brought it up. Almost. Gwen decided long ago that Theodore was just a momentary thing, a fling, something physical, even if he overestimated himself and made the faux pas of popping the question about living together.

Ann was slower to decide. There was a lot she liked about Theodore. The lovemaking for one. The boy came fully equipped and he knew what to do with it. And, well, the lovemaking for two. His humor; he was sort of witty. No, he was convenient, really. Although he was right for a fling, he was definitely not living-together material. And he was unhygienic and far too possessive.

"Theodore, I don't need you to pick me up after work," she said in that newscaster voice. "Yes, I know it's late when I get off and I know I could save the cab fare, but it's easier. I have two cab drivers who are regulars. I call when I'm ready to leave and they're outside the door waiting for me. I get in, we come straight here, they wait until I'm inside and everything is safe. Theo, I know you don't mind but you don't have to wait around for me."

"What?" He still didn't get it.

"I'm staying late tonight," she continued. "No, I'm not sure exactly what time I'll be finished . . . I'll just catch a cab . . . No, Theo, I won't call you . . . I'll catch a cab and talk to you in the morning . . . You'll be sleeping when I get in . . . I'll call you in the morning . . . Theodore, don't call me at 1 A.M. . . . What do you mean where will I be? . . . What do you mean what do I mean? I mean I can take care of myself . . . Obviously you don't know it."

Gwen had seen through Theodore weeks ago, peeped his program very early. The shower door opened. Theodore stepped in there with Ann. He was naked except for his sarcasm, which he didn't wear well.

"You mean, when I urinate, you want me to sit down like when . . .
I, uh . . . defecate," he asked wickedly. "Is that what you mean?"

4.

The answering machine in Ann's bedroom carried Theodore's latest
pleadings. "When I saw you bleeding, I knew I'd messed up real bad. I
don't know what got into me. I mean, you know me, I'm not really like
that. I mean, I was crazy or something. Ann? I'm sorry. I'm sorry. You
want me to beg? You want me to crawl? What? I've sent you letters, I've
called you every day. This hurts me too. I don't know what else to say. I
mean, I know I did something really, really wrong. And I know it will be
hard for you to ever trust me again, but I love you. I really love you. I
mean, it's serious. You make me feel like a man . . . a real man."

5.

It was the same old song, the begging, pleading, and tears. Ann
didn't even listen to the whole tape. Why couldn't he be a man and
let it go? No decent woman respected a whimpering, begging man.
None. A punk. A chump. He talked to her machine for twenty, sometimes thirty minutes or more. Sometimes he just said, "I'm gonna
keep calling until you talk to me." This went on for over two weeks.

Fortunately, the erase mechanism was fast.

6.

It's about a year and a half later. Theodore is married. Yes, he sent
Ann an invitation. When she didn't go, he wasn't surprised.

When Ann got the invitation, she felt sad for Theodore's new
bride. He wanted a wife but he wasn't prepared to deal with a
woman. She left the invitation on the table in the hallway, the table
that held the telephone and answering machine, beneath the mirror.
The invitation was stuffed back into the envelope. Ann did not wonder why it had ever been sent. Gwen didn't even care. A casual toss

and the invitation landed with a slight rustle atop a small stack of junk mail. Ann didn't mean Theodore's invitation was junk mail, but she had no intention of attending.

Later that day, she sat sketching herself. Clarity. In the mirror was Gwendolyn Ann Turner, a thirty-year-old, unmarried black woman. She knew, she knew she would never marry. And she could live with that, was content to live with that. Gwen smiled. She smiled because she appreciated that Ann Turner was becoming less interested in Ann Turner and more devoted to developing Gwendolyn Ann Turner.

Never marry. God, what a thought. But not really. Even though she had been raised to marry. Even though it seemed like the whole world was wondering when she would marry. And have children. In a flash, both Ann and Gwen realized that neither one of them had ever really wanted to be married, not once they were mature enough to honestly face themselves. Ann just didn't want to be alone. Although sharing board was out of the question, Ann could and would find someone to occasionally share her bed. An overnighter penciled in for sexual maintenance, but nothing smacking of a permanent partner or husband. Ann accepted the cost. She could pay the bills. And Gwen. Gwen was happy, she gave thanks to be alive and thriving. And writing; her new novel was almost finished.

A spray of red roses sat eloquently arranged in a bright black vase. "Our vase," the women called it. Gwen had found it while wandering through the French Quarter. She was drawn to the pear-shaped container without knowing why or how she would use it.

As she'd walked along with the trendy shopping bag which held the vase swaddled in newspaper, she'd passed a florist. Roses were on sale: $9.99 a dozen, and so began the floral addition to the sketching ritual. The fragrance of the flowers would radiate through the room while the young woman deftly drew her monthly self-portrait. And as was usually the case within the last few months, Gwen would be smiling a generous smile, all was good. Smiling to her beautiful self. Now, she understood as never before, with a startling clarity, the necessity of the thorns on roses. That everything beautiful must protect itself.

Cayenne

Eric E. Pete

Hot and spicy, with a cinnamon aroma. I didn't know the perfume that covered the secret letter, but it drove me wild. I'd been sniffing the intoxicating piece of paper off and on that day, closing my eyes and letting my imagination run uncontrollably. Wild, erotic thoughts concerning its author's identity took over most of my waking hours and a lot of my sleeping moments as well.

Being a newlywed by most people's standards, I shouldn't have let something like this get under my skin. I'd taken the plunge a year ago in a big ceremony at Gallier Hall, where Mayor Morial and all the other bigwigs were in attendance. Just six months ago I'd passed the bar and become one of the hotshot lawyers that the law schools in New Orleans crank out each year. Some of us were destined to dwell on the lower level of our trade, fighting over business, but I wasn't going to be one of them. I came from an okay-by-New-Orleans-standards family and had married the right girl from the right neighborhood with the right skin tone, etc. In high school, I had attended St. Augustine and she had come from Xavier High. In New Orleans, it wasn't about what college you attended but rather what high school.

Don't get me wrong, I truly loved my beautiful Melanie, but something was lacking in the romance department. Even when I put forth the effort to suck on those tiny, pretty toes or lick the kitty, Melanie just wasn't *there* with me. It seemed like most of the passion and zest had faded out in the first few months of our marriage, so I channeled that energy into being a provider and leaving my mark on the world. The miscarriage Melanie suffered also seemed to leave her numb and distant to my touch.

Now here I was sniffing fumes off a piece of paper until my nose burned. I had to learn whose words these were that made me shamefully nervous, but at the same time excited me to an instant erection.

The sweetly scented letter read:

Antonio:

> *Do you like games? Do you like the winning that "cums" at the end of a good game? I've been watching you and I think I've got what you want. Think you're man enough to play? I sure do. Whenever I see you, you make me so wet that I have to take care of myself some nights. I long for your touch, inside and out. I want to feel what it's like to have you tasting me all night long. All my glorious curves, hips, lips and kisses, I offer up to you to do with as you desire. Interested? You look like you could use a little spice in your life, so here I am . . . if you find me. I'm not that hard to find though. I'll be all the woman you've been waiting for . . . I'm here, right in plain sight.*
>
> *Now,*

Cayenne

The typed letter had been left on my windshield in a sealed envelope while I was down at the courthouse one day. When I was in court, I always parked at the same lot, in the same spot. There were ladies at my firm who had dropped subtle hints about what they would do if they had me alone for a few minutes, but most of that was harmless office flirtation Nothing I would take seriously. This letter was bold, and written by someone who knew how to turn me on. I thought I knew who wrote it but she denied it. It must be Larissa.

You see, Larissa was the law clerk for Judge Bolden at the Civil District Court. She was originally from somewhere in Mississippi, where she attended Jackson State, but now she was in her last year of law school at my alma mater, Loyola. I had a special friendship with Larissa and we had exchanged a couple of winks and smiles while I was in court and over a few downtown lunches.

Larissa was the color of straight coffee, with a smoothness to her complexion. She was five-foot-six to my six-foot-one, which meant everything lined up where it mattered. She wore her reddish-brown hair in a neck-length frizzy, natural style with spiral curls. When out with Melanie, I rudely snickered at some women who tried wearing their hair like this, but Larissa had the attitude to pull it off. Her attitude probably had as much to do with her brains as it did her sculpted body, which she defiantly displayed for all to see. I remembered all the days in court, watching her long, smooth legs and thick thighs extending from her skirt as she approached the bench. I would often find myself daydreaming about bending her over the rail by the witness stand and feeling her firm ass backed up against me and taking every last inch as I probed deep inside her wet confines.

Those thoughts weren't as clear as they were when I met her once after hours. On a Friday last month, a bunch of the black attorneys at my firm decided to go out for drinks after work. We ended up at Vincent's in the east, where Michael Ward was performing. Larissa was there with some of her girlfriends. Both of us were glad to be away from the job and spent a lot of the night hugged up in the corner. We shared a few of Vincent's special fruit punches. She laughed as she fed me a cherry from her glass.

I remember one of the older brothers at the firm, who saw us together. "Antonio, you have the whole world on an oyster shell, bruh," he said, smiling. "Just put some Tabasco sauce on it, suck it all up, and deal with the repercussions later."

Things didn't go any further between us that evening, but my conscience messed with me as I returned home, kicked our dog out of the bed, woke Melanie up, and fucked her uncontrollably the rest of the night until the cartoons came on Saturday morning.

✿   ✿   ✿

I couldn't wait to call Larissa at the start of the work week. I held myself back from calling her during the weekend. Didn't want to seem too eager.

"Clerk's office," she said as she answered the phone, sounding official.

"Hi." I almost hung up but instead picked up the receiver to take her off conference call.

" . . . Antonio."

"You know my voice."

"Of course. How could I forget it? You forgot about that night at Vincent's already?"

"No, no. I've . . . just thinking about that."

"That was fun, huh?"

"Very."

"You're working late tonight. What is it? Six?"

"Yeah, but I'm billing someone for the hours. You'll learn that once you get your law degree. Heh, heh."

"Trying to teach me bad habits already, Antonio?"

"Just those you're willing to learn."

"What if I want to be the teacher?" She was very quick, a nimble mind.

"I guess you could do that too."

"Ooooh, you give in too easy! Haha! So what's on your mind?" That little voice in my head said: *fucking you.*

"I was just checking to see how those pleadings we filed were going."

"Well, I can't say much, but Judge Bolden is looking them over. You know how he is."

"Yeah, I do; I used to clerk for him, remember? So, what are you doing there this late? Judge Bolden keeping you captive?"

"Hell nah! He's been gone. I got some case studies for school, so I'm staying here late this entire week to have some quiet time. Just me and the metal detector and security guard downstairs. Too noisy at my apartment and my boyfriend's getting on my last nerve."

"Oh, I didn't know you had a boyfriend."

Larissa loved wordplay, loved to toy with her opponent's mind. "Relax. It's nothing serious. He doesn't bite . . . *but I do.*"

"That information might come in handy one day."

"That's a secret for just me and you and the walls of my office."

"I won't tell a soul, but don't trust the walls over there at court."

"Hee, hee. I'll remember that." Her laugh was light, bouncy, and addictive.

"Well, I guess I'll leave you to your studies."

"It's been an entertaining break. Bye, Antonio. Stay sweet."

"Bye."

I left my office before I could pick up the phone and call Larissa back. Melanie was already home from her job at Xavier University, where she worked in administration, so I picked up some Popeye's chicken and something to drink for us on the way home. Nothing like homemade daiquiris to spark up things between us.

"Anything happen at work today?" my lovely wife asked later that evening as she took her daiquiri from the fridge.

"Yeah. A whole lot of bitchin' and complainin'."

"Just a regular day, huh?"

"Feel like doin' anything tonight?" In my mind, I could see Larissa's blouse falling open and her undoing her bra. Large, dark brown circles around her nipples waiting for me to dampen them with my tongue.

"Nah, I'm kinda tired. Want me to rent a movie for you?"

"No, I think I'll watch Leno." That was that.

I heard Melanie typing in our den as I half slept, restless with my forbidden hunger. She'd probably brought some work home with her. Later, she joined me in the bed and curled up next to me. I really did love her. I figured as long as I kept saying that to myself I'd be okay.

The next day passed without my calling Larissa. That didn't stop me from thinking about her. My excuse came when I volunteered to hand deliver some papers to court for Judge Morrow to approve for his reelection campaign. There she was in the second-floor hallway. Her navy blue business suit contrasted with the splashes of red in her curls, her head raised high as she laughed with colleagues. I smiled at how blessed we, as black men, were to have such magnificent queens to behold. I should have been thinking about mine, but my thoughts were of plundering another, and they became more carnal the longer my eyes stayed fixed on Larissa.

She saw me and her smile changed, became more pronounced. As I made my way through the crowded corridor, she ended her chat and headed toward me. We stopped in front of the door to Judge Morrow's office.

"Come to visit me?" she asked me, with a tiny bit of tongue peeking through her teeth.

"No," I answered, knowing that wasn't what I wanted to say. "Going to see Judge Morrow."

"Oh. How have you been?" she asked as she gave me a sizzling body hug. My free arm wrapped around her small waist. She extended both her arms around me and pulled me into her. Even under her jacket, her breasts felt firm, pushing into my chest . . . just like I knew they would.

"Wha . . . what's that perfume?" With one intoxicating whiff, I knew what it was, but I needed its name.

"Baxter for Women. New perfume. Expensive but worth it, don'tcha think?"

"It's nice, real nice," I replied with a straight face.

"A little strong, but I think it suits my personality. Macy's had an introductory sale on it a couple of weeks ago and women were swarming to buy it. Matter of fact, when I bought it, I think I saw your wife and an older lady in there."

I pulled away on reflex, remembering that Larissa had seen my wife before at one of my firm's parties. "Yeah, that was my mother-in-law with her. They were shopping for wedding gifts for her cousin. Look, I gotta run. I'm kind of pressed for time, so . . . ."

"Don't let me hold you up, Antonio. Run along. I'm sure we'll be talking."

I held my breath for fear of inhaling more of her lure and just losing all manner of the common sense my momma said I was blessed with. It was another night of dreams filled with images of our sweat-drenched bodies and Larissa laughing wildly as I licked and tasted her, just as she'd described in the letter.

The following day, I was greeted with another letter. This time it was dropped off at the front desk at my job and marked "confidential," for my eyes only. The envelope was covered faintly in the fragrance, her fragrance, as well. I closed my office door and held it near my nose. I shut my eyes, inhaled its scent, and reached for the letter opener. The tearing of the envelope released the seductive perfume into the air, wafting it up into a cloud that seemed to surround me.

Antonio,

I'm surprised you haven't figured it out yet. Or maybe you're just scared to find what ecstasy awaits you on these lips, in my arms, and between my legs. You know where to find your love. It's always been here waiting for you; maybe you got lost along the way. Just show up. Don't keep me waiting tonight.

Now . . . More than ever,

Cayenne

Issues, issues, issues. I thumped my fingers on my desk repeatedly as I contemplated a rendezvous with Larissa tonight. As long as she had desired me, I had probably felt the same powerful feelings of desire for her equally, but had just been afraid to admit it. There was safety and love in what was already mine, but what was burning in me was undermining my loyalty and fidelity to it. If only Melanie was willing to address my passion and save me from my downward spiral to betrayal. But I knew that wasn't going to happen. It was a waste of hope to still believe that. I knew what I had to do.

At four, my assistant peeked into my office to alert me to an incoming call.

"This is Antonio."

"Hi honey."

"Hi." My voice carried the strain of my burden.

"What's wrong? You sound down." She picked it up right away.

"No, I'm just a little distracted, Melanie. Job stuff. A new case that's been assigned to me."

"Oh, I was calling to see if you were about to leave for home."

"No, I'm going to be pulling a long night. You know, this case . . ." I had been sitting at my desk for the last three hours doing absolutely nothing but fantasizing about my meeting with Larissa. The throbbing and lust throughout my body was a symptom of the release I so desperately needed.

"Good," she said, catching me by surprise. "I knew it was my night to cook, but I have some errands to run before I come home. So you'll get something to eat?"

"Yeah, I'll eat something tonight before I come home," I said in a daze, not caring if I ate or not.

"See you later, honey. I'll stay up for you."

"Okay . . . bye."

At seven, I was still wrestling with my demons, but in truth, they had already won. The parking lot across the street from the courthouse was empty. The day attendant was being relieved when I drove up. I drove around downtown aimlessly for over an hour, taking side streets, getting ever closer to the spicy, burning heat of Cayenne.

With my briefcase full of my previous day's work, I walked through the metal detector on the first floor. The security guard nonchalantly watched the X-ray machine monitor and handed me my watch and cell phone, completely unaware of my intentions on this hot, humid evening. On my way to the elevator, the sound of a cleaning person dumping a garbage can startled me. I laughed nervously, telling myself that everything would be alright. I could feel my heart pumping hard as I reached up to knock on the door to Larissa's office.

"Come in," she said, as if she had intuition and knew it was me. Before entering, I loosened my tie because it felt more like a noose with each passing second.

"Hi. I . . . I just stopped by to check on you."

"This time of night? That's so sweet of you, Antonio." She was studying some papers and books at her desk. With a pen in her mouth like a clerk, she surveyed the bulge in my pants that I couldn't hide and smiled approvingly.

"Yeah. That's when things happen . . . at night. Studying?"

"Looks like it, huh?" she chuckled. Her jacket was off and she had several buttons undone on her white blouse, either to cool off or as an invitation for the fun to begin. Hot summer nights in New Orleans and old buildings without air conditioning didn't go well together. I could feel perspiration gathering under my shirt. It was stifling in the room. I had wanted to leave my suit coat down in the car, but it was necessary to keep it for the sake of appearances. I wanted to seem like everything was strictly business.

"So . . . what's on your mind?" Her voice had the same effect on me as her perfume.

"Love," I said after a very long second, an eternity. "Is this where love is? I can't fight it anymore. You win. You told me to come . . . and here . . . here I am. Show me the love."

Larissa appeared stunned by my words and leaned back in the antique chair. She watched me walk closer to her with veiled eyes.

"I can't stop thinking about you or your perfume," I said with a note of desperation in my voice. "Larissa, you're haunting me. If . . . if all of this has been a game or if I'm misunderstanding things, just tell me. If not, then . . ."

She leaned forward and there was no mistaking what was in her eyes now. "Close the door. Lock it."

As I followed her instructions, she closed her textbooks and removed herself from her chair. I turned to find her tugging at my shirt as she reached up to kiss me. The first touch of our lips was hard and forceful, as if we had to release the anxiety of the moment. It was quickly followed by the wet softness as our mouths came to know each other. Her long tongue darted into my mouth like a snake looking for its home while her hands began gently removing my shirt from the waist of my pants. I grunted as her thigh pressed up against my manhood.

Sensing my approval, Larissa clenched me through my pants, outlining the length of my sex with her fingertips, while continuing to unbutton my shirt with her free hand. Hot kisses and small tender bites peppered the side of my neck. "Is this dick for me, Antonio?" she whispered into my ear.

"Yessss, all yours." My jacket fell to the floor and my shirt wasn't far behind.

"You want to fuck me bad, huh?" she teased as she moved her mouth across my chest, stopping to lazily lick my nipples. My hands were finally feeling the firmness of her flesh, caressing those wonderfully soft thighs and those curvy, childbearing hips that screamed out to be tamed. She wore nothing underneath her skirt, causing me to smile.

"It gets hot while I'm in here alone, so I take them off," she cooed in that sexy siren purr that heated me to my core. "I've fantasized about sharing that with you, Antonio."

That thing she referred to had been the burning object of my obsession since the very first letter and now that pearl lay before me. Any doubts I may have possessed about her being my mysterious letter writer vanished with that comment. Thinking about all that was said in the letter whipped me into a frenzy. I wanted her. I wanted to experience everything promised by Cayenne on those perfumed pages. With my eyes locked on hers, I tenderly slid two fingers into her moist sweet pot and I backed her onto the antique desk. My fingers found that precious ridge just beyond the opening and went to work.

"Stop, stop, stop," she gasped, fighting for breath. "You're driving me fucking crazy!"

"You don't want me to stop," I casually replied, sensing no real resistance.

I unfastened the remaining buttons on her blouse and unclasped the catches of her white bra, which came off with a pop, freeing her magnificent breasts. Some of the biggest, most succulent nipples I've ever seen begged for me to kiss and suck them. I obeyed their command willingly, causing her to writhe and wiggle atop the hardwood desk.

"Kiss me, kiss me all over, kiss me everywhere," she commanded, knowing that was exactly what I intended to do.

I climbed on top of her, starting with another long kiss to those lips as she caressed my back and ass with both hands, stopping only long enough to drag her manicured nails whenever it got too hot for her. I trailed my tongue under the sensitive areas near her ear, down her silky neck, across her chest to the peak of her cleavage, where I stopped to inhale the hot, spicy scent that should have been named Cayenne instead of Baxter for Women. The throbbing of my erection increased in intensity, straining its ramrod length. Gently, I cupped a breast in each hand and sucked and lapped at them, switching back and forth. Her head fell under the weight of a chorus of moans.

I left my hands there while I ran my lips across her belly, down to her newly unwrapped treasure that I was soon to claim. Claim in my name and my name alone. It was wet, wetter than that of any woman I'd ever known. My ego was feeling pretty good as I dove in to taste her essence.

As I concentrated my tongue on her clit and outer lips, Larissa erupted into a series of cries: oh shit, oh shit, day-um! She must've climaxed seven times at least before she begged me to stop. I obliged her and helped her to sit up on the desk while I caught my breath and worked the crick out of my neck. She looked at me with a smile of disbelief, then stood and slowly walked to me. Kneeling, she pulled down my pants and briefs, exposing my hard dick, ready for her. She took its head into her mouth, running her tongue and lips over it, then along its length, before gripping it firmly and swallowing it whole, embracing it with the warm insides at the top of her throat. I was getting weak in the knees from the strumming and humming when she suddenly stopped.

"Follow me," she said, leading me from her office to Judge Bolden's chambers. "My back was killing me on that hard-ass desk."

I watched her lay her stately chocolate frame in the dark onto Judge Bolden's large leather couch. Her next words, low and raspy, could barely be heard. "Now . . . come kill this." I knew exactly what she meant.

Balancing on one hand, I lowered onto her body and entered her. It was hot, pulsing and tight. It dared me to break it in and reshape its contours, which I promptly did. She squealed passionately on my first full downstroke, her knees instinctively rising as I continued to pump into her in controlled thrusts. Our breathing became more intense as we settled into a savage rhythm, totally in sync. The familiarity of our dance was scary. We went at it like horny newlyweds, not giving a damn about anything, oblivious to the outside world. The puddle of sweat forming under us on the leather made unusual, almost unearthly sounds in addition to the more natural ones coming from us, two people locked at the pelvis and rocketing toward ecstasy.

"You're . . . you're amazing," I stuttered, catching my breath. I pulled out of her and she guided me with her hands on my ass until my dick was near her mouth. She covered it with her lips and sucked it to a steely hardness.

"Now, give me the dick, Antonio," she shrieked, pushing me back into position. "Give me the dick, fuck me until I can't stand it no more! Fuck me!" I was in it, back snapping, hips going side to side, all on it. She shouted something else, something that made no sense, just before she lost all control of her body. I felt the rush of her sweetness as it drenched me seconds later and I collapsed onto her with our climaxes peaking in unison. I felt the tremors rippling her limp body below me and tried to move but couldn't.

Minutes later, Larissa revived and spoke, brushing wet strands of hair from her face. "Lawd, yes," she giggled, finally getting back her breath.

"Uh-huh." That was all I could muster.

After ten minutes of recovery time, we cleaned up the best we could in the restroom adjacent to the judge's chambers. She found a can of air freshener and sprayed a few blasts before we tidied up her employer's things and left. I escorted her to her car. There was nothing we could say about what had just happened. The mutual satisfaction in our faces, in our smiles, said it all. We both understood the course we'd taken and what it meant to our lives. This was something new. There was no turning back.

"So, I'll see you later?" I asked as Larissa started her Maxima. The song "Seven Days" by the British singer Craig David was playing on the radio.

"If you want," she replied with a wink. "As much as you want."

"Let me get one last whiff of the real thing," I said, leaning over to place my face in the middle of her breasts. The combined scents of her perfume and my sweat were intoxicating. A new fragrance which would linger with me for days. She giggled and pushed me away, giving me a short but sensuous kiss. A good-bye smooch.

"Bye, boy!"

"Bye, Cayenne." I watched her drive away, my body still humming from the workout.

"Huh?" she said as she backed up, pretending not to know I was referring to her. Still with the games, I thought.

To cover the evidence, I blasted the AC and turned all the vents on me during the drive home. Fixing my clothes would not have helped at this point. I considered calling one of my buddies to bail me out with a change of clothes but I didn't see the need to involve anyone else in my affairs. I didn't need to let someone all up in my business, not this kind of business.

I was going to be a man and try to sneak in. It was after ten and I prayed that Melanie would be asleep. I cursed at the sound of the alarm chime that announced my arrival at the door. Strangely, our dog was nowhere in sight.

The coast appeared clear so I let out a sigh and took off my jacket. The hallway light was out as I quietly walked to our bedroom. On the tiny table where Melanie liked to put her scented candles one was lit this night, bathing the hallway in an amber glow. While the candle held my attention only briefly, what I saw placed near it stopped me dead in my tracks and made me back up. A familiar envelope lay on the glass. My heart skipped a beat as I nervously picked it up. I'd thought that both letters from Larissa, or Cayenne or whatever she called herself, were still back at my office, but now I wasn't so sure. Panic set in as I slowly raised the envelope and took a whiff.

Oh shit, I thought to myself. How could this be? Had Melanie somehow gone by the office and found the letters? I yanked the letter out and read.

Antonio,

I'm glad that you've figured out my little secret. All these days, I've been waiting for you to find your way to me. I told you not to keep me waiting . . . but I guess the wait has been worth it. Hope you enjoyed the other letters. I knew you needed a little spice in your life. That time is here, now.

From the hallway, I saw more light flickering from our bedroom. It wasn't until then that I realized the candlelight was casting a long reflection. My head was spinning from both panic and confusion. What would I do? For unknown reasons, tears welled up in my eyes. I took slow, deliberate steps, unsure of what awaited me beyond the cracked bedroom door.

Please God, I prayed like any good sinner would. Let her be asleep. Let this all be a simple mistake. Then it hit me. Right as I walked in. That familiar aroma was in the air, filling the space of our bedroom.

Hot and spicy . . . with a trace of cinnamon.

"I've been up waiting for you all night, Antonio. Like my new perfume?" she asked. Our room was filled with candles, all shapes, all sizes. Melanie was clad in nothing but a see-though lace robe. A red wig covered her jet-black hair, making her look mysterious and even hotter. "It's called Baxter for Women. I picked it up at Macy's a few weeks ago when I was shopping with my mom."

"God no!" I didn't mean to blurt that out.

"Baby, I hope you enjoyed my teases. I know I've been distant lately, but I decided to do something different, spice up our love life. I love you, Antonio."

"No . . . no . . . no." I shook my head. What a fool I'd been.

"Sweetheart, what's wrong? You look like you want to cry," she said as she seductively sprawled across our bed. "You don't like what you see? You mean you don't want any of this Cayenne?"

The Apostle Charles

Tracy Grant

The word today will come from Jeremiah Nine, starting at Verse Three."

The congregation turned their Bibles to Jeremiah as Rev. Holland instructed. His eyes scanned the large audience to make sure they were paying attention.

"They make ready their tongue like a bow, to shoot lies; it is not by truth that they triumph in the land," he read.

"Teach," said a woman from the back of the church.

"They go from one sin to another," Rev. Holland continued. "They do not acknowledge me, declares the Lord. Beware of your friend, do not trust your brothers. For every brother is a deceiver."

"Yes, sir!" shouted one of the deacons.

"And every friend a slanderer," continued the preacher. "Friend deceives friend, and no one speaks the truth. They have taught their tongues to lie; they weary themselves with sinning. You live in the midst of deception."

"Deception!" a woman shouted.

"And in their deceit," Rev. Holland read, "they refuse . . . to . . . acknowledge . . . me . . . declares the Lord."

Charles Holland delivered the rest of a heartfelt sermon, using scripture to tell the congregation that lying and backbiting among friends were, in God's eyes, counterproductive, and nothing good would ever come of it. He had been particularly moved by the spirit that Sunday and his sermon reflected it. He enjoyed the choir's hymns, the supper, and all the other ceremonies of each service, but connecting his congregation to the word of God was most important to him. The way he peered out at everyone before reading a verse, one would almost think they were in a classroom and not in church.

As he did each Sunday, Rev. Holland stood at the church entrance to greet everyone after the morning service let out.

"Fine service today, Reverend," Mrs. Jenkins told him as she left.

"Thank you, Mother Jenkins. A compliment from you sure makes me feel good."

Mrs. Jenkins beamed. "You stop it, with your handsome self." Rev. Holland smiled at one of the elders of Providence Baptist Church. She shooed him away with her arm, but her smile was as bright as the sunshine. A younger woman helped her down the steps.

"Wonderful service, Reverend," another woman told him.

"Thank you, Sister Parker."

"You truly felt the spirit today. Reverend Thompson would be proud, God rest his soul."

"He taught me what I know. I wouldn't be a pastor if not for him."

"Well, he certainly prepared you well."

"Thank you. You get home safe now."

Rev. Holland continued to greet the congregation. The older women showered him with praise and he playfully flirted with them. He contained that charm when the younger women gave him compliments; he didn't want his wife Joyce to get the wrong impression. The wives of pastors were usually not far away when pastors greeted the congregation, but Joyce Holland chose not to do this. Once in a while she would stand by his side after service, but usually she mingled with the church officers or the staff. Still, Rev. Holland behaved when the younger women came on to him; Joyce was never anyplace where she couldn't see him, and no matter what she said, he knew she was watching.

Hours later, Rev. Holland led the afternoon service, trying to preach with the same passion that he'd had during the morning service. Providence Baptist Church was far less crowded in the afternoon, and Rev. Holland liked to think that those who came later were only there for the word. There was no social value in the afternoon service; one couldn't see the latest church outfits or who was with whom, because most of the congregation was home or elsewhere by then. To get a glimpse of the latest goings-on among black folks in Davidson County, Providence Baptist was the place to be. But not during the afternoon service.

Joyce was waiting in his car, a navy blue Chevy Malibu, after the second service. Charles walked across the parking area toward the car, overcome with love for his wife. He loved the fact that riding in an ordinary car didn't bother her; she had an old Toyota Tercel and when the time came for him to buy a new car, he got the Chevy. He could have bought something much nicer, but he wanted to save for their future. Joyce had to put up with a lot of flak from women in the church about the average-looking car, but she never complained.

"Sorry to keep you waiting," he apologized as he got into the driver's seat.

"That's all right, hon. You were working."

Charles leaned over and kissed her.

"What was that for?"

"That was 'cause I love you."

"Well I love you, too! Remind me to wait in the car more often!" They shared a laugh as Charles started the car. Just as he pulled out, he heard a man's voice.

"Reverend Holland! Hey, Reverend Holland!" Charles could see Edward Chase, the fifty-eight-year-old chairman of the Deacon Board, walking briskly toward the car. He was almost dragging a young, attractive woman with him. He tapped on the passenger window and Joyce lowered it.

"I'm sorry to hold y'all up, but I wanted you to meet someone. Reverend and Mrs. Holland, this is my wife, Beverly Chase."

Charles looked at the woman and was stunned. *Beverly?* he thought. *No! It couldn't be!*

"Nice to meet you both," Beverly said, shaking hands with Joyce. Charles composed himself and shook hands with the woman, grinning, but saying nothing.

"I know y'all done heard about my new bride, but she was visiting her mother the last month or so."

"She's not doing too well," Beverly offered. "Diabetes."

"We'll certainly pray for her," Charles replied.

"Thank you."

"We're in prayer," Edward added. "But I'm sure glad to have my baby back. Reverend, I just wanted her to meet you."

"I'm glad you brought her by, Edward. Beverly, it was a pleasure meeting you."

"You as well. I'm sure I'll be seeing you in church."

"Yes, uh . . . we hope so."

Moments later, Joyce was shaking her head as they drove.

"That woman could be his daughter," she said. "Deacon Edward ought to be ashamed of himself. Don't you think?"

"Honey, you never know. They *are* adults, and he certainly seems happy."

"Please. Just like a man to take his side. You know it's not right, I don't care what you say."

"Maybe not." Charles was happy to agree with her. As long as she didn't suspect the truth, he would indulge her opinions all day.

That evening, Joyce prepared Charles's favorite dinner—crab-cakes with mixed greens, wild rice, and Caesar salad. Charles, who had a healthy appetite, was pleased. He thanked God for the home that Joyce had made for the both of them. He paid the bulk of the mortgage on their modern, two-story brick townhouse, but it was Joyce that made it feel like home. And she sure could cook. By most standards, the Hollands were a middle-class family—not wealthy, but not at all starving. Davidson County, Tennessee, had a considerable number of upwardly mobile African Americans, and Beulah, the smallest town in the county, was no exception. Charles had always been smart with money, saving regularly and rarely overspending. Because they had been thrifty, if they wanted the Hollands could now keep up with the "Joneses" of Beulah, with cars, jewelry, and fine art collections. They didn't. And even if appearances had mattered to them, Charles's social status was ironclad; he was the newest and, at twenty-eight, youngest pastor at Beulah's oldest and most popular church. It made no difference what the Hollands had in the bank. Charles, and Joyce by association, were practically royalty in Davidson County.

Charles sat at the table stuffing his face.

"Honey, this dinner is delicious," he told his wife.

"Thank you. You're eating like I never feed you at all."

He chuckled.

"Enjoy it," Joyce advised. "I just felt like cooking tonight."

The phone rang and Joyce got up to answer it.

"Hello? Oh, hi Ryan!"

Charles looked up, shook his head, and waved his hand. Joyce got the message.

"I'm afraid Charles isn't here right now. But he'll be glad you called. Okay . . . bye now."

Joyce hung up the phone and returned to the table with a disturbed look.

"You know I hate doing that. Why don't you want to talk to Ryan?"

"He wants me to hang out with him. He doesn't understand I'm not into that anymore."

"Maybe he just wants to see you, Charles. What's wrong with that?"

"Nothing, if he lived in the real world. But Ryan still thinks we're in school."

"You were inseparable in college," Joyce said, her voice trailing a bit. "Both All-Americans, winning state championships together. You two were the heart and soul of that football team."

"Yeah, we put the Tigers on the map," he said, referring to the Tennessee State football team. "But that was almost ten years ago, Joyce. I've moved on, Ryan hasn't."

"What makes you so sure?"

"He still can't believe I don't watch football on Sundays. I tell him I still love the game, but I don't have time to sit around and look at sports all day. We just don't have that much in common anymore."

"That's too bad, for Ryan anyway," Joyce said. She got up from the table and came around to where Charles was sitting. She planted herself in her husband's lap. Joyce was slender, but her behind was as round as a basketball and she knew right where to put it.

"Now you and me, we have a lot in common, don't we?"

"Yes, ma'am." Charles felt himself becoming aroused.

Charles could hardly wait to get Joyce upstairs so they could make love. The dishes and food were still on the dinner table. Charles laid on his back in bed with his wife, who was nestled under his muscular arm. It had been voracious, hungry sex and Joyce was still shuddering every few seconds. She put her head on his chest, breathing deeply for a moment before speaking.

"I don't know what just got into you, but I like it."

Charles smiled. "I'm still a man, honey."

"I never said you weren't. That's your hang-up, preacher man."

"Oh, I see. Well I'm glad you enjoyed yourself," he told her.

"I did." Joyce began to rub his wide chest, softly scratching him and playing with his chest hairs. Then she kissed him on the chest. She kissed his chest over and over, then she moved to his stomach. Charles was surprised when she moved down because Joyce almost never did that kind of thing. This time she kept going, slowly passing his stomach, gently stroking his stiff erection with her hand. When he felt her lips, it was all he could do not to shriek with delight. She was good.

After Joyce fell asleep, Charles laid in bed staring at the ceiling. He had always enjoyed making love to his wife, but that night she had been extraordinary. He hadn't felt this whorish since college, long before God called him to the ministry. When Charles went to the seminary, he'd thought the only way he could study effectively would be to change his sexual inclinations. His friends had all teased him that preachers didn't do it doggy style, and they certainly didn't receive oral sex. Good preachers, that is. Charles had believed them, and he had played the field for a few months before he began his studies. Multiple partners, strip joints, and freaky sex had never been a part of his life, even at the height of his football career. But before he went to seminary, he did it all. Then he became a minister, calmed down, and married his true love. Joyce had always been sexually conservative, and Charles thought it unfair to expect anything else from her. She had married a minister. So what had happened tonight? Did she suspect something about Beverly? Did she know? Charles stayed up for hours trying to figure out his wife, until paranoia finally let him go and he fell asleep.

The next morning, Charles and Joyce went through their normal routine: coffee with a pastry, checking the weather report on the morning TV news, a kiss good-bye, then Joyce rushing off to Davidson County High School, where she was a guidance counselor. Charles headed to the church to catch up on some paperwork. His predecessor and mentor, the late Henry Thompson, had built Providence Baptist into a powerful force in the community. In addition to the standard choirs, bible studies, and youth groups, Providence provided adult learning, job training, day care, a scholarship fund, a food service ministry, and low-income housing. The church operated a federal credit union and a bookstore. Charles and his staff were in charge of all of these services.

Charles had been working at his desk all morning when someone knocked on the church office door.

"It's open," he shouted, figuring it was the church clerk. Then he regretted the words as soon as they left his mouth. Somehow he knew who it was before even looking up.

"Hello, Charles."

"Beverly." When he looked at her, his mind went back to senior year when they were lovers. She hadn't aged at all.

"I hope I didn't put you in a tight spot yesterday. I didn't know who Edward was bringing me over to meet."

"Right, so he didn't tell you, huh?"

"I didn't know until he pulled me away. I would never want to say hello like that."

"I suppose that's why you're here."

"Yes." She came around the desk and put her arms around his neck.

"It's nice to see you again," she whispered.

"Nice to see you too," he said, pushing her arms off him. "Edward talks about you all the time. I didn't know it was you."

Beverly laughed. "Funny, I was thinking the same thing."

"You knew I was studying to become a minister."

"Yes, but I didn't expect you to be the pastor for a church so big. Not so soon, anyway."

"Reverend Thompson's death caught us all by surprise. But he said in his will that if something were to happen to him, he wanted me to take over."

"From what I can see, you've done a hell of a job. Oh, excuse me!"

"That's all right."

"You've done a fantastic job."

Charles forced a smile and they faced each other in silence. He could think of nothing other than Beverly's build. She was shorter than his wife, but it didn't matter. Everything was the same; shapely legs, full breasts, plump backside, all in a form-fitting black dress with matching heels. She saw how he was looking at her. He cursed himself.

"Why didn't you tell me you were married to Edward?"

"Charles, I didn't know you were in Beulah. I didn't even know you were the pastor!"

"Bull, you didn't know. You think I don't hear these women gossip? You've been the talk of the Usher Board for over a month!"

"I don't care what these hussies say about me."

"Is it true what they say? Have you been sleeping with other men behind Edward's back?"

"What do you think?"

"Stop with the games, Beverly! Is it true or not?"

"I don't think we should talk about that."

"For God's sake! That man loves you! It would kill him!"

"Don't believe everything you hear, Charles."

Charles was fuming, but he gathered himself after this comment. "Oh. I'm sorry."

"It's okay. Look, I haven't always been perfect. But I have been honest. Edward knew what he was getting when he proposed to me. And I don't think he's that concerned with what I do when he's not around."

"Give me a break," Charles muttered.

"I'm telling you what I know," she retorted. "But I didn't come here for that. I came to let you know you won't have a problem with me. When I saw your wife I was . . . disappointed, I'll admit. But I respect you and what you're doing here. If anything, I hope you'll consider me a friend."

"*Edward* is my friend."

"And he's my husband. If everyone minds their business, it'll stay that way."

"Yeah. Listen, I've got some more work to do."

"I understand, I won't hold you. I've got to get to work myself."

"Where's that?"

"The hospital. Administration."

"Good for you."

"Thanks. I'll let myself out."

Charles waved from his desk and looked down at his paperwork.

"Charles?"

"I'd like it if you called me Reverend Holland."

"Oh, excuse me. Reverend?"

"Yes?"

"You look great."

That afternoon, Charles got a call from Joyce. She asked him to pick her up because the Tercel had to go to the repair shop. Charles drove over to the high school, where Joyce was waiting at the front entrance.

Joyce got in the front seat and gave him a kiss. "Hi sweetie," she greeted him.

"Hey baby," he said, pulling off. He could tell Joyce had carried the relaxation of last night through the day. Guilt was rising in him. "Did they say when they'd have the car ready?"

"Friday," she told him. "I'll need a ride to work until then."

"You got it."

"Thanks. Did you get any work done at church?"

"Oh yeah, very productive. Everybody on staff works together, making my job easier."

"Are you ready for Bible study tomorrow?"

"Of course. I can't wait."

"Maybe I'll come tomorrow night."

"You're always welcome," he said, acting unaffected. "In fact, it would be nice."

Charles and Joyce enjoyed an early dinner. They didn't talk as much as they usually did. Charles studied his wife while she ate; her prolonged silence meant she wanted to discuss something.

"Something on your mind, honey?" he asked.

"There is, but I'm not sure if you want to deal with it."

"Of course I do. You're my wife. Your troubles are my troubles."

Joyce looked him and practically melted. "You don't know what it means to hear you say that."

"I love you."

"And I love you, Charles. That really takes a load off my mind."

"So what is it?"

"I'm ready to have a child."

"I see. You're, you're not . . ."

"No, Charles, I am not pregnant. But I want to have a child this year."

"Okay."

"Charles, you don't seem too thrilled with the idea."

"It's not that, hon, I'm just a little surprised, that's all."

"We've talked about it before."

"Yes, but you seem to have made up your mind already."

"I'm thirty years old, Charles. Neither of us is getting any younger. You're the head of a successful church, our bills are paid, we've got a few pennies saved, why not?"

Charles had no answer, and he didn't necessarily disagree. But his silence spoke volumes.

"See, this is why I didn't want to say anything," Joyce said, her eyes tearing.

"Come on, honey, you just—"

"Just nothing!" she cried. "You don't want to have a child with me!"

"Baby, that's not true!"

"Then what's holding you back? If you're not ready, Charles, then why?"

Joyce slammed her hand on the table, got up, and stormed out of the room. Charles was left with the silence that had gotten him in trouble in the first place. He had heard that silence was golden, but nothing could have been further from the truth at that moment. After a few seconds he chuckled to himself. There he was, known as a talented orator, but he couldn't come up with any words to comfort his wife. He had done nothing to calm her insecurity.

Charles tried to console Joyce that night, but she was still hurting and she didn't want to discuss the matter further. She was cold and distant in bed, a far cry from the fiery woman Charles had made love to the night before. He knew Joyce was sensitive about having a child and her impending age, though she didn't look a day over twenty-five. She'd caught him by surprise that night, and his awkward silence had confirmed her fears. He might have been ready with an answer if he hadn't been thinking about Beverly. Charles wanted a child, maybe two, and he loved Joyce. Her question—what was holding him back?—was a fair one. Charles lay in bed wide awake, full of uncertainty. It wasn't that he didn't want children. The fact was, Charles was no longer sure he was ready to be married, and he'd been married for three years. The very thought shook him, and he knew it would never have occurred to him had he not seen Beverly. Beverly. Steadfast under trial, he thought to himself. *Steadfast under trial*.

The Tuesday night Bible study at Providence was packed; there were nearly a hundred people, more than Charles had ever seen. Joyce had still been inconsolable that morning, but instead of being angry with him, she moped around and kept her head down, making Charles feel worse. He would have preferred the standard anger. Still, they had agreed to talk about children after tonight's Bible study. Charles approached the rest of the day positively, starting with his clothes. For all his work at Providence Baptist, Charles Holland also had the stereotypical trait of the black preacher man: style. He was naturally handsome, taking his father's boyish face and his mother's flawless, coffee-colored skin. He was six-foot-three and in tremendous shape. Then he was, as they said in Davidson County, "sharp": always neat and coordinated, even in sweats, and born to wear suits. Folks in church said the boy hung a suit better than the dry cleaners. This wasn't unique at Providence—men were taught from boyhood that a good suit was one of their most important possessions. However, unlike some of the other men in town, Charles wore conservative suits in traditional colors. There was no chartreuse, turquoise, peach, or lavender in his suit collection. Nor did he "freestyle" with shirts or ties; there were no patterns or designs here. With his shirt crisp and white every Sunday morning, Charles looked more like an MBA than a resident of Beulah.

He had stayed home that morning and read scripture, making notes in his study. Reading scripture was a way to let God speak to him. He had to tell himself not to rely on his own intelligence to lead, but on God's wisdom, and he could only do this if he was receptive to the word. This wasn't always easy, but Charles made sure he was as "open" to God that day as possible.

He arrived at church at five o'clock, two hours before Bible study. Thankfully, no one else was in the sanctuary and he walked around by himself. He admired Rev. Thompson's work on the interior; tall stained-glass windows, marble columns, velvet, rose-colored carpeting and ropes, beautiful oak pews, and an oak pulpit. He'd seen all kinds of churches just like it, but this one was his. A painting of Jesus Christ hung from the rafters in front of the church. It struck Charles that in the painting, Jesus looked like Michael Jackson; long-haired, pale-skinned, benevolent, a black man made to look white. He made a mental note to look at some other Jesus paintings.

So, with his mind clear, Charles began a spirited Bible study that night. Just as she'd said she would, Joyce had shown up and he was pleased to see her.

"Last week we said we'd look at the Book of Romans, Chapter Eight," Charles told the congregation. As usual, he waited for everyone to find the verse in their Bibles.

"This was Paul's letter to Rome, and he talked about faith. I thought it would be useful to start at Verse Five. 'Those who live according to the sinful nature have their minds set on what that nature desires,'" he read. "'But those who live in accordance with the Spirit have their minds set on what the Spirit desires. The mind of the sinful man is death, but the mind controlled by the Spirit is life and peace.'"

"Yes, Lord," shouted a woman from the pews.

"What does Paul mean by the 'mind of the sinful man' here?" Charles asked.

"Sin," answered a young man. "Someone thinking about sin."

"What kind of sin? What do y'all think?"

There were murmurs from the group, but no one spoke up.

"The mind of the sinful man is set on the flesh, beloved," Charles told them. "The words 'nature' and 'desire' are the clues. Living according to the sinful nature means thinking about the desires of that nature. Lust is a desire, and it's physical. From Verse Seven now. 'The sinful mind is hostile to God. It does not submit to God's law, nor can it do so. Those controlled by the sinful nature cannot . . . please . . . God.'"

"Yes, Lord," shouted a woman. Just then, Beverly walked in, wearing a cream-colored blouse and a loose, medium-length, pale green skirt. Charles had to fight not to look at her tan, stocking-clad legs, looking like caramel against the pale green.

"We all have sin inside of us," he continued.

"Yes," said a woman from the pews.

"But the challenge for us, beloved, is not to be controlled by that inner sin."

"Teach."

"Paul never said it wouldn't be there, Jesus never said it wouldn't be there, but we have to control it!"

"Talk about it now," shouted a man from the back.

"We can't let base desires control us. If our mind is set on the flesh, then we are controlled by that mind. That's why you have to keep your mind on the Spirit!"

"Yes, Lord!" another woman shouted.

"Not just your heart, but your mind!" Charles pointed to his own head. "That takes effort, beloved! That's why we come here every Tuesday, isn't it?"

"Yes!" shouted a woman from the back.

"We've got to keep our mind right! Because the sin is in us! It's in all of us, y'all."

"That's right," agreed a man sitting in front.

"There are no exceptions. Human beings are the same. The sin is in us. Don't matter if we in church every day, it's in us, y'all."

The study group laughed. Charles allowed himself to smile. "But we have to control our mind. We can't have the mind of sin, that's what leads to the wrong decision. We've got to keep our mind in the Spirit. Actively in the Spirit."

For the rest of Bible study, Charles faced one side of the pews, opposite where Beverly was sitting. The quick glance he'd had was enough to give him an erection. Beverly's legs were crossed, and one of her high-heeled shoes was almost off, hanging from her toes as she moved her ankle. As much as he tried to ignore her, Charles couldn't always divert his eyes from her. Nor did it matter that she was across the room; Beverly gave him super vision. As he enlightened the study group, he caught quick glances at her skirt, the loose, paper-thin pale green. The way that pale green fabric fell across her lap and accented her thighs, she may as well have been naked.

When Bible study concluded, the attendees did their usual mingling in the church lobby before leaving. Charles collected his jacket and briefcase, locked up the church office, and walked through the sanctuary to the lobby, where Joyce was waiting for him.

"I enjoyed that, Charles."

"Thanks, honey. Let's go, I'm starving."

Charles led his wife to the door and quickly followed her out. Beverly was at the foot of the steps.

"Excuse me, Reverend Holland?"

"Yes, hello, ah . . . Mrs. Chase."

"Hello. I wanted to tell you how much I liked tonight's Bible study."

"Thank you," Charles said, trying to hurry along. Beverly followed behind them.

"I've been to quite a few, and I must say that no one else has ever interpreted the word that way. Nobody."

Joyce craned her neck and shot the woman a nasty look.

"Perhaps you should come to church more often."

"Oh, I plan to," Beverly answered. "Good night, Mrs. Holland, Reverend Holland."

"Good night," Charles said, forcing a smile.

Joyce slammed the car door when she got in. Charles braced himself as he drove out of the parking area.

"Goddamn tramp. Who the hell does she think is? Think I don't know when someone's trying to catch? *My* man? Bitch must be out of her mind."

Instinct told Charles to keep silent, but silence had failed him the last time Joyce was upset.

"I understand, honey."

"Yeah," she fumed. "Where was Deacon Edward tonight, anyway?"

"He had to pick someone up at the hospital."

"Hmph."

Charles changed his mind and decided to keep his mouth shut. He figured the incident might blow over before they got home. He was wrong.

"Do you know that heifer, Charles?"

"Huh?"

"I said do you know that woman Beverly." He could feel Joyce's stare. Silence was not an option.

"She looks familiar, but I don't think so."

"You don't think so?" Joyce shouted. "Do you know the woman or not?"

"No. Not personally, anyway."

"Where do you know her from?"

"I don't know her, honey, but I used to see her around school."

"Something you want to tell me, Charles?"

"No!" Charles felt his temper rising. "Absolutely not," he lied, composing himself. "She did look familiar when Deacon Edward brought her over, but I didn't know her."

Joyce turned away and looked out the window, dissatisfaction all over her face. Charles knew she was still thinking, but he could live with that. He had provided nothing to which his wife's suspicions could take hold.

In an attempt to keep the peace, Charles ate dinner without saying much and retreated to the living room afterward. Usually he read or worked out in the basement, but tonight he tried to relax by watching television. He ran through the channels with the remote until he found *Cooley High*.

"Honey?" he called. "Your movie's on." A night on the couch could be just what they needed.

"What movie?"

"*Cooley High!*"

"I'll be there in a minute."

After clearing the table, Joyce joined Charles in the living room. He pulled her close to him and she seemed to relax, laughing all over again at the classic film. After about an hour, she looked up at Charles.

"You know, we still need to talk."

"Honey, don't worry about Beverly."

"I don't care nothin' about that ho, I'm talking about having a baby," she spat. Charles sighed, knowing he had upset her all over again. Where was his divine wisdom now? Where was the pastoral guidance that everyone raved about?

"I'm sorry. I didn't forget."

"Charles, I don't understand why you're not ready."

"Baby, I am ready, spiritually and emotionally. It's just that Providence is still new to me and I'm just getting adjusted. I didn't expect children to be an issue so soon."

"We've talked about it, Charles," Joyce retorted. "You never had any problem before. I don't see how the time could get any better. And you didn't say that the other night, you just sat there looking dumb. What's the matter with you?"

"Nothing. I don't know, maybe everything is happening too fast."

"Too fast? Charles, this is what you've always wanted. You're following in Reverend Thompson's footsteps, you're doing everything God wants you to do. Except make me a mother."

"Come on, Joyce, that's not fair."

"Maybe not, but I didn't hear anything about moving too fast when you agreed to take over Providence. It wasn't too fast when I had to leave my school and move to Beulah. Now all of a sudden, everything's moving too fast."

"That's not true."

"The hell it isn't."

"Stop that cussing," Charles spat.

"I will cuss when I damn well please!" Joyce jumped up. "You don't want to come clean, I'm cussing. Some hussy steps to my man, *in my face*, I'm cussing." She stormed out of the room, then came right back.

"Listen," she said, pointing her finger right in front of Charles. "I understand your position. But I also know how women are in this town. The rumors, the pettiness; all of that's beneath you. I trust you and I love you, Charles, but you're acting different."

"What are you talking about?"

"I can't explain it, but something's wrong."

"Nothing's wrong," he muttered, growing irritated.

"I hope not. I don't know if I could take you being dishonest with me, about anything. I don't think I could take it." Joyce walked out, leaving Charles alone, oblivious to the boys of *Cooley High* laughing and having fun.

Charles had another cold night in bed; although Joyce was there and even a bit affectionate, he felt lonely. He certainly couldn't sleep, because the truth was jabbing at him like a boxer in a prizefight. He realized, in fact, that two truths were attacking him. Firstly, though he loved Joyce, Beverly's arrival had given him a smidgen of doubt about whether Joyce was the last woman he ever wanted. He could still be honest with Joyce and end the marriage at this point, though she would be devastated. If Joyce were to have his child, however, walking away would be even harder, and he would surely fall into disfavor with his congregation. This fact brought Charles to another truth: with all the church ministries and groups running like well-oiled machines, he would be hard to replace. So hard, in fact, that he could be forgiven for indiscretions that would end another pastor's career somewhere else. Divorcing Joyce would be bad enough, but divorcing her with a baby, on the other hand, couldn't be forgiven in *any* church that he knew. Therefore, as long as Joyce didn't have his child, he could taste Beverly again. With Charles's lust came an overwhelming sadness. He thought his love of God and the ministry was enough to overcome his weaknesses, but for the first time he saw he was wrong. Rationalizing a means to have sex with Beverly was twisted thinking and he knew it—Satan was doing his thinking for him. But all of his sadness and remorse wasn't enough to take Beverly out of his mind—her soft, warm skin, her sweet perfume, the crazy, rhythmic way she moved her hips when he was inside her. His penis was erect again, urgent, stretching his very skin. Charles said silent prayers over and over, trying to put his mind back in the Spirit.

Charles continued to pray throughout the week and he stayed as busy as he could. He talked to Joyce and tried to listen to her, but he had heard her the first two times. She was forlorn and aggravated, until he finally agreed to have a child that year. At first she thought he was conceding defeat, but Charles convinced her that he had thought about it and that he wanted a child also. Joyce was overjoyed; she even broke down and cried a couple of times. Charles felt warm inside and he regretted ever thinking about Beverly. By committing to having a child, he had forced himself to resist the best lover he'd ever had. He had also invigorated his marriage in the process and provided his wife with the happiness she deserved. When the weekend rolled around, Charles was confident that his mind was right. Regardless of his lustful thoughts, he was back in the Spirit; the congregation and Beulah were none the wiser.

Charles arrived at Providence Baptist at 6 A.M. the following Sunday, giving him some extra time to meditate and look over scripture. The church was quiet and the morning sun brought orange rays of light through the windows. The only noise to be heard came from the birds in the trees outside. Charles imagined the birds were singing about the glorious day ahead. He read the Bible in his office for nearly thirty minutes, then he heard a knock.

"Oh no," he whispered to himself. Charles sat silently, hoping the person would go away. Again, he heard a knock.

He didn't move. Again, a knock.

Charles got up to lock the door, but it opened. Beverly stood in front of him, wearing a short tan dress, snug enough to display her fabulous physique.

"Leave," Charles told her.

"I'm sorry, Charles."

"Just leave," he said sternly.

"I had a feeling you'd be here," she replied as she walked in. "But I wasn't sure. I figured if you weren't here, maybe it wasn't meant to be."

"I don't know what you're talking about. Now get out."

"Charles, you're fooling yourself. I saw it in your eyes. I bet it's there now, that's why you're turning away." She walked toward him. Charles backed up and inadvertently shut the door.

"You have no business in this office," he told her, almost whispering. "I'm trying to get ready for service."

"I'm trying to get ready for service too," she said with a smile.

"Out, Beverly. Right now," he ordered.

"No, darling. Not until I get what I need."

"I'm not playing with you, woman. Get out." Charles opened the door.

"There hasn't been a man who could satisfy me since you."

Charles shut the door.

"I'm sorry, that's the way it is. I gave them all a chance, Edward included, bless his heart. But only you can do me right." She approached Charles, backing him up against the door.

"You're the only one, Charles. And you know it. Stop fighting me."

"Beverly, please."

"Stop it." She put one hand on his crotch and the other behind his neck. She tried to pull him forward and kiss him, but he resisted.

"Don't fight me, Charles." She unbuttoned her dress, keeping her other hand on what was now a healthy erection.

"No!" Charles shouted, shaking his head. "No!"

"Yes." She pulled him by the neck again, and this time he smothered her, kissing her neck, pulling down her bra to lick her nipples. She unbuckled his belt and his pants dropped.

"That's my baby," she said, clutching the back of his head.

Charles pulled himself back.

"No, no, this isn't going to happen," he said, his voice cracking. Tears were welling up in his eyes.

"Oh yes it is," she told him. She reached into her purse. Charles's eyes grew wide with horror at what he saw.

"I know you remember this."

Beverly had a small bottle of honey in her hand. Sitting on top of his desk and leaning back, she unscrewed it and poured drops of it on her breasts. Back in college, Charles had told her that her nipples were like silver dollar pancakes. He would always lick them clean, and Beverly brought him back to his old ritual, licking and slurping like a thirsty puppy. Beverly giggled and squirmed, becoming more aroused by the second. Charles licked his way down to her stomach, nuzzling her navel and pulling on her panty hose with his teeth. Beverly pushed him off with her knees.

"Me first," she commanded. She got to her feet, then got down on her knees and pulled his underwear down.

"Beverly, no," Charles pleaded. He could hardly catch his breath.

"Yes," she answered before taking him into her mouth. When he tried to push her away, she bit him until he stopped.

"No," he cried. "No, no, no!"

Beverly picked up the pace when she heard the no's, and Charles was right back in college. Before long his right leg was shaking.

"No! No!" He felt stress and incredible arousal all at once. Charles was certain that it wasn't him but God Himself who moved him to push her away. Knowing his strength would overcome her, Beverly bit him as hard as she could when he pushed her off. He let out a terrible scream.

A line of blood ran down the side of Beverly's chin. She spat out a piece of flesh.

"Charles, why'd you make me do that?"

His whole body was shaking as he checked himself. Charles saw some blood and couldn't look anymore. Delirious with pain, he could only make grunting noises.

"Charles, what were you thinking?"

"Aaargh!" he screamed. "You bit me!"

"You should have let me keep going. You were right there. Who are you, Bill Clinton?"

"Get out! Get out before I kill you, you crazy bitch!"

Charles was enraged, but he couldn't move quickly without inflicting excruciating pain. Beverly pulled her dress up and snatched her purse before Charles could catch her. She was out the door before he could touch her. The honey and Beverly's bra were left behind, along with several drops of blood on the floor.

Charles spent the morning in the emergency room and he received stitches. He had driven to a hospital in the next county. He was barely conscious when he arrived, but no one there knew him or his wife. He called his associate pastor and told him to deliver the word that morning, claiming he had to see a dying friend. He asked his associate pastor to call Joyce; she would probably wonder why he himself hadn't called, but he was willing to deal with that question. Though he was very sore and sensitive, he returned to deliver the sermon at the afternoon service. Looking out at the congregation, Charles saw Joyce beaming at him. He also saw Beverly, in another outfit, sitting near Edward and the rest of the deacons in the front pew. He had been comfortable at the pulpit for years, but that afternoon he was utterly lost. He took a deep breath and began.

"Lift up your heads, O ye gates; and ye be lifted up ye everlasting doors; and the King of glory shall come in."

"Who is the King of glory?" asked the congregation in unison.

"The Lord strong and mighty . . ."

His sermon was calm and deliberate as always.

"The word today comes from the second book of Corinthians,

Chapter Twelve, Verse Seven. The apostle Paul. You all know Paul, don't you?"

"Yes sir," a man called out.

"The apostle Paul. Paul had a thorn in his side to keep him humble. He said, 'To keep me from becoming conceited because of these great revelations, there was given me a thorn in my flesh, a messenger of Satan, to torment me.'"

"Yes, Lord," a woman shouted. Charles studied the congregation, larger than usual for the afternoon service. Beverly and Joyce looked at him, utter devotion on both their faces.

"Three times I pleaded with the Lord to take it away from me," he continued. "But he said to me, 'My grace is sufficient for you, my power is made perfect in weakness.'" Charles felt tears trickle down his cheek. "Therefore," he continued, "I will boast all the more gladly about my weaknesses, so that Christ's power may rest on me. That is why . . ." he paused and wiped his face.

"That is why," he said between sobs, "that is why, for Christ's sake, I delight in weaknesses . . ."

"Teach!" someone shouted.

" . . . in hardships . . ."

"Talk about it!"

" . . . in persecutions, in difficulties." Some members of the congregation clapped their hands and shouted while Charles tried to pull himself together.

"For when I am weak," he continued, "I am strong."

"Yes, Lord," shouted a woman. The shouts of affirmation continued for the rest of the sermon.

The Rumor

Alexs D. Pate

She has followers yet. People who move around her like so many bugs. Like insects. She is always fanning them, shooing them away from her. Stupid idiots. For a smell of mischievous perfume they flail about her as if she knew something special." Jake sat in his spot behind the Cozy 73 Bar and Grill. He was thinking about one of his two living mysteries.

"Oh yes, women and men alike. It doesn't seem to matter. They are all the same. Little doo-dads hanging on. Like purple gushing swirl. A laughing peek between the covers. A shout out loud." He looked around to see if anyone was watching him. It wasn't likely in the shadowed alley, but you could never be that sure.

"She don't stand for nothing though. Nothing I can see. Comes waltzing around here like there is something terribly pressing about her life. As if she secretes some kind of wishful ambience. A trifle. A mere little nothing."

Jake swallowed himself in a short breath. Coughed. The creases unrolled from his scalp, unwinding until they touched his eyebrow. He smiled a dark, empty smile. His teeth were wretched. They reflected a touched canvas.

"This ain't no vendetta. She is a world I have come to know for its mystery. I cherish a mystery." He spat. His spit hit a patch of dirt and oil on the ground in front of him and rolled up into little dirty beads. Unthinking, it sat there. Later, when the noonday sun gleamed, it would die. Death by nonmovement.

"I'm just a spectator for you. Ain't nowhere I got to go. Nobody I got to see. I just be watching, that's all. Then, bam! This picture came running in here like she was water color. She just went to throwing herself all over the goddamned place."

Jake had reptile eyes. Even as words came from his mouth, his eyes pulled themselves forward and swiveled. And as he talked, his tongue, pale pink, almost white from dryness, would slip quickly into the air.

"But colors came off that woman like the moonlight off the Caribbean. Warm, shimmering." Jake coughed again, wiped his chin, closed his eyes for the briefest of moments.

"Don't love her though. Can't stand her. She gets to kissing all these little flies around her. I seen her. Kissed them one by one. Placed them in envelopes and mailed them somewhere. A feisty, gutsy kiss that worked the seams off their lower bodies. Put some of them in deep pain. But they would fall off and regurgitate on themselves and get right back up in her face."

The sun was now rising, the night glow sadly faded. Above and around him, people, exhausted from the life that trampled them, deep in sleep, were scattered as far as his mind could imagine. Figments of their own reality. What did it take to be happy? To know yourself? To care? Questions he'd long ago stopped asking. He'd stopped going through the motions because he'd discovered the answers. All you had to do was quit sleeping, at night anyway. A man had to sleep sometime, but it didn't have to be at night.

You had to stop sleeping and you had to find and fight the Rumor. The Rumor was nourished in the night air and crept about the city. You had to be awake to see it. Jake had come face to face with the Rumor on many occasions. He'd followed it as it slipped into people and made them moan. He'd stumbled on the Rumor escaping through an open window thirteen days ago and had stealthily followed it. He had seen how under the cover of darkness, the Rumor had spread and reached thousands of people. Jake had watched the writhing bodies, fitful and agitated in their sleep. Felt their sweat. He'd stood back and watched the Rumor play with them.

Jake pulled a cardboard cover over his head and let fatigue embrace him. Another night gone and the Rumor had not been sighted. No moans. No Rumor.

He wanted to sleep but it wasn't easy. He couldn't stop thinking about the woman who haunted him nearly as much as the Rumor did.

"Her friends clatter around here like castanets. Their feet sound like beads on a string, banging against a hardwood floor. She'd come strolling along right past me. Like a brazen woman. Flash me that smile. I could see the eyes of small fish in the corners of her mouth. I could see a clear river cascade by her ears. But I didn't say nothing. Nothing to say really. But, after a while, I started getting kind of ticked. She comes through here throwing herself all over. Like a pinwheel. Moving out, and coming back on herself. Spraying this glowing light here and there and never losing that much energy. Finally, I said, Wait a minute. How long is this gonna go on? There's such a thing as fairness you know. How come you get to have all that?" Jake's face was a distant image, a vague replication.

He remembered how once she'd dropped something right at the mouth of his alley. Ten steps from the front door of the Cozy 73 Bar and Grill. He was just sitting there like he almost always was. But she'd seen him. Actually looked in his direction. "She just kept smiling. And all them little would be's was just buzzing around me. Wondering who I was and what I was doing here. I told them this is where I am. I'm just sitting here waiting and watching you. Hell, I told them, you the best show that comes around here. I ain't been nowhere and I ain't going nowhere. This is my spot. You the folks that should be telling me who the hell you are."

His eyes grew tired. The flattened remnants of the cardboard box shielded him from the brightening sun. He sank deeper. His eyes no longer moved by themselves. They required direct orders from his skylarking brain. Then, new sounds broke over his head like a serenade. The air jarred time and again by the gushing of automobiles. Things happening. People walking by. Deep within his twilight, he could vaguely hear them talking. Horns and sirens. Backdoors clanked shut and garbage cans were dragged against the cement.

Then there was the odor. As the morning rose from the grass that grew between the cement blocks of the sidewalk, a smell of sweat, exhaust, and fresh-cooked bread. All of this was going on about Jake as he slept.

Jake never dreamed. When he slept, nothing special went on in his head. What occurred without him went unwritten, unmarked. It was his world. He ruled it completely. When he slept, the dictionary went blank and nothing meant anything.

He didn't even dream about her. He didn't even know her when he slept. He had never met her. She had never existed.

This went on all day. He slept comfortably in garbage throughout everyone else's life. But as things became tired and started to lose that purposeful look, Jake began to flinch. The more things slowed and stopped, the stronger Jake got, until near dusk, when there was enough inactivity to motivate him upward.

He stretched, yawned, shut his eyes tightly, and felt the momentary thrill of disorientation. It was a high, indeed the high point of his day, this stretch and yawn. He relished it. It felt like minutes before the blood again slowed to its former pace and he slumped back into his chair of garbage.

"Two things on my mind today. I want to see that woman and I want to catch up with that Rumor."

2.

Jake checked out his surroundings. Not much had changed. More refuse perhaps. But mostly it was the same. Yesterday buried beneath the crumbling remnants of today with shrinking space available for the forthcoming future. Ashes unto themselves. Garbage remarking the past. This was his life. Rivers of water derived from places and processes unbeknownst to him. He could not identify one puddle as being rainwater and the other urine. Still, in his life, it was water all the same. It was wet. In the winter it would freeze. In the summer it would stink. Change was chemical. Objects existed and were useful. They slowly but surely degenerated.

His eyes reached out for the smell of darkness. They pierced the shrouded shadows. He rustled in his garbage. Banana peels enveloped in soft white jackets, putrid colors permeated the air. "That woman keeps such a racket when she ain't here. I don't like her much, but when she ain't here I gets to wondering where she went. I can't get used to the way she just erupts into this world and creates this mystery out of thin air. Definitely don't love her. Almost can't stand her. It's just the way she does things. Swirling and twisting like she knows a tune we can't hear.

"And when she's around here nothing else is moving. Just her and those insects licking her heels. Spelling out her needs in graphic signals. Telling me secrets about her to stimulate me. Whispering things inside my head which tell me it's a sham. That they're really in love. They've lost their sight. They only see what's important to her. I just can't live like that. You can't go around buzzing off of someone else's energy. Even if she's got so much they ought to try her for unlawful possession. You just can't survive that way.

"What happens is that someone will come along and see you flying all over someone else and they'll laugh at you. Just like I laugh at them. Just insects."

The moon was off to the right, at a distance that would make the average person feel insignificant. But Jake was a man inflated. His purpose described itself in visions. And when he turned to face the moon, he did so with a sense of forgotten grace.

"Two things of major consequence, that damn woman and that weather-changing rummy they call the Rumor."

3.

The alleys run dark gray behind stores, vacant houses, dry cleaners, and restaurants. In this city, where the darkened streets contain momentary slits through which the flash of light sometimes appears, the streetwalker faces the known side. The facade of life that is seen

by all who pass that way. Whether moving swiftly by, as in a motor ve-
hicle, or walking, perhaps strolling thoughtlessly along, there is only
so much to be seen from this vantage.

But, as is true with all facades, the other side presents the thrill of
difference. Ruled by rodents and creeping fear, the alleys welcomed
no one, not even their residents. To be there, in that world of slippery feelings and foul smells, was to be enveloped in a nightmare of
uncharted dimension. It was felt by everyone. For those, like Jake,
who spent their time there, scrounging food, sleeping in garbage,
drunk or spaced out, it was like living outside oneself.

It was as if one only had a history, not a present and not even the
whisper of a future. It was possible within the murk of this existence
to be distended and vague. Streetwalkers and passing motorists
would occasionally see and be repulsed by those of the alleys, but for
the most part, they lived in near isolation.

4.

"A fashionable folly, this need to affix oneself to a mess like this.
People asking questions all the time. Women looking at me. Smoke
trailing off into the thin air. Just goes up that way and bends around
in circles. Takes itself up there and moves along." In leaping gasps,
he took in his air. The taste warmed him. It was hot. The creeping
night surrounded him. Its stillness added to his growing strength.
His sense of life grew like discarded bones at a family barbecue.

And, just as Jake was about to lose himself in the deepening night,
he saw the streetlights dim. She was near. He couldn't see her yet.
Didn't know which direction she'd come from. But he knew she was
close by. Besides the fluctuating surges that buzzed and popped all
around him he could also hear the growing volume of her heels as
she clattered his way. He sat up straight. Craned his neck, made himself a lighthouse, his eyes the searchlight. And then he saw a shadow
bending itself around the corner of his alley. He pried himself up
from the ground and struggled toward the street. He'd only taken
two steps when a bright light walked past him. There were no bugs

buzzing, no hangers-on, nothing flitting about. Just the clack-clack of her shoes and the swirling energy that was always present around her.

He started to call out but thought better of it. Instead he muttered to himself, "You think you got rights the rest of us ain't got. Every damn day. I see you." Suddenly his world stopped. She stopped. The light about her cooled. Everything stopped. She turned, perhaps to confirm that she'd heard someone talking. Their eyes met.

Jake wanted to sit right back down in the space he'd just vacated. He couldn't stand under the weight of her gaze. But, even as he reeled on his heels, with their eyes locked in the moment, he wanted to tell her how much he thought about her. How well he knew her. But before he could do anything she smiled.

In a flash, the alley lit up like a baseball field at night. Air flowed effortlessly throughout his body. He felt spry. Spry. Like he could jump if he wanted. Or skip. In his head there was nothing but laughter. Not his own, but other people's. Lots of people laughing. Not derisively either. But pure joyous laughter ringing in his head. He raised his hand to say hello, but in an instant she was gone.

"Go on then. Think I care?" He stumbled forward, searching out the trail of sparks she left in her wake. And he knew, as he left the alley and turned onto the street, letting her vapors guide him, that he was entering the other world. He knew there would be people watching him the way he watched them. He knew he would be forced to feel diseased. He knew people would try to act like he wasn't actually on the same street with them. He had a story just like they did. The only difference between his and theirs was that his was purely his. He'd managed to simplify his life to the point of ennui. The only thing that threatened him now was her.

He pulled his tattered coat closer to his body. His lower legs itched but he didn't want to stop walking to scratch them. The people who watched him would be repulsed by the sight. A large, lonely, dirty, battered black man bent over in the middle of the sidewalk scratching his legs. Someone might even scream. So he tried to walk in such a way that his legs might rub together.

Jake passed through the sheer veils of consciousness that separated one place from the other. On one block he'd feel the arms of Africa enfold him. On another he knew he'd better walk fast and avoid eye contact. But that was difficult because he had to keep searching for her. He didn't want her to get so far ahead that he'd never be able to catch her. He didn't know where he was following her to, but something was pulling him forward. Every now and then, he'd see the flutter of her brown hair as it lit fire to the air, pointing him to his destiny.

Jake was careful not to slip into her line of sight. Careful not to move too close. "I could care less where you go. I know you got the power. I feel that. Pulling me along like you normally do those fleas and flies that follow your smile. But don't expect me to be like them. That's not what I'm doing." He sounded breathless even to himself. He wasn't used to talking and walking.

"Where ya goin', Jake? Where ya goin'?" It was the Rumor. "I know where you want to go, but where ya goin' fa real?"

Jake immediately stopped talking. He'd almost forgotten about the Rumor. It had never spoken to him before. Had never slowed down enough in Jake's presence to be anything more than a half-assed truth. Jake had been chasing the Rumor for years. If it weren't for that woman with her auras and such, the Rumor would be all that Jake desired.

But the Rumor never stood still and slipped into nothingness. "Damned rummy. I almost got you that time. You goddamned mystery." Jake paused, searching once again for his path. He realized that people were watching He was walking again. Itchy legs and all.

He turned a corner and saw her slip into a doorway. "Ah. I see you don't take them insects into the house with you." He crossed the street and approached her house from the other side, hoping he would be able to see. And he could. Her blinding shadow drew an outline on the window covers. He sat on the ground directly across from her. And then he saw a man's outline join her there.

"You can say hello. That's right. That's what I'd do too. Say hello just like that." Jake smiled. And suddenly Jake saw that the man was aglow in the same way she'd been. "He's not one of them bugs she drags around with her. He's like her. Damn. There's more of them than I thought." It made him feel good that she wouldn't give up her stuff to some doo-dad. "Yeah, that's right. You deserve more than a damn Rumor. That's for sure."

The two figures kissed. Jake leaned back on the wall behind him and sighed. They were kissing. How sweet was that? And he was touching her. Holding her. And her hands wove themselves through his burning dreads. Ropes of fire caressed by fire. Sounds like a chorus of woodwinds and harps, coming not from their mouths but from their bodies. Jake watched as the man obviously spoke flowers to her. The man placed his hands between her legs, touched her, setting off a cascade of yellow sparks, then their bodies joined at the middle. The man became her and the woman became him. They moved against each other with force, beyond primal, so strong that the earth seemed to tilt. Jake could almost see them through the veiled window. Without a sound, the pair coupled in shadow, dancing against the other, until their glows merged and brightened to their limit. At its peak, the light was blinding as she rocked against the man, seeking to satisfy her desire, impaling herself on his flesh. Then the miracle happened. Lilies and birds of paradise, crocuses and gladiolas bloomed right under their feet and stained the air with their wondrous smell. Which Jake could smell. Around them rose petals rained.

And now, as they held hands, they stepped back from each other, with the man obviously smiling a smile broad enough to part the window curtains. He loved her. He loved the sound of her voice. The way she moved. The way she looked. Jake knew that the man loved her as much as he did. And she blushed blue all over the room. She loved him too. "Damn."

They stood like that for a long time. Maybe they were talking, maybe they were just looking at each other, Jake couldn't tell. And then they were together again. Body to body. Light to light. It brought tears to Jake's eyes. Not just a moistness. But a real, rolling cry. He hadn't cried in years.

But before his sobs completely overpowered him, he could see through the stream that they'd gathered their coats again and were reemerging to the street. And then they were at the front door, still hand in hand. "Going back out into the world with all that stuff they got. Damn."

He quickly jerked his head down and tried to disappear. In his mind he was like a chameleon. He was brown red now, like the bricks on his back. And they, their brownness now beginning to glow again, were swept away. "Hope she didn't see me. Don't want her thinking she got something I want. 'Cause she don't. She was just one of the things I had to do today."

Jake stood up and stretched, wiping his eyes as he brought them down from the sky. "Now I'm ready to find that no-account Rumor. Put an end to that, right now."

Wallbanging

Brian Egleston

Maybe you have some idea, but I have no clue how I'm supposed to seek leniency from the Chinese government for two people caught screwin' each other's brains out in broad daylight at one of the country's most infamous attractions. Hundreds of people were watching. Wait, I'm getting ahead of my story here. I'm Thaddius Clark, and in the eastern part of the world, Asia more specifically, they call me a liaison, a middleman, broker if you will.

During my tour of duty, or *tours* of duty I should say, there's been some desperate people come my way. Take for instance the time I had to rescue these two fellas after they'd been makin' posters of penises and selling them as fetish replicas of the god Mandingo down in South China. By rescuing, I mean I was able to get them five years in a Chinese prison instead of twenty-eight.

Then I recall when this idiot from Chicago tried to establish a sex enhancement business over in Singapore—with monkeys. Tried to convince people the apes were from an island where a goddess had placed her spirit and sexual potency in animals because the men on the island didn't have enough stamina. One meal of the beasts, roasted with a special sauce, supposedly made you able to go all night long with no let-up. A man became tireless, frequently leaving the woman physically exhausted and hospital bound. Turns out the monkeys were rare and the advertisements all a lie. Ludicrous, I know, but people fell for it. Oh, I was able to get him a public caning instead of life in prison.

You see, I represent those imbeciles that the U.S. embassy refuses to acknowledge as American citizens due to their stupidity. Of course you've never heard of me or someone in my position. For the most part, folks come over from the States, have a good time, never get into trouble, and head back home. But then there are the rare cases that I happily call clients. Just plain old morons.

This one couple, however, they were just normal upper-class black people—over here on vacation—who happened to get caught humpin' like wild animals . . . I'm getting ahead of myself again.

The minute I heard about the incident, I knew my phone would ring soon. And it did. On the other end of the line was Darius Williams, a loquacious publisher, accomplished poet, and the male half of the sexual exhibitionist team. You should have heard this guy talk. Desperate and long-winded. I immediately arranged a meeting so we could discuss the facts and weigh his options—if he'd have any. We met at a holding center in Beijing, with the local officials watching our every move.

"How in *the hell* did this happen, Mr. Williams?" I asked of the nervous black man seated before me.

"Well, it all began when I put my hand in my wife's panties at the Top Ten Club and—"

"What! At the Top Ten Club! Are you insane?"

"Do you want to hear the story or not?"

"I'm not sure I do," I answered, scratching my head and popping a piece of candy. I knew this would be trouble. I birthed a gargantuan sigh. "Go ahead."

"I don't have to tell you how aroused one can get in the Top Ten Club with that . . . you know, the rule they have."

"But it's the rule that should have given you some restraint."

"Are you gonna keep interrupting me? Just let me know so I can put in some commercial breaks for you. Last time I checked this wasn't a free service, and I do believe I'm your customer."

I should have left him right then. Left him and his sex-crazed wife for the communist buzzards. I had a mind to walk out right then, but of course there was the ten-thousand-dollar retainer he'd given me—

in cash. My pride was banished by the sheer intrigue of having a client who had the gall to put his hand in his wife's panties at the Top Ten Club, of all places, and the nerve to walk around in China with ten thousand dollars in cash. So I did what any person raised in a capitalist society would have done. I shut up and listened.

"I'm feeling my own protrusion as soon as I walk in the door. My wife has this erection radar. Says she can tell when I'm aroused just by watching my facial reactions. She smiles and gives me the look of torture. The look of, *I know you want to consume my insides and you'd open me up on the first flat surface we could find, if I'd let you.* Seductively, she crosses over, barely grazes my zipper and confirms her suspicion; I'm bulging. Her smile is gleaming now and she whispers in my ear, *It's okay, I'm a little excited myself. I dare you to put your finger underneath my faucet.* The "t" danced on the end of her tongue and it traced the contour of my ear, swerving, winding, and brushing until it landed on the bottom of my lobe. She traced my crotch lightly again and swaggered away to a table, leaving me there at the door, bulging. I followed her, sat, grabbed a menu, and placed it over my embarrassment, as if anyone would have noticed, let alone care.

"Now, my wife is not the most slender of women, but I guess that's one of the reasons I'm so attracted to her. She's not fat, mind you, just full-figured. A real woman. With meat on her bones. Not like the artificially sculpted bodies on the newsstand racks. My wife is a . . . she's a regular woman that you would see on the street or at the shopping mall and wonder—if you had any imaginative desire— how does she like it? Top or bottom? And that's why I can't keep my mind from thinking of throwing her down and making love to her every chance I get. Well, there's another reason, but, er, huh, I'm getting help with that."

"How do you mean?" I asked him.

"Never mind. So she's at a table and the teasing continues until just before the club's second performance begins. Ever been down to Tianjin and seen the Top Ten Club's show?"

"Sure, plenty of times."

"Then I don't have to tell you about the lights bouncing off the curves of the dancers. How the waves of green cast shadows against their jiggling breasts, making you wonder about the sizes and shapes beneath the feathers and fabric. It's a tease; the dark green disguises the reality. Suddenly a contraption turns on from the ceiling and the light goes red, shows everything. The red is so brilliant you can see the roundness of each body part, every curve of every backside, every turn and twist of their gyrations on the floor. Isn't it fascinating that green makes the fantasies stop but red makes the fantasies go?"

"Yeah, but what does this have to do with your—"

He shot me a look that shut me up.

"Just as I was waiting, hoping that the next color would be yellow and expose more flesh, my wife grabbed me. When I say grabbed, I mean she reached over and took hold of my erection like it was a handle. My attention was taken away from the dance floor as my wife transitioned from grabbing to caressing. And she has this . . . this stroke that feels like a blanket of sensation covering and surrounding me. This is with my clothes on, mind you. All I could give her was a moan and a smile. She went again to my ear and says, *I was serious, I dare you to put your finger under my faucet.* She meant it. I told her she was crazy. Sexy but crazy. There was no way I was doing that at a table in a club in a foreign country. That's when she pointed out the rooms in the back of the club."

"No way! Don't tell me you took your throbbing wife into one of the back rooms. Do you know what those are used for?"

"Just let me finish. Please! Jesus sakes!"

I couldn't tell if Darius was getting flustered because I was interrupting his story or his fantasies.

"So off we went to one of the back rooms. And you know, of course, there are people usually already in there. Other couples. You can imagine the stares we got, being the only Americans in the room and also black. We were practically celebrities, or lepers. I couldn't quite interpret the looks. There we were, in one of the back rooms with five or so Chinese couples who were all staring intently at the television screen. I couldn't believe what they were watching. It was all baffling to me. Of course, my wife didn't seem to care one bit. Didn't care if there was a television in the room at all. Again she starts that sensual stroking and then comes that dangerous tongue lacing my ear with the whisper: *If you don't touch me, I'm going to pull you out right here right now in front of all of these people.* As proof, she unzips my pants and reaches in. I turned into a squeamish embarrassment trying to get away.

"Now don't get me wrong, if I have a favorite activity, it's being passionate and making love to my wife. But when she gets turned on, she's like this . . . this orgasmic parasite and I'm the host. I remember just before we got on the plane on the way over, we were in the first class waiting lounge. Before I knew it, we were running to catch the plane, zipping up my fly and straightening her skirt. But that's another story.

"Finally, I moved her hand and took her up on the dare. She was wearing one of those silk knee-length skirts that fit her curves the way a peel protects its fruit. The elastic near the top was expandable enough for my hand to glide down her skin without discomfort. A few fingertips below her waistline, I felt the vertical cotton ridges of my favorite pair of panties that she owns. You see, we've got this game. She lets me put my hand in her clothes and guess what style, brand, and color underwear she's wearing just by feel. It makes her so erotic. Or hot, sometimes drenched. She loves that I pay attention to her so much, that I can see her beauty even if others are blind to it.

"I felt the ridges, went down a few fingertips further, looked at her with a sinister smile and said, *Victoria's Secret, low cut, black . . . am I right?* She let loose a loud moan and pushed my hand down further. I maneuvered her panties and moved the part covering her crotch, giving me full access to her bountiful faucet, abundant with its drips of pleasure. It was overflowing, running down my fingers as I tried to make it burst by touching its source. I knew the spot exactly. Just below the trim of hair and just above her own protruding satin petals. Caressing was the vice. Always in slow, tiny circles at first, and then gentle strokes back and forth over her vulva. She was moving and moaning and talking now. *Yes my love, touch me right there. Let's get the party going in this room. They've been waiting for someone to go first, I'll bet.* My strokes intensified with speed but still remained as gentle as ever. Repetition. The circling of my fingertip over her throbbing source and her moans became barely controlled shouts. With her eyes closed, she opened her legs wider and I paused from escalating her passionate rapture and took a glimpse around the room. Others were beginning to move—away from us. I wanted to tell my wife that people were looking at us with peculiar eyes.

"The instant I tried to take my hand away, she grabbed it, saying, *Don't stop! I'm almost there.* The stroking continued, this time as fast as I'd ever caressed her. Later she told me it had felt like a hummingbird fluttering against her flower in search of tasty pollen. I was rapidly trying to get her to come because the room had been cleared unbeknownst to her as she neared a trembling climax.

"Controlled shouts became sporadic screams and she clawed her fingers into the seat, grounding herself, so that she wouldn't waft away with the rush of her orgasm. Her screaming became this siren, getting louder with each second. The conclusion was coming and so were the authorities. And that's when we found out."

Darius paused for the first time and looked like he wanted me to interrupt.

"Found out what?" I asked.

"The rules of the Top Ten Club. They oughta have the rules posted or pass 'em out with menus. What do they expect in an atmosphere like that? They wouldn't even give us a chance to explain. Without even asking questions, they just threw us out."

"Well, if it's any consolation, you're not the first Americans to be thrown out of that club."

"Club? They threw us out of the damn city!"

"Are you serious?"

"Hell yeah, I'm serious. How do you think we wound up in Beijing? We were escorted back to our hotel and monitored. They demanded that we check out and leave Tianjin immediately."

And that's how Darius and his wife found out that the Top Ten Club was not a strip joint, but the closest thing the city had to offer. The rule was strictly hands off and clothes on. All serious touching was forbidden. The back rooms, as unbelievable as it may seem, were used for men who rented girls as companions while they watched television. Usually CNN or a soccer game. Where Darius expected to see porno, he saw stale peace treaty coverage with NATO negotiators in Bosnia. The couples were all neatly arranged at tables around the room. A girl would be paid eight hundred yuan, or ten dollars, to simply sit and keep a gentleman company—watching the news. If she wanted to be adventurous and break the rules, she might touch his hand. But that was it. The dancers never showed breasts, never revealed buttocks, and never climbed a pole. And this, of all places, was where Darius Williams chose to give his wife a screaming orgasm.

"This ain't gonna be easy. Not easy at all," I confessed. "I thought you guys came over just to see the Great Wall."

"No. Well, I mean yes, eventually, but we wanted to golf all week in Tianjin. Now we had to come over early, get new hotel reservations, rearrange our whole itinerary."

A sigh was all I had to offer him.

"So you wanna hear how we got arrested?" he asked.

"I really don't. I really and truly don't, but I guess I have to. For whatever it's gonna be worth."

"Early Saturday morning, I was blowing on my wife's nipples at the Forbidden City, so—"

"Ohhh God. Mr. Williams. What . . . How . . . Why?" I offered an even longer sigh.

"What? You gotta hear the details."

I waved him on to continue, mentally formulating the lies I would offer to the Chinese officials.

"I mean come on, Thaddius. Even you must admit that the Forbidden City is somewhat of an aphrodisiac. It's the emperor's palace for God's sake. He had at least ten concubines. What guy wouldn't get turned on from the spirits alone?

"We were standing with the rest of the massive crowd and she kept saying how hot she was . . . I mean hot physically, not sexually. So we went off to try and get away from all the people and ended up in one of the off-limits quarters. I tried blowing cool breath down her back, her stomach, and eventually I wound up at her breasts, which makes her hot—sexually not physically—and we both agreed it was time for a 'session,' as we like to call them. But before we could even exchange kisses, we were spotted, and, of course, thrown out of the Forbidden City.

"By this time we figured we'd better see the Great Wall of China before we were deported from the country."

"Good idea."

"Excuse me?"

"Nothing, keep going, please. I can't wait for more," I offered with sarcasm.

"Thaddius, we got to the entrance and I have to tell you . . . you been to the Great Wall?"

"Oh yeah."

"Is that not the most amazing thing you've ever seen?"

"It's something to see, alright."

"When you look out over the majestic mountaintops and see this winding wall riding the mountains like a never-ending dragon, it just makes you marvel at the engineering ability of humans. And we were simply in awe the entire time. For the most part we just walked up and over. Some of the wall's inclines were so steep we had to hold on to the side for support. We must have walked for at least a quarter of a mile up and down parts of the wall. Of course we ambitiously set out to walk the entire wall, until we learned that it was over fifteen hundred miles long. That, coupled with the burning sun and thin air, altered that little endeavor. Then we had to take a break because my wife wore a skirt; why, I have no idea. In some areas, the wall was too narrow for people to stop and stand so we kept walking further and further out until we reached a section closed for repairs. Finally, we found a spot in one of the lookout towers and we rested. Turns out,

Mongolian soldiers fought in some spectacular battles near those towers. Amazing, huh?"

"And that's where it all started?"

Offended, he paused. "You wanna tell the story or should I?"

Ten grand, ten grand, ten grand, I had to keep reminding myself.

"We're sittin' in the tower and my wife sits in the little window about three feet from the ground. I can see she's in agony from all of the walking. When she gets irritable and uncomfortable, there's nothing she likes better than a foot massage. Gets me lots of 'get out of the doghouse' points. I go to work rubbing her soles and stretching her toes. Must be the altitude, 'cause she's really enjoying it. I ham it up a little bit and get on my knees, asking her, *Is there anything else my Queen desires?* Just as she says, *Make sure you rub my arches real good,* she changes positions and I catch a glimpse. Her faucet was uncovered. I said, *Uh, honey, did you forget something?* She thought I meant bottled water until I extend one stroke of the foot massage along her calf muscle and up her inner thigh. My whole arm had been swallowed by her skirt when I said, *You didn't want me to guess your panties today so you didn't wear any, huh?* All she said was, *That's not my foot you're touching.* God, she's quick-witted! My hand descended back down her leg. As soon as the foot massage continued, she tugged at her skirt and made the material rise above her knees, her thighs, and finally her hips. It was like . . . it was like the curtain was going up because the show was beginning. She removed her right foot from my hand, placed it on my shoulder and raised her left leg over my head, resting her left foot on my other shoulder. Staring at me, in all its beauty, completely exposed, was that damn irresistible faucet, already dripping.

"Before I could even ask, I mean before I could even think of a sexy sentence, she shot me with, *Are you thirsty?* I mean, she is so quick it's unbelievable. Was I thirsty, she asks. Hell no, I wasn't thirsty. As soon as I'd noticed there was nothing between her skin and skirt, my mouth began watering. So I lied and told her, *I've got cotton-mouth.* Her hands started gliding over the crown of my head and down my neck. Then came the gentle gesture of tugging. Pulling me in closer. I moved the rest of the way toward her and kissed her. Kissed the gentle coolness of her raining insides.

"You know something? When you love someone, I mean really love 'em, everything about them is good. Their nagging is cute. Their bad habits are of no concern. Their illnesses are temporary and their flesh tastes like sweet serenity wrapped in a layer of buttered beauty. I can't understand why a man who claims to love his woman wouldn't kiss her in the deepest part of her femininity.

"I make it a weekly ritual, and all that practice has made me a clitoris connoisseur—of my wife, that is. The tip of my tongue met her tip. I tasted in circles and she grabbed hold of the wall, screaming and sucking in gusts of the thin air. A high-altitude breeze rushed in and it was almost like the elements were bringing us comfort. The wind was too much and it began to dry her fountain. I had to forego the tiny circles in exchange for rapid swirls dancing across her tip and gliding down her lips. My head was swerving and bobbing between her legs while she tried to find a grip on the wall. Each time she moaned and reached for steady support, tiny rocks and dust crumbled at the end of her fingertips. I put my hands against her lower back to offer what little support I could while still concentrating on the tip and lips and swerving and bobbing. Always make sure the queen is supported and comfortable while serving her on the throne. Remember that, Thaddius.

"Now that I've got my arms wrapped around her waist and hands planted on her back, I thrust her toward me, placing my tongue into the depths of that overflowing fountain. *God*, I love my wife!

"How lucky am I to find someone who's as hot as I am? I know this writer who told me he saved himself for his wife. Never had a piece a day in his life until his wedding night. Then, two months later, his wife had no desire for him. She'd screwed everything from linebackers to light bulbs, and now she's worn out. Is that not the saddest thing you've ever heard? Seems he's writing a novel about it entitled *Alterations at the Altar*.

"But anyway, of course by now, my wife is pulling off bigger pebbles. Dust from the wall is all in my hair. I can hear the wail of the siren telling me that her orgasm isn't far away. So I stop."

"Huh?" I asked him. Was he kidding me? Hell, I was all into the story now. Wanted to give my own wife a call and guess her panties' color. "Why'd you stop?"

"That's exactly what my wife said! I asked her, How many people can say they made love on the Great Wall of China? She smiles and looks at me with this seductive look and says, *Fill my insides*. I got ready to take off my pants, and she covered my cheeks and my neck with soft kisses, allowing her tongue to pierce through her lips and brush my skin at the end of each kiss. The kisses grew hotter and stronger and her tongue moved along the length of my neck with gentle vertical flicks. I had to start taking care of business before she made me explode simply by her kisses. I rose up over my wife and she placed her hands behind her. Her skirt was up around her waist and completely out of the way. Her knees were touching and suddenly she just . . . just slowly spread her legs and unfolded that inner beauty. I walked to within seven inches of her and our tips traded touches. My erection lowered to her entrance and the first touch shook us both as we exchanged moans. We were both so close to climax it wouldn't have taken much. She put one hand on my hip and pulled me inside.

"That breeze returned. The breeze that had found its way through the carpeted mountains of China, and ridden the rails of stone and brick to find its way to us. Its soft currents danced in the high altitude of the ridges, and I swear it was like the breath of clouds. Her hair was being tossed around and my shirt was blowing like a flag in a monsoon. God, it was awesome. That first contact of my offering and her insides was . . . it was . . . Her fountain just engulfed me. I could feel every piece of her surrounding me. Before either of us could move, we simply reveled in our contact with each other. I didn't want her to lose the momentum of passion, so I danced inside of her. Long and short movements, first with ease then with intensity. Ease then intensity.

"The breeze slapped my back like it was giving me added strength for the all-consuming movements. She braced herself because she knew that I knew that she was close and it would take all of my stamina and strength to raise her passion to its apex. My dance was fast now, and each thrust made her give short guttural shouts as loud as the wind smashing against our ears. I had to close my eyes in order to finish. If I look at my wife while we're making love, her expressions, that pleasing look of satisfaction turns me on even more. To know that she's feeling the ultimate physical joy, it just . . . just makes me explode. My eyes were closed and I gave her every inch. Every minuscule cell of my elongated skin that wrapped tightly around my manhood was given to her—with forceful repetition. Deeper thrusts. I could hear the destructive but comforting wind and the cries of joy from my loving wife. I could feel the softness of her dripping womanhood splashing out of her and down my shaft. I could see, in my mind, her breasts heaving with each anticipated breath of her orgasm . . . But I couldn't see us moving toward the edge of the wall.

"The dust gave way to the pebbles, the pebbles loosened and shook the rocks. The rocks fell out of place and disturbed the section that we were sitting on. My wife's siren peaked and so did she. I was about to burst, so I gazed down at her convulsing body, but she was moving away from me while screaming with satisfaction. At first I thought it was visual disorientation, having had my eyes closed in the high altitude for so long. Then I realized the wall was still but we were moving. We'd knocked loose a stone in the lookout tower about three feet wide and it was falling out of place. My wife was still gyrating from the aftershocks of pleasure and it was like a rhythmic jackhammer making small thrusts against the weakened rock. Thaddius . . . for a second all I could see was my wife falling to her death. I swear I thought I'd died for an instant.

"The wind stopped. I couldn't hear anything. My wife was frozen in space and even the clouds weren't breathing. All I could do was grab her and pull upward from her fall with every shred of strength I could find. She finally felt the rock moving. It was a few inches away from the edge. She screamed, with fear this time. The panic made her lose balance, and as hard as I tried to pull, she fought to grab on to me. For God's sake, Thaddius, we could have been killed! The brink of living and dying. You know that midpoint on a see-saw where you can go down or up, where you can balance yourself if two kids weigh the same? It's called the fulcrum. We were on the freakin' fulcrum of our lives! I pulled back as hard as I could. God, I swear I had tears in my eyes. And then it came back. The clouds breathed on us again. That comforting wind rushed over us and I felt the biggest gust I'd felt that entire day. It came from behind my wife and pushed her toward me. She fell on me and into my arms.

"We cried. Sat there for a few seconds and cried, allowing our insane heartbeats to quiet themselves. Then we started laughing. Laughing like two kids who'd been caught doing what they had no business doing in a place they had no business being. We laughed for a few seconds until we heard it. That's when I almost crapped on myself.

"The wind had pushed my wife out of the window but it could not hold the falling stone. It had fallen and crashed down some three hundred feet into the scaffolding used for the wall repairs. If it had been a weekday, workers would have been there and probably died. But that day it was empty. The large stone smashed the structure and caused it to shatter. Not only did that section of scaffolding break, but it also caused a chain reaction because the entire repair system was linked. It all came crashing down and the heavy steel structure crumbled and splintered like a child's falling Lego blocks. A repair structure seven feet high and five football fields long—destroyed by two people making love on the Great Wall of China.

"That's when it happened. We looked down the wall to see if anyone had noticed the genesis of the disaster. Imagine how we felt when we saw a quarter of a mile of Chinese people pointing at us. And of course the authorities came at once. They let us get dressed, then rushed us off to the holding area. Some guy from the U.S. embassy gave me your number, and here we are."

If I hadn't seen it on the news, I would not have believed one single word. But it was all true and I had no idea where to start.

"Mr. Williams . . . may I ask you a question?"

"Sure, that's what I'm paying you for, isn't it? Ask questions so you can make a case in our defense."

"But you've been . . . never mind. Anyway, here's my question. What were you thinking?! How in *the hell* could you do that to your wife in broad daylight?! How am I supposed to present this? Are you serious?! I'd have a better chance to get you off if you had humped the prime minister's pet dog on live television! Were you even thinking at all?"

Darius unwrapped a piece of my candy and bit off half of it. He placed the other piece in his breast pocket. Staring down on the table at the cracked candy crumbs, he spoke with a lowered voice, in shame.

"I guess we don't think much about making love or sex or whatever you want to call it. You see, Thaddius, my wife gave me the ultimate gift on our wedding day. She gave me her purity. She'd never been touched until that night of consummation and she hasn't stopped giving herself to me yet. She hit her peak and stayed there, and doesn't show any signs of slowing either. I love her more than life. Do you understand that? I'll do whatever it takes to please her, to make up for my lack . . . for my impurities. My illness.

"You wanna know if I was thinking at all? No, I wasn't. I don't think about sex. I just do it. It's how I was raised. You wanna try my case? To do that, you must try my father's case. Try the case of a man that forced his son into sexual perversion. Try a man who taught his son the ways of the world by making me watch pornos when I was seven years old! I am a sex addict. It's my father's fault. He should be in this fucking jail, not me."

Darius wept for a few breaths while I painfully watched him.

Funny thing about language barriers. Words can be translated, but understanding can never be duplicated. As knowledgeable and as fluent as I am in the Chinese language, it was difficult to convey to them that with democracy come freedom and choices. And with choices also come perversion and sickness and abuse. For them, communism meant discipline, stability, and morality. So there was no way they could possibly understand the motives of my clients and why they indulged their passions in public. But I tried. I did my best.

If you're ever in China, there's four things you gotta do. The first is to stop by the Top Ten Club, watch some great shows, and sit with nice people in a room watching television. The second is to visit the Forbidden City. The third thing you gotta do is walk the Great Wall and see those carpeted mountains and feel that breeze Darius was talking about. Fourth thing you gotta do, and this one is important. It, uh . . . excuse me. It, uh . . . makes me feel better about the job that I did. Or didn't do well enough. If you're ever in China . . . sorry, this is tough for me . . . stop by and see Darius and his wife. Just, uh . . . just ask for prisoners number 34-982 and 45-300. They'll be there for the rest of their lives. Tell you this much, I've never seen a man love a woman like that.

The Question

Brandon Massey

This was the question: Would he tell her the truth?

He didn't know. They sat in his Mustang in the parking lot of Walgreens, the air conditioner humming softly on a humid July afternoon. During the drive to the pharmacy, they had been silent. He hesitated to speak because he didn't want to risk saying anything that would derail this event that he had been inching toward since puberty. He didn't understand why she was quiet, but he could guess. It had been two years since her last time; she was probably nervous.

It would be his first time. He was what he often considered to be the rarest of breeds: a twenty-eight-year-old black man who had never been with a woman. A bona fide virgin, partly by choice, and partly by chance. Things had just turned out that way and he could never give an answer that fully explained his virginity.

But she did not know that about him. She believed that he was experienced, that he'd had more partners than she. He'd maintained the lie for their entire five-month relationship. It began as a comfortable, almost casual dishonesty. He automatically lied to every woman that he met, having been burned several times when he revealed the truth. You're a virgin? Yeah, right! Why? What's wrong with you? Or: I like you, I like you a lot, but I don't want to be your first. If I have sex with you, you'll get curious about how it might be with another woman, and you'll leave me, you'll go buckwild. Or: Your first time needs to be special, and I don't think I'm special enough for you. I'm sorry . . .

Before, lying about his virginity had had no visible consequences, because his relationships with the women he'd lied to had never grown serious enough to progress to the bedroom. But soon after he met her, he discovered that she really was special . . . and by then he'd already planted the lie. It continued to grow like an indestructible weed, entangling his words whenever they discussed sex. Yes, if you really want to know, I've had partners in the past, of course. The last time was eight months ago. Sure, I've always practiced safe sex. Of course. He was such a smooth liar he wondered if he'd been a con man in a past life.

He hated to lie. But how could he stop? She was the first woman who'd ever said she loved him. He told her that he wanted to marry her one day, and he meant it. Their relationship was as charmed as if a love spell had been cast on them, and he feared doing anything that would dissolve the magic.

But that afternoon, in the heat of kissing and touching, she finally said she wanted them to make love, and the weedy lie slipped tightly around his throat, and the question gained critical urgency.

Would he tell her the truth?

He took her soft brown hands in his. Her large dark eyes shone with love. Trust.

A vise pinched his heart.

"Are you sure you're ready for this?" he asked her.

She nodded slowly. "Yes. Yes, I am. Are you?"

He raised one of her hands to his lips, kissed it softly. He had once written her a poem about her smooth, beautiful hands, and when he'd read it to her, she had cried.

"Yes," he said, and slipped out of the car.

He walked through the pharmacy as though in a dream. He had never purchased condoms; there had never been a reason. He looked around warily, wondering who might be watching and noting his inexperience. Sometimes he felt as if he wore his virginity on his chest, like a giant, red "V."

You aren't the only black man in the world who's a virgin, one of his female friends had told him one day. He'd been able to confide the truth to her because she was unavailable for him to date.

I know I'm not, he'd said. But there aren't many of us, I bet. We have to keep a low profile. It's embarrassing.

Why are you embarrassed? You should be proud. Shit, I wish I was still a virgin.

You don't get it. Most brothers start getting busy when they're teenagers. A grown man is supposed to be expert, smooth. What woman wants to fumble around in bed with a man who doesn't know what the hell he's doing?

If the woman loves you, you'll work it out just fine. You need to tell your girlfriend the truth. She'll deal with it—if she loves you.

She loves me . . . but, I don't know. She always tells me how afraid she is of getting close to a man. She's really lowered her guard with me. If I confess that I've been lying all this time—

You're making too big of a deal out of this. Tell her the truth. Being a virgin is a wonderful thing. Unless she's crazy, she'll love you for it even more.

I hope you're right, but I don't think it's that simple. She seems really fragile sometimes. I'm worried about how she'll react if I tell her that I lied . . .

He scanned the boxes of condoms on the shelf. There was a large selection, and none of the labels made sense to him. Okay, he'd heard of Trojans. And the spermicide stuff sounded good. Someone had told him to buy that brand.

At the cash register, he expected the clerk to give him a knowing smile or a smirk, but the woman rang up the purchase as if he'd bought an item as ordinary as deodorant.

Back in the car, he handed her the plastic shopping bag. She looked inside, nodded with approval. She worked as a nurse and had an insider's knowledge of how to practice safe sex.

He sighed. He'd passed another test, added credibility to the lie. No virgin bought the right brand of condoms the first time, did they?

"I love you," she said suddenly. "I'm glad we've waited this long, because I really, really love you."

He forced out his response: "So am I. I love you, too."

She squeezed his thigh, smiled lasciviously. "Now let's hurry up and get home."

Anticipation spread like hot oil across his loins, and he realized that he was not going to tell her the truth. Not yet. He'd tell her afterward. Yes, he would, he vowed.

Or was he now beginning to lie to himself?

In the cool, quiet bedroom of her apartment, they slid out of their clothes. They had been nude together before, during their heavy-petting sessions. But this was different. The box of condoms sat on the nightstand like a time bomb, ticking down to a moment that would change their relationship forever.

They pulled a thin bedsheet over their bodies, and dove into each other's arms. Her tongue darted into his mouth, warm and liquid, and he sucked on her sweet lips. She traced her fingers down his chest, down to his groin, and cupped his erection. He moaned.

"You're ready, aren't you?" she said, her breath hot. "So am I. Feel me."

He slid his finger into her and felt her sex wet, throbbing. He'd become adept at fingering a woman, stroking her to orgasm. That was the weird thing: all of his experience had been with foreplay, and he'd mastered it. But now that he was finally moving past foreplay into the real thing, he had no idea what he was doing and prayed that some ancient sexual instinct would take over and carry him through.

"Put it on," she said, and her muscles contracted around his finger tightly enough to make his pulse race. "I want to feel you inside me."

He reached behind him and grabbed the single condom that he'd taken out of the box. Tore open the package. His hands shook.

This is where the truth starts becoming obvious, he thought.

He examined the condom. He didn't know which end to roll over his penis. It was like trying to figure out how to put on a contact lens; there was only one right side.

"It's been a while," he said. He chuckled. "Always have trouble with these things."

She raised up. "The lubricated side, remember? Here." She took it from him and expertly rolled it down his erection, snugged it down tight. Then she maneuvered on top of him and lowered herself against him, taking him inside her fully.

Oh, my God. So this is how it feels. No wonder folks go crazy for sex.

He sucked in a short breath. She smiled down at him, her breasts jiggling gently. He cupped them, stroked her dark nipples. She began to rock, and he raised his pelvis in time with her motion, grinding against her.

But after only a few minutes, he slid out of her.

"Uh-oh," she said, and quit rocking. "It's not in there anymore."

Heat flushed his face. "I know. Damn. Let's try another position."

"Okay. You on top."

She lay beside him. He raised up and straddled her.

"You aren't hard anymore," she said. She was right; his erection had diminished.

He forced a chuckle. "Guess I'm nervous."

"Let's not force it. Lie down and let's just talk."

They lay side by side, their faces only inches apart.

"This is kinda funny," he said. "We've waited months, and now we're awkward with each other."

"We'll work it out. We have time." She kissed his nose. Her brown eyes were so clear, so understanding, so kind.

This was the moment to tell her the truth. The realization pressed down on him like a weight, so sudden it nearly expelled the words out of him without his conscious effort.

"Sweetheart, I have something I need to tell you."

She propped her head on her arm. "What is it?"

You need to tell your girlfriend the truth. She'll deal with it—if she loves you.

He played his fingers through her hair. "Remember I told you that I've been with other women before? Well, that's not totally true. I've been sort of intimate with other women, but I've never had sex. You are . . . the first."

Her eyes grew large. "You're a virgin?"

He swallowed, unsure of the extent of her reaction, yet it was too late to stop. "Yes. I'm a virgin."

She stared at him.

"I'm sorry I lied," he said. "I never meant for it to go on this long. I wanted to tell you the truth, but I was anxious about it. I mean, a man at my age who's a virgin is—"

"You lied to me all this time? Oh, my God, I don't believe it. I don't believe it!"

She sprang out of the bed. She snatched her houserobe from where it hung on a nearby chair, and wrapped herself in it.

He got out of the bed. "I'm sorry, I really am. But I love you. We can work this out."

"I loved you, trusted you." Weeping, she suddenly came into his arms, and he held her. Just as abruptly, she pushed away from him. "I told you everything about me, all my secrets. I trusted you!"

"You can still trust me. That was the only thing I was ever dishonest about, I swear on my father's grave. I'm sorry."

Crying, she fled the bedroom. She rushed into the bathroom across the hall, slammed the door.

He stood there, butt naked, staring at the door.

I don't believe how she's reacting to this, he thought. This is crazy.

He'd hung his own houserobe in the bedroom closet. He put it on. He went to the bathroom door.

He heard her weeping loudly—uncontrollably, even. She was talking to someone, between heaving sobs. Damn, she had already made a phone call? His first guess was that she'd called her mother.

This was getting out of control. He had to try to steer this back to level ground.

He knocked on the door. "Can we please talk about this? Open the door. I want us to talk and work this out. Please?"

She didn't respond. The lock clicked into place. He tried to turn the knob, no luck.

He knocked against the door. "Shutting me out isn't going to help us work through this. Please, open up and talk to me."

"Get away from the door, you bastard!" she shouted.

He flinched at the virulence in her tone. A chill coursed down his back.

By confessing, he had pressed some deep, disturbing button in her psyche, triggering a reaction that defied explanation. He'd expected her to be upset, disappointed, hurt. But not to this degree. He suddenly felt that he didn't know this woman at all. This woman that he'd courted intensely for five months, that he drove three hours to see every weekend, that he spoke to on the phone four times a day, that he had introduced to his family, that he composed poems for and brought flowers and had professed pure, deep love for, that he was certain that he would marry . . . this woman was as alien and strange as the dark side of the moon.

He wished that he'd kept his damned mouth shut and never admitted the truth.

He sat on the bed, waiting for her to come out of the bathroom. Twenty minutes later—which felt like twenty hours later—she opened the bathroom door. Her eyes were red and puffy. Instead of coming out, she stayed beyond the threshold.

"I think you need to go home," she said. She sniffled.

He stood. "What?"

"I need time."

"Time for what?"

"Time alone. I need to think about this. This hurts me. This hurts me a lot. I need time."

"You want me to drive all the way home? Three hours? Why can't we talk about this?"

"Because I need time. Please. Go home."

"Sweetheart . . ." He started toward her. She moved deeper inside the bathroom and poised to slam the door again.

"Please go," she said.

"I'm sorry," he said, and he could think of nothing else to say. "I wish this had never happened."

She only watched him, warily, as though he were a stranger. Funny, he felt the same way about her. To shift from lovers to strangers in a matter of minutes was dizzying. He felt vaguely ill.

"I loved you more than I ever loved anyone," he said. "I just want you to understand that about me."

"I need time," was all she said.

"Yeah," he said in a shaky voice. He dragged his hand down his face. "So do I."

A half-hour later, he was on the highway, driving home. He drove with the stereo off, unable to endure his usual driving-to-see-his-girlfriend music. He was left with only his uneasy thoughts and his searing memory of the incident that had just happened. Their relationship was over. He didn't want to accept it, but he knew it was true. She would never trust him again. And now that he'd seen her reaction to something unexpected, he was afraid to trust her, too.

He could not quit asking himself: Had they ever truly loved each other? Or had they both been living a lie? Could genuine love shatter as easily as a vase?

The dark highway stretched in front of him endlessly, and he knew that even if he drove forever, he would never find answers to those questions . . . especially when the truth could hurt so much.

Anita
(An excerpt from *All-Night Visitors*)

Clarence Major

I had just gotten in, was tired and nervous—imagining all sorts of possible punishments or deaths for myself, but was going to read a little before going to bed. It was about two o'clock in the morning when the knocking came.

I went to the door and asked, "Who's there?"

"Anita."

I was overjoyed. She was a shapely Afro-American, the color of a Chinese. She was very together. I hadn't seen her since returning from Vietnam. She didn't look much different now than she had then, except she had gained some charming weight.

I remembered all those miles of delicious pussy, the *tupu* goodness of her! *Shmo!* Her thick, protruding clitoris, trimming her, her inner lips, but most of all—what an expert she was at handling my *coke*. How she had milked, milked me, milked, milked, milked me! And she wasn't as mean as some black chicks. She had a spongy goodness, was getting into herself, last time seen, in a way, but . . .

But there she was!

"Come on in, baby!"

"Thank you." Pause. "How are you?"

That last convulsive night, her sensitive voice: "I'll just have to get someone else," Anita said ingenuously. "Sure, I guess you will," I answered. "You see," she countered, "I can't go on like this, Eli. As I imagined you cared for me. I mean, I'm human, you know, I need certain things, and well . . . you're not giving me what I *need*." The night was tinged with mist. A socialist poster was trapped on a brick wall, a kind of American infraction. I strolled beside her, silent, bestial. The heaping stink of this urban captivity wedging in like her words. Her mouth, a cove. Her red dress, black in the encroachment of night. Her heels slapping the sidewalk. Unrequited love! What a thankless bastard I had been! Three boys went by with the word "Warrior" impressed on the cloth of their backs, a kind of justice for them. Some legacy! I saw a bat circling slowly inside a werewolf's medieval dwelling of the mind. She was a deep blue brink. "But of course, we're still friends." "Somebody else?" "No, Eli." I frankly didn't accept that. I couldn't feel self-righteous, but I craved it this instant. Our footfalls. Her hands in her trench-coat pockets. Her long eyelids, still. And my hands, the tips of my shoes.

Anita's face was the kind that is difficult to remember because it possessed a kind of universal beauty, that is, by any standard. There was film of white-yellow overtone to the deeper red-brown of her complexion, so that she came through, usually, depending on the light, as caramel creamy rich, a glowing darkness suggesting ancient rapture. Her eyes were deep brown. If I was angry with her about something, I picked on the stupidity in her eyes as justification for my violent moments of intense hatred for her whenever it was obvious that she wasn't devoting her entire life to boosting and accentuating my essence in the world. Her mouth was large and juicy. A few teeth in the back missing. Its wetness, hollowness, was an excellent aid to her fellatio skill. She had no academic argument pro or con to inhibit her overwhelming self-confidence and spontaneous ability to enjoy lovemaking with the sense of fulfillment an artist knows through creating pleasurable art. Her head was the only slightly offbeat component of her face: it was rather flat, with a kind of bulbous skull, pronounced, high cheekbones, a firm, protruding chin—a softness altogether that detracted from the unfortunate nose.

She now stood facing me in my living room. I was, for the moment, speechless. I had thought of her quite a lot lately. A sad half-smile on her face. She lifted a finger, pointed it at me. (Goddamn! That finger—suddenly it came back to me: at the orphanage *that bitch!* The Warden used to push her finger into my face between my

eyes, jabbing; her mouth going yakety-yak!) "You're really—Oh, forget it!"

"What's wrong, Anita?"

She had her face covered. I went to her. She was trying to cry, her
shoulders shook. I held them.

Finally she lifted her face. "Have a drink with me, Eli?"

"Sure."

Strange that I could later almost forget her.

Outside, the night air was thick and damp, but warm, like walking
through a green pool of dark water. Peaceful because she *wasn't* the
world to me.

Anita, beside me, was murmuring: "This time, Eli . . . I think I've
found him. I'm really nice to him, too."

"You mean your man?"

"Don't say it like *that*."

"What other way is there to say it?"

"Well, anyway, on Sunday, I cook him all kinds of wonderful
meals. You should see some of the nice—"

"Why should I see them?"

"There you go, getting mad already!"

"All right! I won't say anything!"

"Well, if you're going to be mad I'll just—"

"I'm sorry, Anita. Go on, tell me."

And she went on: "He loves salads! You never cared for them, did
you? He loves all kinds of salads . . . You know, onion, lettuce, toma-
toes, grated cheese—real salads."

"I'm guilty of a crime."

"You are, indeed."

"I tried my level best."

I detected in Anita's tone a high wind over a cellar of frustration.
Just how deeply unhappy was she, and to what extent would she go
to cover it? Why tell me? He would soon cause my fists to ache.

In any case, we went to a modest bar and ordered scotch on the
rocks. Her face, in the great shadows of silky purple hair, seemed
gently in a furious unhappiness. And she was still a lovely woman.

But what was happening to any woman? What were they letting the world do to them? Not just black women, all women! That great hump rump bang ugh bang bag they were in, selling body. The idea of body, a commodity.

I didn't want a woman who was going to do too much moralizing about anything. At this time, I wanted in a woman complete femininity; this I found completely necessary. Other times, my relationship to women had been hypothetical. (In Vietnam, I hadn't bothered them. They seemed so sad.)

". . . I have a nice place now. He helps me—Harold, I mean—with the rent and groceries."

"Do I hear wedding bells?"

"I doubt it. He's—well, I won't say . . ."

"Live with you?"

"No, we have an arrangement. What's your girl's name?"

"I don't have one."

"Ah come on! *You?*" A tempered laugh.

"I want you." Want the flesh but what else?

She finally said, "I have scotch at my place."

Unlike in New York, you cannot hail a taxicab on the street in Chicago any time and any place you want one. Only theoretically in New York, I stepped inside a phone booth and called a taxi.

Anita's key opened the door into a very colorful room, drenched in soft lights. The couch was a very simple affair, extremely orange in color, and the few lamps in the room were low, made of wood, while the coffee table was one round sweeping feature of oak with limbs of stud roots seen clearly beneath the varnished surface: the two armchairs heavy, simple, like the couch, one deep green, the other a screaming yellow, while the plush rug was gray in contrast with the Chinese white walls. "You like it?" She was watching my eyes. There was, nesting in one corner, a fifteen-thousand-dollar-looking TV/record player/tape recorder, dull finish.

"You've come close to it?"

"What'd you say, Eli?"

"Forget it. This is beautiful."

Anita. There was the early marriage, big church wedding. Display in the *Defender*. The failure of it, the child that died at birth, the fussy parents at 86th and Drexel; their values she violently questioned. Her husband had turned out to be a big, empty, self-deceiving yella nigger. From a pretentious love for African culture to a confused cross between a radical socialist and a giggling pussyhappy clown. She had her problems too. "I'll show you more."

I followed her into what turned out to be the bedroom, which was done in shades of blue; the furniture itself was early American, the color of the center of a sunflower. There was a spindle-backed rocker, like the one President Kennedy had owned and used so often, and there was a little writing table, a dresser with ruffles (sexy) around it, and a cherry (virgin) bench with its (hard) nightstand.

I laughed. "Wow! He bought this stuff?"

She smiled. "It's all mine." Pretty pride.

Quickly and timidly, I kissed the corner of her mouth. Good Anita, who could have gone to the University of Chicago had she been able to pass the entrance exams; though for most of us at Roosevelt, it was an economic condition. I kept looking at her, trying to imagine what she'd look like without affectations, makeup, etc. Social habits, a different set of inhibitions, or none at all.

But she was bright! For her, Easter was a dress-up day but it was also simply the beginning of the planting season, which meant fewer clothes, brighter clothes.

But she had *no black anger*; she was like any middle-class white girl. She could rave with anger about napalm and death under the buckram palm leaves in Vietnam, without having been there; she could demonstrate against the war, but she could still laugh.

The kitchen was ultramodern, L-shaped, with a thirteen-cubic-foot refrigerator, looking like a sterilized monster dedicated to a sparkling function. A note on the table said simply: "sugar toilet paper." The tile on the floor had a pattern which reminded me of syrup and butter whipped together. Fresh flowers on the table. Everything spotless. Anita's movements were studded with pride as she directed this tour.

We went back to the front. The superglamour of this place floated into my senses, playing volleyball with my mind as I, against my will, measured its essence alongside the formation of artifacts (held together by warmth) I called home. The class struggle, said the May Day people.

She sat on the couch with her legs beneath her, running fingers through her hair, the grease. She had turned on the music. Soul volume, black magic.

"Ice?"

"Yes," she said.

I sat there silently drinking and watching my lady of affections and melodrama, so easily defined by her Calgon bath oil, her high school English teacher's way of smiling, or the sudden easy way she drops the information on the price tag of her latest apparel purchase, or by the fact that she buys Armour Bacon Longs . . . It was very sad to realize that I had come back to the wrong person—but there was no one else.

The bullwhip of time already driving the pain and joy of another journey into my giant gypsy soul . . .

Anita was not a black woman who emphasized the blackness of her beauty. I mean, she went to her beauty shop to have her hair fried, oiled, and curled, or straightened to make it look Lady Clairol; she was a shadow of a blonde, she believed blondes had more fun, once she even dyed her hair blonde; she used bleaching creams though she was already lighter than the average bear; she was a devoted reader of *Ebony*—she believed in its philosophy, especially its ads.

At the orphanage I didn't come in contact with many girls. There were women. A thing like a woman, too: the Warden. There were Red Cross broads who used to come there, being nice. I dreamed of pussy a lot. Tried to see it under dresses. We all did, you know that. It's the way boys are. We had masturbating contests. We had visions, and there were hero shows. Anything to prove ourselves, into something.

A fantasy of a black grown woman with bog muscles serving food in the chow hall, I could come a lot to her musical attention . . . Her breasts were like huge symbols of security.

They were also frightening.

Anita was a broad of some busy concern for material luxury; she was also the kind of chick who rapped: "Listen—you're the man, *you're supposed to do for me! I'm the woman . . .*" But she had no idea that I hated her attitude, felt that she was wrong in her choppy bullshit philosophy that that thought was unique. We didn't just eat each other, we went to all kinds of restaurants and shit, ate food and stuff. Had fun though. She dug window shopping too, ate it up. Loved to eye those garments; she had to see everything, especially *prices*, along the way.

But there was one thing she would not talk about: racial problems. She would not discuss civil rights or Black Power or riots. The realities in the world around us. She absolutely refused to become engaged in any kind of discussion even remotely related.

Later, in her wet grip, I rode . . .

Anita is whipping her tight pussy on me like mad! We are in her dark, beautiful apartment, with a little wine that has warmed her, I think, more than it has me. "I want the light on," I say and get up; the shock of my sudden movement, leaving her, stuns her. I come back, the bright three-way lamp, a new dimension on her caramel-colored, firm, lean body. The taut, little tits with their large, rich dark red berries, some sweet nipples. The gentle yellow lights drive mathematical light sets, beautiful *tupu* sounds of Coltrane. My spongy sore moist sword, I come back to bed, dripping her juice along the way, the sweet goodness of it all soothing my limbs; I happily pat my stomach, singing a couple of bars from something new by James Brown as I jump on the bed, over her now, growling like a dog, "GGRRRRRRRRRRRR," and imaging, even how it looks graphically in cartoons, or here, which is a kind of cartoon of love, my soft black dick, by now completely stunted into a virginal softness, hanging there, and Anita goes, "Lazy nigger, you!" And her wide mouth, those big eyes, sparkling, her white *white* teeth glowing, spotless, virtuous teeth. "I'm dog—GRRRRRR bow-wow! BOW-WOW! BOW-WOW WOW WOW!" I am in her face, and her head is turned sideways, she's looking at me with those big Lil Armstrong–jazzdays eyes at me, as if to say, "Who're you supposed to be *now*? What kinda new game is this, little boy? My, my men are always boys! Boastful, silly, self-centered little boys, who want somebody to jack them off all the time!"

She giggles, the unclear voice of Donovan carries its weight equal in space, timing our sense, from the FM radio. Her big red tongue shoots out, touches my nose. It is good that I am able to enjoy these moments with Anita, despite all the past contamination between us! She runs her long (she has an extra long, extra red, extra active) tongue around my cheeks, quickly licks my lips, but I am still a pompous dog ready to bark again, when her hard, long, firm hand intrudes in the soft, baggy, damp, hairy area of my semen-smelling fruit picker. The conduct of her dry hand always astonishes me, as it delights. She is still giggling. I am delighted, of course, whenever she touches my dick, I like it in a very civil way, not just a natural magnet, magic way. She puts me in large swimming pools of myself weighty with supreme delight, despite the slight roughness of her hand. Anita's hand is not rough because she's been washing dishes, sweeping floors, or ironing clothes—they're rough in a natural way. She's a creamy thing, hard all over. Her little tits are stiff cups that stand firmly, like prudent sentries, looking with dark steadiness in opposite directions. Her stomach is firmer than any stomach, male or female, that I've ever seen. There isn't one inch of fat on her anywhere unless we consider her earlobes fat. Donovan is doing "Mellow Yellow"; as I gently let myself down beside her, she's saying, "Lazzzy lazy nigger, humhumhum," still holding my soft copper-headed dick with a kind of playful sense of disgust. For a moment I feel slightly ashamed that my bonanza detector remains, even in her active hand, serene. She is simply shaking it back and forth, and now asking, "What's this?" She smells clean, fleshy clean, she always does. So gently soapy-smelling, not strong with some overdose of peakily cheap perfume!

She is already on her elbow, looking down at me by now, smacking her lips, going, "Tut tut tut—What am I gonna do with you, nigger, huh? You're a mess—won't it get hard?" "Be nice to it, Anita, baby, it'll do anything you want it to do . . ." Yes, it has been a long time since she's given me that sacred rite she is such a master at performing. I'm thinking, Why should I torture poor Mr. ex-Perpendicular any longer, tonight, in her dry hole? She gets up to her knees, and I deliberately say nothing because I know from past experience that Anita does not like for me to ask her to suck it, though when she volunteers, she has proven to be unbeatable at getting the essence of the act. I remember now as she is about to suck it, she knows that at least turning it around in her mouth, swiveling it, whirling it, rotating it with her thick, long tongue, makes it hard as bookends, and vigorous, so powerful, in fact, that I've rocked and almost unhinged her torso from such long, pithy, severe sessions of pure slippery fucking, pushing one juicy hour, to the rhythms of music, into another, right here in this bed. And I suspect now she thinks she'll get me hard and then stretch out on her back, her brittle little pussy hairs twisting together there, damply, at the mouth of the jewel, hiding that ruthless, hungry, merciless gem! That gobbles and gobbles, eats at me—rather, lies more or less in repose, as I, out of deep meanings of the self, feel compelled to work to death, so to speak, to fill up its crater! But that ain't what's happening this time—she doesn't know it yet, but she's going to swivel it, rotate it, nibble it, lick it, gently chew on it, playfully bite it, turn and turn it in the spitkingdom of herself, dance it with her tongue, spank it with juice, excite it to huge precipices without bursting it out of its tense axis of delight; she's going to hold it in honor with both brown hands, as it dips, tosses, as it ascends, in all oh all ranges of mind states! Yes, it is my mind! Equal, that is, to every level of myself . . .

I know I can turn her off I say One Word now. That's the last thing in the world I want to do now as I feel the weight of her knees adjusting between mine. "Put this pillow under you—" She's being clinical; OK, if she wants to be that way, it'll still be good. I feel how I deliberately relax every muscle I can consciously focus on with my mind. She wiggles her firm ass, adjusting it somewhere on her heels, her arms inside the warm soft area of my thighs, I feel the hairs on them. She takes a deep breath; I can smell the air of the ruby we drank drift up to my nostrils. Sound: the slow wet movement of her strong red tongue moving over her lips, mopping away the dryness. Like most of her body's exterior, her lips are usually very dry. Only two spots, exceptions, I can think of: the areas around the edges of her scalp, the crevices between her thighs and where the mound of her pussy begins to rise, are usually warm and moist. As I lift my narrow ass, holding myself in a loop, she slides the big pillow beneath me, I sink down into the conquering softness, her busy automatic-acting fingers tickle the rooty area at the base of this selfish generative Magic Flute of mine, pull and squeeze my sagging sensitive balls. She coughs, clears her throat. I hear the smack of her tongue between her lips again. I have my eyes closed, soon I'll feel the slow, warm, nervewracking sweet fuck of the pensive mouth beginning.

The hesitation. I know it is coming. Her mouth has not yet touched the ruby head of my dick. The moment of waiting, the anxiety of it builds like musical improvisations in my bones, my membranes, the heat, blood energy in me; I continue to try to keep it all very still, cool, I am not even trying to concentrate on hardening up my ecstasy-weapon, this dear *umme* to the emissive glory of life itself! And for once Anita doesn't seem impatient, she isn't pumping it, bungling, and jacking it, trying to make it instantly hard—I suspect she's going to make it really great this time. She can be absolutely wonderful, when she wants to! The anticipation of these moments, of a kind of antagonism of sweet memory of the best times, is overpowering. It takes all the will in my being to lie here, still, the corporeality of myself, in the spit-slick heady memory of it . . .

(It is only at these moments, of course, that this particular "movement" of the symphony of life is so beautifully important, all-consuming . . . Equal to the working moments when I am excited by the energetic, rich growth of a concept I am able to articulate! Or my sudden ability to construct bookshelves, or create a silly wacky painting, equal to anything that I do involving the full disclosure of myself! I hesitate to say equal to my ability to handle those firearms in Vietnam, against those nameless human collages that fell in the distance, like things, but maybe even equal to that, too . . .)

The hot nude hole of her mouth, *oh God it is so gooooood!* Slides now, caressingly, dry at first, but she's excreting saliva, like pussy juice, her firm hands stretching out, in slow motion, sliding up my flat stomach, my gentle spongy dick blowing up, expanding at a pace equal to the tension in her lips behind the root of her tongue, getting hot as the crevices of her gums, the slow-sinking of her mouth still coming to the very base of my seed-giver, gently but firmly engulfing it, in all of its lazy softness, the nerve-ends of my whole ass, my nuts, my thighs are fructifying! The meaty warmth of her velvety-lined interior begins to climb just as slowly: Mr. Prick is anxious to quickly reach the full and painful proportion of its promise, but I fight that drive by applying more and more deliberation to my restraint, under the magic, almost weightless touch of her fingers as she adroitly guides them down, tripping through the hairs of my stomach. She need not hold my *uume* with her hands any longer. "He's trying too hard to make headway in his headiness!" He holds himself up; I refuse to let the progressive bastard gristle up to the prolific point where he is like some giant tendon, though Anita might (if she weren't unusually patient right now) like that; O motion, joy, oh shit, this is TOO MUCH!; the still missiling motion of the circle of her tight mouth, restrainingly prolonged, up—up! I can feel the inelastic cords of my inner tissues pulling in a complex of nerves, pulling, as her strong big Black Woman, Mighty Nile, African energetic tough lips, the muscles in them quivering, the lengthy moist spongy-porous tongue gently milking the base of my valve, Mr. Hammer's underbelly, milks fruitfully, in a slow rhythm. My eyes are still closed, I am trying not to settle my mind anywhere, it tries for a moment to drift to the greasy magazine of a gun I was examining one day, sitting propped against another guy's back, at the edge of a rice paddy, and I don't know why. I want to stay right here, with her, focused on every protrusion, every cord, abstract circle of myself, of her every "feeling," every hurling, every fleshy spit-rich convexity, mentally centered in all the invisible "constructs" of myself, right here, where she and I now form, perform an orchestra she is conducting in juicy floodtides; stay in her woman's construction, her work, her togetherness, the rich procreating-like magic of her every touch as—more and more against my will—my *kok* protracts, swells, lengthens, perpetuatingly jumpy with fertility, as her permeable mouth decreases its gentle grip in exact ratio to Dick's eminent strong polarity. I love her for her reflective, melancholy approach to this fine art! So seldom does she take this much care to do it properly . . .

My serpent is just fatty-hard, but extra long, reduntantly so! It is best this way, if I can manage to keep it from stiffening to the point where the nerves are minimized somehow. I feel the mouth-motions of her workings, the salivary warmth of her slow, pensive chewing at the acutely sensitive head, where the loose skin has slid back, the rich, thick nerve-ends in the thin layers of this loose skin, she lets spit run down slowly around this Bridegroom in his moment of heaven, the warm secreted water from the prolific glands of her taste bud–sensitive mouth, I feel these oh so slow careful and skillful movements, the deliberate soft scraping and taking of her beautiful strong teeth across the tender texture of the rim of the head, gently bathing with spit the prepuce's densely nerve-packed walls, which rub these ends of my luckily uninhibited penis. She is concentrating on the head of it, and she can do this so long it drives me mad with porous, beautiful pleasure. She will nibble me here, suck one or two times, stop, let it rest limp, aching, in the soft warm cave of her rich dark "construct," saliva mixing easily with the slow sebaceous secretion, my own male liquid lubricant, smegma, washing around in her grip—a gentle but well-controlled clasp! Then, as she might take a gentle but playful plunging down, straight down, down, sinking down faster than she's so far moved, the dick head exploding up into all that wet, warm slime, it's running down, profusely, the tunnel-sinking sense of it, the sounds of the cool capful of wind speeding away, giving way to this cravefeeding, just the hallelujah-warm, narcotic feeling of the drop, as my dick thickens, pushes out—the lengthy pole emitting into her muscles, and tonsils, the juicy soup of my penis glands, the sheath, now in this plunging motion stretching in this hymn of heat to frantic, mad ends! Two more strokes like this and she can finish me. I would shoot a hurricane of seeds into her, falling out convulsively, palmus, in nervous-twitching; but Anita isn't trying to finish me off this time, get it over. She's going to be good to me, but I cannot keep myself from the submissive fear that she might bring it to an end, and it can be very painful if it is done incorrectly. Instinctively, Anita knows this. This knowledge is in the very pores of her skin, she is the knowledgeable Mother of a deep wisdom, intrinsic in her every chromosome.

Yes.

God!!! Yes! She can sustain me, even as I lie pitched on this brink, she controls it all. The way I'm beginning to whimper, groan, beyond my control, she controls it all. With her mouth, she is screwing the head of my dick, around and around. She is worrying it now, from side to side, clasping it, increasing and decreasing the pleasure, the circles of my mind follow some rhythm she is leading, in this voracity. My ass already is beginning to throb under the acute, tremendous, mesmeric workings of her facsimile-pussy, which has the irresistible kind of skill the lower mouth of ecstatic agony, also a spicy feast, with good lips, does not have, because it lacks this mobility. I lie still, the rich body-pungency, the fuck-fragrance of ourselves in my senses, the dry taste of my tongue, as I lie here, my palms face up, the smell of rich black sweet pussy filling the room, the door to her mouth, the wet-smell of my own pungent body fluids that escape her jaws, dripping down into the hairs around this cylindrical, pendulous totem pole, Anita's rhythm upon it begins to increase . . .

I worry. Please baby! Take it easy; but I am not speaking. A few muscles of fear harden in my stomach but I manipulate them back to peace. *Be quiet body*, but she now masculinely grips it, the excited columns of its interior pressed together, the cavernous tissues throbbing, like my head is throbbing, the roots of my hair, my toes are twitching, like this wonderful stand-up organ she is holding in its wet harmony, as she treats the head like it's a Popsicle. Anita has her hand just below the bulbo-cavernous muscle, wrapped in an amorous squeeze there, which serves as a kind of pump, and a restrainer. As she licks the edges of the dome now, lifting her mouth completely up, air currents rush in, refreshingly stimulating; her hand continues to milk my *coc*, setting a pace, otherwise the explosion would come. She knows. She rests. I rest it, I open just the slits of my eyes to see that she has herself in a very relaxed position, so that she can last, without getting tired. I whisper the first words thick like *cum* in the air, "Baby, it's great, beautiful, oh I can't tell you how much—" But I don't finish, I feel her mouth's downward movement, engulfing the bulb as it relaxes from some of its previous excitement. She can detect its state by its throbbing, meaning to be very perfect, she eases the pressure of her hand, the cylinder somewhat dried where her hand has been pressed. I can even feel the sperm, free, push up, the quickening exit, though it is still very slow, still under her control, I am helpless. I am almost unconscious with the pleasure of it. She rotates her heated seminal-stained mouth five times swiftly on this meaty pendulous organ, *umme* . . .

Fighting my tendency to explode, she plans to shift the pace of her work, she uses no method for more than one second, for fear of tipping me off the delicate whimpering thin-skinned "construct" I'm being balanced on. She chews at it, with the gentle crunching of her teeth, tongue working, like she's chewing the juicy texture of an apple, she does this three times—it's so effective, so deeply sinewy good, closing distance between us, a kind of suspended liquid oneness holds us, I am in her, I am one, in her . . .

Home Alone

Curtis Bunn

I met my wife at the movies. I had just come from seeing *Heist* at Buckhead Backlot in Atlanta, and was standing in the long bathroom line that extended into the lobby. In the women's line, I could see Priscilla struggling with her young twin sons, who did not want to go into the ladies' room to pee.

"I'm not letting you go in the men's room by yourself," she said, trying to pull the kids along. "You have to stay with me."

"Don't make us go in there," one of the little fellas said.

"We can hold it," the other said.

Understanding the mother's concern and also the boys' reluctance, I volunteered to be the kids' chaperone, so to speak. "I'll watch them in the bathroom," I said to Priscilla, "if you're comfortable with that." Priscilla looked me up and down and then glanced down at her sons, who were nodding in approval. "OK," she said. "You can go with this man right here. But no playing around."

"I'll take care of them," I said. "Don't worry."

I volunteered because, even at thirty-one, I could remember being four years old like they were and being in that same position. It was usually just me and my mom, and that meant using the ladies' room when I had to go away from home. No boy wants to use the ladies' room, and at four years old you already start to believe you're big enough to go on your own. So I offered to help. That was my only motive. There was no ploy to gain the mother's attention; I hadn't even really noticed her. But after she let the twins come with me, I looked back at her and offered a reassuring smile.

Her smile back at me was what first caught my eye. It was full and warm. And thankful. I could tell she did not want to take her sons into the women's bathroom, but she was not about to put them in a position where harm could come to them.

The kids were delightful, energetic boys who were well mannered and full of life. I could see that even at four they enjoyed being with each other and enjoyed being out and about.

They used the bathroom, and I directed them to the sink and helped them wash their hands. I didn't even use the bathroom. I was focused on completing my good deed.

"Here they are, safe and sound," I said to Priscilla.

"Thanks so much," she said. "They just did not want to go into that ladies' room. They are growing up."

"I understand," I said. "They seem like good young men."

Priscilla smiled and said something about the movie they were about to see, *Harry Potter.* I didn't really hear what she said because I was checking her out. She was tall with a medium-brown complexion, and jet-black hair that sometimes hung over her right eye. There were slight dimples on either side of her face and lips that were full and shapely. I had no idea that my noble intentions would lead me to someone that would capture my imagination. I even liked her voice, which was confident and smooth. We formally introduced ourselves to each other, and her handshake was firm and warm.

"Well, I guess we're going to go in and get our seats before the theater fills up," Priscilla said. "Thanks again."

She was about to turn and walk away and I felt sort of panicked. I needed to not let her get away without finding out how I could see her again. The only thing I could think of was this:

"You know what," I said. "You should let me know how the movie is. I'm planning on taking my niece. She's a big Harry Potter fan." Then I pulled a business card out of my back pocket and handed it to her. "Please call me when you get a chance," I said. Then I shook her sons' hands and they walked into theater number four. I watched them—watched Priscilla, really—and I felt an excitement I had not felt in a long time. I went to the movies by myself as a respite from work, and, well, life really. And I ended up having my imagination sparked. I left there feeling good, hopeful that I could get to know Priscilla Evans.

After two days of not hearing from her, my enthusiasm faded. I was so caught up I didn't even consider that she might be married; didn't even check to see if she was wearing a ring. Or she could have had a man.

When I thought about it that way, I resigned myself to the notion that I would never hear from her. But that same day, when I came in from a fraternity meeting in downtown Atlanta, there was a voice message that made my blood rush through my veins.

"Hi, Joe, this is Priscilla. You met me and my sons at the movies the other day. I've been meaning to call you before now, but it's been hectic. Anyway, I want to tell you about *Harry Potter*, as you asked. My home number is 678–706–1906. Take care. Bye."

That was our beginning. Although it was ten-fifteen that night when I got the message, I returned her call immediately. She had just gotten Lee and Roy to bed and we talked for nearly two hours.

Our first date was that weekend—dinner at Food Studio. I admired her from across the table near the fireplace. She was a red-wine drinker—Pinotage from South Africa especially—and we downed a bottle and engaged in lively, warming conversation.

Over the next eight months, her sons became an important part of my life. They felt like my sons. When I knew I wanted to marry their mother, I explained it all to them—that I loved their mother and that I loved them and that we would become a family that grew together and shared all the great things life has to offer. And when it was time to propose to Priscilla, I included the boys in the event.

I coached Lee on what to say as we all sat in Priscilla's living room one Friday night. I entrusted Roy with the two-carat emerald diamond engagement ring. With everyone in place, I told Priscilla: "This right here is perfect for me—me, you, and your boys. I can't ask for more than this."

Before she could respond, I nodded my head to Lee. "Mommy," he said. "Joe loves you and he loves us. Will you marry him?"

A stunned expression came over Priscilla's face. "What?" she said.

Then I nodded to Roy. "Here, mommy," he said, handing over the ring.

She opened the box and quickly closed it. "What's going on here?" she said. "Is this real?"

"Yes," the boys and I said in unison.

She reopened the box, took out the ring, and slid it on her finger. Then I pulled the boys toward their mother and we all participated in a group hug.

"I love you, Priscilla, and I want this to be our family."

"Yes," she said. "Me, too."

On February 19th, we were married. That was nearly one year after we had met that evening at the movies, and the date is significant for more than matrimony for us. It also was the first time we ever made love.

Before Priscilla, no one could have ever told me I could be with a woman eleven months, get married to her, and not have had intercourse with her. But that's exactly what happened, and it turned out to be a beautiful thing.

What happened is, over that time we achieved and then mastered a lost art: we made love to each other's minds. And that helped us fall so deeply in love, because we touched the core of each other's souls. We were intimate—kissing, hugging, caressing—which made it even harder to not seduce her to physical fruition. But it was so fulfilling to be with a woman for her heart and spirit and caring and mind and understanding and compassion and empathy and intellect—all the intangibles that really are at the heart of a person's being.

Really, we sort of stumbled into the no-sex thing, and stayed there because it felt right. We both had circumstances in our lives that called for a new approach, a careful approach, and it turned out to be the galvanizing force that cemented our relationship.

For me, I experienced the kind of drama that can either make or break a man. My last girlfriend told me she was on birth control and so we repeatedly had unprotected sex. After about two months, she told me, "Something's wrong with you. I've been off the pill for about six weeks and I still haven't gotten pregnant."

Of course I was livid. Silly girl, she was so disappointed that she did not achieve her underhanded mission that she did not even care that she had divulged her evil scheme. "What? You mean you've been trying to get pregnant? What's wrong with you? How can you do that?" I said.

Her response was typical of her distorted mindset. "Well, you don't have to worry about it because I didn't get pregnant."

When I finally got beyond the anger enough to give the situation some thought, I realized I needed to get a checkup to see if something, indeed, was wrong with my juice. And sure enough, after a series of tests, the doctor told me I was sterile. I would never be able to have children. I was crushed. And I was emasculated. I didn't feel like a man. I felt like . . . I don't know what I felt like. My desire for women stopped, and I *really* became sterile. I mean, I could not get an erection. And the worst part about it was I didn't even care to get one.

Priscilla and I had grown so close that I shared that news with her, news I'd shared with no one else. She was her typical caring and reassuring self. I actually felt better after telling her.

Then she shared some news with me that made me understand better her willingness to abstain from sex.

"About a year and a half ago, I was engaged to be married to Lee and Roy's daddy," she said, her Texas accent becoming more evident, which was an indication that she was speaking from the heart. "He was from Philadelphia, and we had planned to move there together, get settled, and then get married. The boys were two.

"He moved up there to get our apartment together and we were coming the next week. I packed up our stuff here and gave my thirty-day notice to move to the leasing office. He left on a Friday for Philly. Everything was great. I was excited. Being from Houston, I wasn't thrilled about moving up north to the cold weather, but we were going to be a family. And as a middle-school teacher, I'd be able to find work up there with no problem.

"Well, I never heard from the boys' father again. I mean, he just vanished. The job he'd said he had there did not exist. His only family—both his parents were deceased—was a younger brother. I called him in Philadelphia, and his number had been changed. Non-published.

"I was petrified, scared, confused, everything. One day went by, two, three, a week, ten days. I called around, called the police, the highway patrol, everyone I could think of. I went to his old job at Georgia Power and even his friends there said they knew he was moving but had not heard from him.

"You can't know how devastating that was to me. I eventually found out that he had moved to New York, but I didn't even want to contact him—for money or anything. He's just a sorry man.

"I could have had a breakdown over all that. Only God and the will He gave me to stay strong for my kids kept me going. I had quit my job, given up my apartment, had a going away party, said tearful goodbyes to my friends here in Atlanta . . . only to have nowhere to go, no future husband, no nothing. Just me and my kids and, most importantly, God. I know now I can handle anything after surviving that."

That probably was our most significant night together. We shared our most intimate, life-altering experiences and came away from it closer than ever. From there, it was a continuing process of growing together. I knew then it would lead to marriage. Some things you can feel. I felt that as sure as I'm black. For me, the biggest revelation was that the doctors were wrong about me not being able to have kids. I wasn't able to *produce* a child, but at the moment I said "I do," I certainly had two sons. And it was such a proud feeling.

On our wedding night, we talked about how far we had come to get to where we were. Priscilla said, "I have a family now. After what happened to me, I never thought I would or that I could even trust that it could happen. Thank you."

And then we made love for the first time. The honeymoon was short—three days in the Bahamas—but it was great. My sterility issue had no impact on my ability to make love to my wife. I'd never

felt more frisky in my life. It was like I had a seventy-two-hour erection, and Priscilla showed me her passionate and freaky sides all at
once.

When we returned home to start our lives together, we found that
we would not be able to keep up the intimacy pace we'd set on the
honeymoon. Life just would not allow it.

Between taking care of the kids and making sure to spend quality
time with them, working, managing things around the house, and
sleeping, finding intimate moments with Priscilla was a chore.

Sex became scheduled, like a meeting. We bought a house in
Lithonia, which created more time-consuming responsibilities. Before I knew it, three months had passed and my wife and I had found
a routine that was satisfactory, but not what we wanted. When we
had the energy after a long day, we would make sure the kids were
asleep, lock the bedroom door, turn the TV up to muffle the sex
sounds, and then enjoy each other. But it was like drive-by sex.

Finally, the end of school came and Priscilla's sister, Yvette, volunteered to keep the kids for a weekend. Teaching and tutoring and
other civic responsibilities had just worn Priscilla out.

"This is my chance to get some rest. I love those boys, but these
two days will be a vacation for me," she said.

I had other plans. We took Lee and Roy to the airport, prayed that
they'd be safe flying alone to Houston, and headed back home. "I
know I said I wanted to go out, but I'm exhausted. Can we just order
out?" I said in the car.

"That sounds good to me," she said. "Let's pick up a DVD from
Blockbuster."

When we got home, I suggested Priscilla take a bath, which she
quickly agreed to. I watched her as she ran the water and filled it
with oils and sweet-smelling bubble bath and lit the bathroom with
candles. She was so beautiful. Not so much physically, although she
was, but more so her spirit. It was alive and free. I was so into her.

She slipped out of her clothes and slid into the tub. Just as she
did, the doorbell rang. I had ordered seafood—shrimp, crab legs,
vegetables—from the restaurant C'est Bon on Panola Road. They

didn't deliver, but I begged and pleaded and promised a big tip, and the manager made it happen for me.

I set up two plates on a tray and carried the food upstairs to the huge, open bathroom.

"What are you doing?" Priscilla said.

"Ever heard of breakfast in bed? Well, this is dinner in tub," I said.

I also had a bottle of Moët Nectar Imperial. I put on a nice Nancy Wilson CD and took off my clothes and joined my wife in the oversized tub. "I can't believe you," she said.

We sat facing each other and fed each other and sipped on champagne. I moved the tray back after we finished eating and proposed a toast. "I love you, Priscilla. Here's to our family—and to two nights home alone."

"Amen," she said, and we tapped glasses.

I set my glass down and pulled Priscilla's legs around my body. She laid her head back as I slowly, delicately ran my hands inside her thighs. Priscilla moaned in pleasure.

My hands worked their way underwater and between her legs. Even engulfed in the hot bathwater, I could feel more heat the closer I got to her pussy—or Li'l Priscilla, as she called it.

I rubbed and then stroked her clit, which produced more moaning from her. She took one last gulp of her champagne and set down the glass. She looked me in my eyes as I caressed Li'l Priscilla with care and affection. Her legs opened wider and I slid my finger in her pussy, her muscles immediately collapsing around it.

She squirmed on my finger and with my other hand I gave her clit its proper attention. Priscilla and Li'l Priscilla were both hot and ready. My dick—or Big Joe, as she called it—was a symbol of hardness. It floated above the water and the bubbles, and Priscilla leaned over and stroked it with an incredible passion.

"Can I have Big Joe?" she said.

I didn't even answer. I just moved my hands along her legs and down to her ankles. She immediately positioned herself on top of me, on top of Big Joe. Her luscious titties were half covered in bubbles and her hair was all over her face.

My dick was so hard that for a moment I wondered how a baby could not come out of what was in there. If nothing else, hard as I was, I should have been able to produce an iron rod.

Priscilla appreciated the hardness. She slowly slid down on my dick, moaning all the way. She started timidly and then increased her riding pace. My arms were on either side of the tub to hold me up for support. She rocked on my dick and I push deep inside her, a sensual, pleasing effort that produced waves of water that spilled onto the floor.

Neither of us gave a fuck. We were into the kind of passion a married couple can only have when the kids are gone. I squeezed her juicy titties and tried to suck them, but the force of her gyrations knocked me back and even pushed my head underwater. Again, I didn't care. In fact, I kept my head underwater for about fifteen seconds as my wife rode my dick like the Texas cowgirl she was.

When I emerged from the water, Priscilla, ever the caretaker, grabbed a towel and wiped my face—all the while sliding up and down on my dick. We both let out cries of pleasure that had been supressed for months for fear of waking up the kids.

Priscilla stopped riding me long enough to somehow contort her body so that she was facing the other way, exposing to me her plump ass that I would sneak a feel on every day when the boys weren't looking.

From this position, she bounced up and down on Big Joe with ferocity, again splashing water all over the place. By the time we finished, the tub was nearly empty and our legs were weak.

Well, I shouldn't have said "finished," because we weren't. We pulled ourselves out of the tub, walked right past the towels and straight to the double vanity. Priscilla grabbed hold of it and bent over, and I entered her from behind—our favorite position.

I flipped the light switch on and told Priscilla to look into the huge mirrors so she could see me stroking her. "Oh, my God. Look at you. Look at us," she said. "This turns me on."

I swiveled my hips and plunged deeper from various angles so as to make sure Big Joe visited all of Li'l Priscilla. My wife screamed unabashedly, so loud that I would not have been surprised if the mirror had cracked.

"Smack my ass," she said, and before she could take another breath I obliged her. I smacked both cheeks, in cadence with my strokes. As much as she liked that, I did, too. It made my dick even harder, which I did not think was possible. Already I thought I could chop down a tree with Big Joe.

As much as I wanted to sex my wife all night, the pleasure of it all was too much to contain. The combination of loving her so much, the juiciness of her pussy, the sensation of smacking her ass, and thrill of watching me do all of that in the mirror drove me to the kind of climax that makes you see stars.

I came hard, and would have collapsed on the bathroom floor if I'd had the energy. Instead, I just filled Li'l Priscilla with my hot gism and held on to my wife and kissed her back and shoulders.

We managed to make it to the bed, where we lay with her head on my chest, right over my heart, where she belonged. During the night I blew out the candles. Out of habit, the bedroom door was locked, and I made sure to unlock it. We were free, at least for two days, so there was no succumbing to the usual restrictions.

The next morning, we sat at the kitchen table and had breakfast. We both wore nothing but robes. It was so liberating to be so free at home without the kids.

We sat on the couch and read the paper and talked and embraced the temporary freedom we had. Priscilla had committed to a school outing for the kids she tutored, and so around five she left the house. I went to the golf driving range and came back home and cooked dinner. Nothing fancy: baked trout, rice, and green beans.

Priscilla called to say she'd be in around nine. When she came through the garage door, she saw the table candlelit with plates full of food—and me standing there naked.

"See, that's what I need to come home to every day," she said.

She dropped her purse and came directly into my arms. My dick started getting hard as she approached. We hugged. "Look at Big Joe," she said, looking down. "I think he missed me."

Then she asked me to wait as she rushed upstairs and took a shower. I rested across the couch, dick hard, while she did. She came back downstairs dressed as I was—in nothing.

"Ready to eat?" I said.

"Actually, I'm ready to taste—taste Big Joe," she said.

"I like that," I said.

I remained prone on the couch and she came to me on her knees and kissed me deeply. Then she kissed my neck and shoulders and chest and stomach and then the throbbing Big Joe.

She kissed my dick as passionately as she kissed me. I rubbed her back as she did, and then her ass, and then pulled her by her leg so that she would lift it up and over me. In other words, I positioned her so that her pussy was right in my face. I wanted a taste of Li'l Priscilla.

So, with it right there, I licked her clit and then softly sucked it and ran my tongue into her moist, hot pussy. She moaned and sucked harder on my dick, which made me lick her pussy more intensely.

In minutes, Priscilla was cumming, and so she screamed out and tried to pull away from my tongue. But I held her firmly and licked harder, sending more sensation through her body.

"Give me that dick," she said. "Put it in."

Who was I to deny her? We got untangled and she rested on her back, panting, with one leg on the back of the couch and the other on the floor. I entered her and she screamed again, and she held me tightly as I stroked hard and deep. I pulled up and grabbed her legs and held them wide open. I grunted sounds I didn't know I could make as I pounded away, making sure Priscilla received Big Joe like she liked it. Suddenly, it was my turn to cum, and I did so loudly, letting out those weird sounds that meant the ultimate pleasure.

I put Priscilla's legs down and lowered myself onto her chest. We hugged and kissed deeply. There was nothing to say and no real breath to get it out anyway.

Several minutes later we cleaned up, warmed up the food on the table, and ate. And then, as we put up the dishes, we made love in the kitchen. I made sure we stayed away from objects sharper than my rock-hard dick.

The message was clear in our passionate exploits: When the kids are away, the parents should play—and anywhere but the bed.

"You know, our lives go back to normal in the morning when the kids return," I said.

"I know, but this was something very special, Joe. We needed this," Priscilla said.

Then we spent the next hour talking about our kids. It was heartwarming.

"You know what," I said. "Please don't take this the wrong way because you know I love you and our time together, just me and you. But I miss the boys. I'm ready for them to come home."

"Me too," she said. "I feel the same way."

A month later, Priscilla came home glowing. "My sister is coming here next week and taking the boys to Disney World," she said.

I smiled a knowing smile.

"But that's not why I'm really happy," she said.

"What is it?"

"Joe, I'm pregnant. I didn't want to say anything until I was sure. But I went to the doctor. About four weeks pregnant."

I was shocked. The four weeks dated back to our weekend home alone. I was also thrilled. "The doctors were wrong about you, Joe," she said. "I always believed that but I didn't want to say anything."

"I *wanted* to believe that too," I said.

We hugged and kissed and called down the boys to tell them they would have a brother or sister. "And you know what," I said to them. "If it's a boy, he'll never have to go into the ladies' room, because you guys can take him."

Wild Thang

Gary Phillips

She was chunky in the hips. This only added to the sensual quality of her shapely body. And given the nature of the venue the dark and lovely healthy woman was showcased in, notions about ideal weight weren't on the minds of the various audiences she was seen by.

The woman wore a mauve bustier with matching lace panties that peeked from below. Initially she was viewed from behind as the camera's shot opened on the middle of her back and panned down to the sway of her hips. The camera tracked her and the firmness of her wondrous butt as she entered the bedroom, swathed in candlelight. She homed in on her destination.

Lying stomach up on the king-size bed with its massive headboard, was a brother who even Stevie Wonder could see hadn't been shorted in the shaft department. He wore only a pair of boxers imprinted with cartoonish grinning devil heads. His one-eyed beast lay outside the slit and was fast becoming aroused as he grabbed that bad boy in one hand and started working his tool.

The shot switched from the handheld to an up-angle side view as the woman sank on the bed next to the man, helping him along with her purple-nailed hand. The shot cut again as the camera pushed in slowly on her profile. She ran her tongue across her bright lipstick, making its pumpkin hue wet with anticipation.

"Day-um," Elrod, the six-foot-eight ship container–built manager of Continental Donuts exclaimed. "That is her, man."

Ivan Monk, the proprietor of said house of sweet breads and licensed private investigator, kept silent. The two men were anchored before Monk's PC monitor watching the downloaded video clip unfold. Beyond the ajar door to his file room, the phone rang.

"That's the judge," the big man joked. "Her radar has gone off and she knows you're in here watching some homegrown porno."

"I'm looking for clues."

"If you need a clue to what she's doing, I feel sorry for you. Really."

Now those orange lips parted as she descended on the man's penis.

"Yeowww," Elrod said.

The veins in the man's enlarged member stood in rigid relief as he methodically, and gently, pumped her mouth. Her head bobbed rhythmically.

"Buddy, buddy," Elrod said. "And this has been up since this morning?"

"Yeah," Monk said hoarsely. "Willie Brant was talking about it this morning at the barber shop."

Elrod's laughter was like rocks tumbling in a clothes dryer. "That's the first time that old crow has been right about anything."

The camera shots alternated from the stationary view to the handheld. Once, as the woman changed position, the shadow of the person taking the shots was briefly thrown against the headboard as one of the candles spat liquid wax. The man took hold of her panties and slipped them off her, kissing and nibbling her stomach as he did so. In her three-inch heels that were now visible, the famous woman straddled the sprung man, inching up until her legs smothered his face. She grabbed the top of the headboard and bucked as the man's head shook from exertion.

Monk gulped. "You damn skippy."

The woman then eased back and inserted the man inside her. She bent over and they kissed as she began to ride him. The muscles in his legs tightened and he matched her stroke for stroke.

Elrod and Monk watched transfixed.

"Ivan," Josette called from the front.

"Huh?"

The clip ended on the woman arching back as she shuddered with pleasure. The screen blinked to black.

"Phone's for you."

"I'm coming." He and Elrod chuckled. "I mean I'll be right there."

"I got to see it again," Elrod proclaimed.

Monk got up from his seat and left the room. Elrod, who'd been sitting next to him on a stacking chair, fooled with the mouse.

"Thanks, Josette," Monk said, picking up the handset after stepping into the front.

She wagged a finger at him. "I'm going to tell Jill."

"The dude in the video is fine."

Josette made a face.

He answered the phone. "I bet you've seen it," the voice on the other end of the line said.

Josette finished taking care of a customer's request for three maple crullers.

"Pardon?"

"This is Alicia Scott."

Josette walked toward the file room.

"Well, yes, I have heard about this steamy video you're supposed to be in." He lied because he was embarrassed at being found out, like when he was 14 and his mother found a copy of *Playboy* under his bed.

"Then you know what I need." Her voice was without inflection, yet the stress was just beneath its surface.

At that moment, Monk realized how it was she'd called him. He occasionally did work for, and was represented by, an attorney named Parren Teague. Though criminal law was his specialty, like his law school colleague Johnnie Cochrane, his firm had branched out into entertainment and sports. And more and more in the big bad city, those areas always seemed to be overlapping.

"There's not much of anything I can do for you, Ms. Scott. The video is out there on the Internet. Whoever shot it," and he paused, catching himself. "That is, I understand this took place inside a room." To admit more would give away he'd seen her and the stud getting very busy.

"Can we meet? I'll pay you your day rate."

"That's five hundred seventy-five." That price wasn't for everybody. But he knew the three-time Grammy winning, multi-platinum-selling singer/songwriter could stand the freight.

She put some sugar in her voice. "At my housecleaner's crib in half an hour? I'm hiding out from the press. She lives in Inglewood."

"Sure." Too bad, he'd wanted to see her house and maybe get to see the bedroom where the alleged penetration took place. Monk grinned and went to tell Elrod where he was heading to make him envious. Thirty-three minutes later, the bemused PI was sitting down with the stressed-out singer. Cups of coffee on the table.

"Thanks for coming."

Be cool, man, he warned himself. Don't make everything into a double entendre. "No problem."

They were sitting in a breakfast nook in a modest house on Sixth Avenue near Hollywood Park, the racetrack. Inglewood was a mostly working-class city of blacks and Latinos people drove through on their way to the airport. Save for years the Lakers used to have their home games at the Forum, no one from Hollywood, not even the hookers, trod its streets. As this was Saturday, the animated mayhem of *Courage the Cowardly Dog* drifted in from the living room where Monk had stepped past three youngsters watching his exploits.

"I need you to do one simple errand, that's all." She was sitting sideways at the table in jeans and crossed her legs.

It took all of Monk's discipline to shut down the image of those bare muscular legs clamped around the man's head as her ass grinded in the video.

He shrugged. "I don't do beat-downs. That is, I don't set out to do thug work."

She frowned.

He spread his hands. "Take care of the cameraman."

"Camerawoman, actually."

It just kept getting better. "Lay it on me . . . I mean—"

She held up a hand. "I know."

Olga Salas stepped into the kitchen. "You two okay? Want more coffee?"

"We're the ones imposing on you," Alicia Scott responded. She crossed her hands to her chest. "I'm just so thankful."

The housecleaner, in her mid-thirties, smiled. "You know I owe you too. More than . . ." and she choked up, unable to go on.

Scott got up and went to the woman and they hugged. Monk waited. The woman mumbled that she was just going down to the store and would be back in a few. Scott responded she would make sure the kids didn't torture each other—much. Salas exited through the back door in the kitchen.

"Olga was in an abusive situation," Scott began, sitting back down and answering the question on Monk's face. "He was a motherfuckah from the word go," she said, lowering her voice so it didn't carry into the living room. "This bastard waled on her while she was pregnant with Rudy, their third one."

He nodded.

"I got Parren to not only get a restraining order against him, but to use some of his connections to get the D.A. to pay him a visit too. He split and now's shacked up with some ho down in Santa Ana."

Monk liked her. She was real. "Okay, so tell me about this 'director.'"

Alicia Scott put a hand to her pretty face and shook her head. She looked at him through open fingers then took the hand away. "She's recorded other . . . things I've done. We've done."

"Well, well." It had occurred to him that personalities like Rob Lowe, Pamela Anderson, even sorry-ass Tonya Harding, had survived their sexcapades being the subject of public titillation. But those were onetime tapes and conventional in a certain way. "There's more than just the usual on these other episodes."

She looked off, then back at him. "Unfortunately."

He almost blurted, You been muff diving? but managed to maintain some decorum. "So this camerawoman, she's a friend, is she?"

"The bitch used to be," she said. From the living room one of the kids yelled at another one, and Scott went in to see what was up. She returned in a few moments. "Look," she resumed, going to the refrigerator and taking out a carton of orange juice. "Let's just say there's other stuff that I don't want—can't have—out there, okay? Can we leave it at that?"

She poured some juice, then said, "Maybe me getting it on with a dude hung like a stallion might be good for sales." She replaced the carton.

He had to ask. "She not only taped, she participated?"

Scott sighed. "I'll tell you this, me and homegirl, her name's Kelly Marie, well, that's what she calls herself now. The name her mama gave her is Mary Stevens. Anyway, me and her go back a long ways— junior high, okay?"

"For me that's decades. For you it's what, seven years?"

"You're cute. It's more than ten even for me." She paused. "The two of us been through a lot."

He helped her take the three glasses to Olga Salas's children. Back in the kitchen Monk said, "So now she's blackmailing you?" He leaned against the tiled counter.

"Yep. Got a little note in my e-mail last night 'bout twenty minutes before the video dropped." Scott snickered. "Damn, I'm talking about this like it was an album. She said in her note she'd release this mild one to make sure I understood she wasn't playing."

"And the rougher tapes would show up if you didn't come across," Monk finished.

"No doubt."

"Tell the police. It's illegal to extort money."

She shook her head. "The less who know, the better. Plus just let me go to the po-po and this mess will leak out for sure." She looked evenly at him. "I need your help, Ivan."

"I'll do what I can. But you don't know, the bloodletting may never stop," he cautioned. "And I'm guessing this sudden manifestation of greed your girl's exhibiting is due to some personal static between you two."

She regarded the dude built like an aging linebacker. "Parren said you're good—and nosey as hell."

Monk wiggled his eyebrows.

"Fine," she smacked a hand against her thigh. "We were lovers and partners in her music video business. We had threesomes and foursomes going on, all colors and all persuasions gender and sexual preference–wise." She crossed her arms. "Happy now?"

"Exceedingly," he said as Olga Salas returned.

Soon Monk was guiding his fly '64 Ford Galaxie up one of the numerous twisting inclines of Silverlake, not too far from the house he and Jill Kodama, his old lady and a superior court judge, shared overlooking the eponymously named reservoir. He'd recently installed a CD unit and was listening to his client's latest album, *Lot 47*. Scott's material was a mixture of R&B interjected with hip-hop flavor. In particular the song playing as his car wound along Berkeley, was entitled "Nightfall." The cut set the mood of the case.

Scott and Stevens/Marie had had a parting over the last music video the latter had shot for the former. But, as Scott told it, this was merely the last in a long line of fissures erupting between the two. The problem, she concluded, was not having enough distance between the personal and their business lives.

"And," she'd added, placing those purple nails on Monk's arm in the kitchen, "I like dick too much." Her kilowatt smile boiled his heart. "Kelly just don't swing that way, and was mad bothered that I did. You feel me?"

He was glad she couldn't tell he was blushing. Now at the house, Monk took in an understated California bungalow of angles and fluted panes reminiscent of Gregory Ain's designs. No one answered the door, and there was no car in the driveway. Monk's job was to scope out the situation, part stakeout and part tailing the blackmailer if need be.

The message Alicia Scott had received last night hadn't been on Marie's usual server. And also funny, Scott had told him, she was to deliver the cash tonight to a drop in Wilmington.

"Why's that so odd?" he'd remarked, halting at the kitchen door.

"Girlfriend's all that with computer and high-tech shit. Got little cameras, fiber optics, knows CGI," she hunched her shoulders. "I figured she'd just have me wire the benjamins somewhere."

Recalling that as he stood on the side of the house, Monk was happy the view from the street was partially blocked by a hedge not trimmed for months. Breaking in could at least cost him his license—if he admitted doing such a deed. Like his work for Teague, he was given certain parameters and how he accomplished those goals . . . well, Teague—and his current client—had plausible deniability if he got jammed up. After all, they never said to do anything illegal. Only it was understood that walking the line didn't always produce results.

And who was to know if no one's home? He had no lock-picking skills, but in this case it didn't matter. Like a lot of side doors in houses of this age, this one wasn't as substantial as the front, and it was loose in the frame. A few leans of his heft against the door, and the lock popped out of its socket. Inside, the house was still. On a ledge over the sink, a clock ticked off the time.

There was something else and it took Monk a few seconds to realize: the number he'd been listening to in his car was on in the house.

A Rod Serling moment he told himself and went forward. The living room was populated with tasteful furniture; North Vermont Avenue trendy. Her home office, Scott had told him, was a second bedroom off a short hallway to his left. On his way there, he took a right to see the master bedroom where the nasty had been done, as Scott had also mentioned.

The door was closed and the old instinct slipped into gear. He withdrew his hand hovering just above the old-fashioned glass knob. Aware that prints could be made of his ear, he leaned in close to the door without pressing the side of his head to the wood. As far as he could tell, nobody was in there getting their swerve on. From inside this room the music emanated. The prickling on the base of his neck wouldn't stop.

"Shit," he swore softly. He couldn't help himself, he just had to get a peek in there. Alicia Scott was a fool for the freaky-deaky as he was for snooping. John Lee Hooker was right, he mused, "It was in 'em, and it had to come out." Monk retrieved a potholder from the kitchen, and twisted the knob. Sure enough, Kelly Marie was laying on the bed, face up, eyes on the ceiling and dead as Jimmy Walker's career. She was in a terry cloth robe that was tied at the waist.

Looking at the corpse closer, he could tell there was an object in her pocket. Some sort of remote control he guessed. He was also cognizant of the woman's rigidity, and estimated she'd been dead since last night. There was a red stain on the robe's side, near her waist. She'd been stabbed through the kidney, probably more than once. A particularly painful way to die. The repeat button had been punched on the CD player. He took a look around then walked out of the room. He didn't shut the door as he'd need it open to go along with his story of coming to the house, finding the back door unlocked and this room open.

In the kitchen, Monk replaced the pot holder on its hook, next to the phone. He began to dial the cops then replaced the receiver. The picture of Alicia Scott working overtime on the hung brother's tool suddenly snapped into his mind. But he wasn't fixating on the act, it was the point-of-view of the shot that intrigued. He went back into the bedroom.

Crouching alongside the bed, he pivoted from the still body of the filmmaker toward the far wall. There were two parallel built-in shelves and on them were some retro toys made of sheet metal. He went over there, then looked back. Monk nudged a couple of the items then picked up a blockish robot replica from a '40s sci-fi serial. There was a clear lens in its chest. The toy also had a rear panel for batteries. Upon opening it, Monk smiled broadly.

Horace Edwards was arrested as he left his apartment in Gardena for his drive out to Wilmington. He was the love machine who'd been doing the wild thang with Alicia Scott.

Edwards was a calendar model, and bit part player used by Kelly Marie in a few of her music shoots. He and Scott got to talking during the shoot of her music video, exchanged e-mails, and so it went.

But Horace had ambitions and shared those ideas with Marie, aware as he was about the pair's recent rift. He figured if she'd filmed him sexing Alicia Scott down that one time, there had to be other tapes.

"But that stupid lez couldn't see what I was talking about," he griped during interrogation. He snorted derisively. "How she and Alicia had a split, but she'd never do that to her friend."

"Now look here," he added. "That crazy broad came at me, hear? I had to defend myself."

The two detectives interviewing him gave each other the big eye. What jury would go for that bullshit?

It turned out that Kelly Marie had wisely hidden previous tapes elsewhere. She only had the most recent one in her home because she was doing an edit of it on her computer. Edwards got a friend of his who knew something about computers to send the tape he stole, after killing Marie, onto the Net. Edwards had moved Kelly Marie's car several blocks over to make it seem she was away on assignment. He'd collect the big payday from Scott, then bounce out of town.

"So Kelly Marie had one of those micro surveillance devices in the robot?" Jill Kodama unbuttoned her shirt.

"Yep," Monk said. "She used shots from that and the handheld digital video recorder to make her masterpiece. Horace hadn't seen the video and so didn't know Marie had two cameras going. When he cornered her at her house, it seems she palmed the remote control that triggered the camera hidden in the toy robot." Monk unbuckled his pants, folded and hung them up.

"She probably got him into the bedroom so she could catch him threatening her on tape, and tell him later to have him back off." Kodama unzipped her skirt. "But he must have gone off and stabbed her."

"All captured in living color. He put her on the bed and took off." He stepped out of the closet, she came over to him. Her breasts, encased in a silky bra, rubbed against his back as she reached around, her hands exploring a body very familiar to her.

"And how did you surmise all this, master sleuth, if you hadn't seen the video?" Her fingers latched onto his stiffening rod.

"Aw, baby, you know me."

"I sure do."

He turned around and kissed her as she walked backward to the bed. They flopped down, he on top of her. "Okay, your honor, you caught me. I did see the thing. Elrod made me watch it."

She laughed. "You must think I believe that like I believe the backdoor to her house was open."

"How about we concentrate on what we're doing right now?"

"Depends on how hard you try to convince me."

They kissed and her hand massaged his balls. And Monk did the best he could to please the court.

Revolution

Colin Channer

Every Friday, after taking tea at four o'clock, St. William Rawle would drive downhill in his blue Ford Fairlane, dressed in a crushed white suit.

Short and fat, with a ring of sunburned skin around his neck, he had flunked out of Cambridge before the war and had returned to San Carlos to discover that fate had sent banana blight and hurricanes to wreck his family's fortune. With a Higher School's Certificate and a letter from the new archbishop, he was appointed headmaster of an all-girls' school, a position that he held until a book by Graham Greene convinced him that his future lay in letters.

Since that revelation, he had published thirty-one books, a volume for each year: thirteen novels, six books of verse, nine books of science, a natural history of the island, a translation of the New Testament in *sancoche*, the local dialect, and a primer on etiquette for unmarried ladies all at his own expense.

He had been married six times, four of them to Rebecca Salan, who had died beside him in her sleep four years ago, in 1971, while he patiently awaited her response to one of his unfathomable questions. But to anyone who offered him condolences, St. William would reply that he was not bereaved, because Rebecca came to him at night in dreams with answers from the spirit world.

Every Friday evening at a quarter to five St. William would sit on a folding chair at the base of the statue of Admiral Nelson, face the public buildings that three-cornered the square, and repeat his demand for the chief minister's resignation.

The square had been designed by St. William's great-grandfather, who had brought from Venezuela a perverse enamoration with arches. So it was with deference that the constables would arrest St. William, who, but for his eccentricities, would have been governor himself, the eleventh in a line that started in 1792, when the English, led by one of his antecedents, had seized San Carlos from the French— who had seized it from the Spanish—and razed the domed cathedral, erecting in its place a parish church whose spired clock was impotent, mute, and arthritic.

On the morning that St. William heard the brick-and-plaster timepiece chiming for the first time in his life, he sat up in his postered bed and made a quick decision. For the last sixteen months Rebecca had been appearing in his dreams in army greens, her eyes replaced by watches.

And so it was, at the age of sixty-one, when he should have been gazing at retirement from public life, that St. William Rawle decided that history had invited him to start a revolution.

St. William lived alone in the Metropolitan Hotel, a Georgian house with cinder-block extensions, which had not attracted guests in thirteen years. The floor planks were damp, and the rafters draped with spider webs that trapped the odd mosquito.

St. William was not a violent man; but in his soul there ran a subterranean stream of anger that erupted into flood with his orgasms. An early riding accident had left him sterile. Still, he had accepted from his wives and many mistresses a brood of eighteen children.

The chief minister was one of them—the youngest and the only boy—and he had caused St. William great embarrassment.

In a recent address on national radio—television would arrive in later years—he had ridiculed St. William's plan to leave the Metropolitan Hotel to the people of San Carlos as a national learning center: a library, a museum, a teachers' college, and an institute for the study of Atlantis.

The property had been in St. William's family for a hundred and fifty years, at first as a coconut plantation. But the chief minister believed the land should be used for public housing.

That fucking bastard, thought St. William, standing at the dresser, whose top was inlaid with mother-of-pearl and littered with composition books, enamel bowls of melted ice and bottles of Antiguan rum. The last time we built them housing they were slaves.

"Estrella!"

By the time the footfalls had arrived outside his door, St. William was dressed in a khaki shirt, a baseball cap, and knee-length water boots.

From his double holster hung a pair of silver-plated pistols that had once belonged to his grandfather, and slung across his shoulder was a bolt-action rifle with a wooden barrel and a clip that held six bullets.

His silver hair was parted and his oval jaw was radiant with the soft gardenia whiteness of an egg.

As he heard the turning knob, St. William swiveled to the mirror to appraise himself, resuming his stance to see at the door not his old long-suffering maid, but a young woman in a calibrated state of semi-dress—white string bikini loosely tied at the side and an unbuttoned vest in iridescent Indian silk that stopped just below her bosom and continued to her waist in a shower of delicate braided fringes hung with colored buttons.

Her hair, which was brown and curly, was parted in the middle and tied in a pair of poufs. She was holding a bouquet of roses. And in her state of shock, her arm began to fall until the petals brushed the floor.

Her lips were dark and pouty, and below her eyes, whose lids were rainbow-shadowed in yellow, pink, and blue, her long cheekbones resembled horizontal bruises.

"Get away from here!" St. William shouted in *sancoche*. The woman leapt backward, and he slammed the door and flung himself across the bed; there he pumped his surge of anger till it burst its banks, erupting in a flood.

Over a breakfast of jackfish and pounded plantains in a little room beside the kitchen, Estrella told St. William that the woman was a paying guest who had arrived the night before, an American with a

New York address who was the lover of the man who had arrived at dawn that morning, hours after he had been expected.

The man was short and slim, Estrella went on to describe, and judging from his face and arms, possessed a body that was tightly muscled. His hair resembled an explosion, and his voice was keen in pitch and edged with danger like a file against the blade of a machete.

The woman's arrival, Estrella gathered, was not in fact a rendezvous. It was an ambush, a surprise. Her voice had been timid when she had requested to be notified the minute that the man called down for breakfast, her intention being, Estrella thought, to present him with something more delectable than bread.

"So why did she come to my room?" St. William asked as the clock began to strike again.

Estrella raised her brow to indicate that she was still wounded by choices she had made in the vertigo of youth, and muttered: "Like every other woman who has ever made that trip, she made a grave mistake."

That day, St. William kept watch through his window, which overlooked the pool, a palm-shaded puddle in a square inscribed by the back of the house and three wings of concrete extensions with row upon row of brown doors and glass jalousies and redwood railings stained black with rot and water.

How many revolutionaries, he asked himself, had been faced with such a monumental choice? If Toussaint had been faced with a woman such as this, would Haiti be French today?

The Spanish influence in San Carlos ran deeper than its name. *Sancoche* was based on Castilian. Old men still foraged for love songs between the wires of the cuatro; and Carlitos of all ages kept an almost sanctimonious faith in the virtues of siesta.

But at two o'clock, after using the pealing bell to mark the terraced descent to the hour of sleep, St. William did not go to bed. If he did, he knew, he would dream of Rebecca, who would admonish him for ignoring the call of duty. And disobeying her, the only person who had ever believed in his greatness, would be a monumental act of treason, surpassing in vileness the affair he had pursued with her niece, Andrea, a teenage seductress who would entertain him by raising her tunic above her breasts, crossing her ankles behind her head and performing tricks of ventriloquy with the lips of her vagina.

At two-thirty, just as St. William's lids began to droop from habit, the woman appeared on a balcony, dressed in a full-length caftan whose neck and cuffs were trimmed in gold. Her hair was no longer in poufs, but had resumed what he assumed was its natural form, a style that he knew as a *makeba*.

She glanced over her shoulder and slammed the door and tipped up on her platform clogs and thumped it with her fist, shooting a remark whose answer was a burst of automatic laughter.

By the pool, she spread a towel on a slatted chaise beneath a palm and lay without moving. To observe her more closely, St. William watched through his binoculars, holding his breath as she withdrew her head and arms into the caftan. She reappeared in a bathing suit whose color matched her skin, its evenness evoking foreknowledge of her body in the nude. On her inner thigh, there was a mole that made him marvel. It was black and slightly raised, and in its center was a single copper hair.

The way the shadows striped her, the wooden slats that pressed into her flesh, the suggestion of her ribs through the fabric like gills, St. William felt the hunger rise inside him, and he wanted to consume her like a fish.

As he thought of this he heard a rusty hinge and changed his view, and saw the man emerging through the door. He was wearing jeans with bell bottoms, and, St. William saw, when the man raised his foot against the wooden rail, a pair of zippered boots.

He was shirtless. In his mouth there was a conical extravagance of what St. William's hairy nostrils told him was imported marijuana; and he was holding a guitar, which he carried by the neck, slackly but with need, like a drunkard holds a bottle.

"Baby," the man commanded.

The woman did not reply. The man chuckled and disappeared inside the room, returning with a vase of roses.

"Baby," the man called out again.

The woman did not answer, and the man began to toss the blooms. As one hit the water, he would toss the next. When the vase was empty, he disappeared inside the room, leaving the door ajar.

When the clock struck three, St. William vowed to take bold action. He would send a note with Estrella. If the woman did not reply in his favor, he would commence his revolution. If she did, he wasn't sure what he would do.

He invited her for tea at four o'clock. And when he arrived downstairs in the drawing room, she was sitting on a hassock trimmed in chintz beside a window whose translucent curtains softened the Antillean light.

Out of habit, St. William was dressed in a crushed white suit. His shirt was blue to match his eyes. And he walked with a silver-handled cane that he did not need but which he carried in case she was the kind of woman whose passions would disguise themselves as sorrow.

"Good day," he said as he stepped off the mahogany stairs onto a Chinese rug. "Welcome to the owner's tea at the Metropolitan Hotel. It is a long tradition here for us to cater to our guests, especially those that bring to mind the exquisite beauty of our local flora."

"I'm sorry for our rendevous this morning."

Her smile, which on one side was clamped with a sarcastic tuck, was otherwise open and persuasive in a way that implied that he had been given accidental insight to her erotic mysteries, which were deep and dark, and usually accessible only to those on the verge of undertaking a journey through the constricted passage that released the soul into the light.

"My name is St. William Rawle," he said in courtly manner, sweeping his hand to invite her to a table, which was set with dull silver and chipped porcelain and baskets of freshly baked scones.

"I'm Felicia Morris," the woman said, passing her hand along her flanks before sitting down to prevent her dress from creasing.

"Have you been to the Caribbean before?"

"Yes," she replied. "Many times."

"And what brings you to San Carlos?"

"To be with a man who doesn't want me."

That isn't true, St. William thought. Such a man, I'm sure, does not exist.

He inhaled deeply, as he had often coached young actors, and hoisted his chin, staring at her down his nose in a way that he believed communicated power. And as he appraised her, the cup dangling halfway between the table and her lips, she whispered that his nostrils were clumped with boogers.

"My goodness," she exclaimed. "How can you breathe?"

Before St. William could recover from the shock of her response, she was standing by his side with her elbows on the table, pressing his nose into a napkin and coaxing him to blow.

As if summoned by the honking, Estrella entered the room.

"I am fine," St. William grunted.

"You won't be when you hear this. Do you know why the bell has been ringing all day?" she asked in *sancoche*, sparing the guest from experiencing an anxious moment. "A band of idiots from Black Well tried to start a revolution. They used the bell as a sign. What kind of idiot would try that in San Carlos?" She raised her arms and showed her palms, which splattered on her thighs. "They tried to take over the radio station, I heard, but the police cornered them and they surrendered. I hope they get some licks with the pistle for their work."

"At least," St. William sighed, "they had a plan."

"What's the matter?" Felicia asked, as Estrella left the room.

"Some fools tried to take over the country. But don't worry. They caught them. There is no excitement. All is well."

"And you were their fearless leader?" she joked.

She brought her elbows to the table and cupped her face. The tucked-in smile appeared again, and with her face framed by her hands, St. William looked anew and saw the freckles sprinkled on her nose, which brought to mind the memory of the mole, which he began to think of as a scar remaining from the scorch of his saliva.

"Your friend," he asked to change the subject. "What does he do?"

"He is a singer."

She told him the name but he did not recognize it.

"And what do you do?"

"Floating around. Hoping to become a writer."

She slid her hands around her cheeks to hide her face; he allowed her this moment of childish indulgence and held his breath through her reemergence, forehead first, hands retracting like the hood that hides the clitoris.

"I am feeling very sensitive right now," she said, arousing his appetite for scandal with a sigh that caused her breasts to heave. "I need someone to talk to. I'm leaving in the morning. So it doesn't really matter."

"That is true."

"I left my husband for him," she said, leaning forward in a whisper, her eyes flitting from the doorway to the stairs. "And this is what I get."

"I saw him throw the flowers in the pool," St. William told her. "I was watching."

"Oh, you must think I'm such a fool."

"It depends. How long have you known him?"

"Today makes a week."

St. William tapped his tongue against his palate.

"And you followed him here and he doesn't want you?"

St. William found this fascinating, for she did not strike him as a woman who was weak. And although he had often been guilty of bad judgment, he instinctively believed in his instincts, which were urging him to offer her his help.

"Would you like me to say a word?"

"To who?"

"To him."

"About what?"

"About the two of you? Remind me of his name again?"

"People call him Bob."

"I must tell you something," he whispered, gathering his thoughts as the bell began to peal again. "I am doing this because I want you, and I know I cannot have you. When you came into my room this morning I was going to start a revolution. But I haven't been able to think about anything since you came into my life. I lay down my gun and took off my clothes and touched myself as I thought of you. I watched you all day through my window. I need to touch you. Allow me please. Can I touch you? Out of sympathy. I am old."

"You could be my father."

"I understand," he reasoned as she laughed, "but that is neither *yes* or *no*. Do you know what you are doing? You are making me feel sensitive right now. You are making me feel old. I watched you and wanted you. He threw you away."

As he listened to himself, St. William was aware that his voice was rising and that his brave appeal had liquefied into a grovel.

But what he was too old to understand was that in those flagrant days of the sexual revolution, when women were still excited by the view from the top, an appeal from the bottom, wet with blood desire and the suggestion of tears, would soak and undermine a woman's will.

"I have to go to my room," Felicia said, with a dreaminess that he mistook for boredom. "Don't worry about dealing with this. I'll handle it on my own."

St. William nodded, and having lost his pride, confided that he had not had a drink all day and would be going to his room to be rum-suckled.

Ascending the stairs, he began to use his cane although Felicia was not watching. His heart was filled with lamentations and his lungs filled with the dust that his repeated sighs had brought into his scoured nostrils.

I have failed myself, St. William thought. He sat on the edge of his bed and gargled with the rum before he swallowed. Through the window, he watched the man, who was sitting on the railing, strumming his guitar and softly singing what sounded from a distance like a psalm, his voice light but keen and edged with a profound sense of longing, as if it emanated from a hole in his heart; and as he felt himself being drawn into the mystery of that hole, St. William put away his bottle and walked to the window and pressed his face against the glass and felt a coolness on his forehead as the rage evaporated out of him into the gash from which that voice had come—that primal place of grief, that wound left behind when the first fruit fell away from the first tree and faced the conflict of survival, the unconquerable knowledge that it too would cause pain when it split the earth to set down its roots.

As St. William watched, Felicia climbed the stairs and the man put down his instrument and draped his arms around her as a bird would fold its wings around its young; and as she opened her mouth and the man's head dipped toward her, his hair like an ignited plume, St. William felt his bones reverberating as if they had been struck by a gong; and in a flash of clarity he understood why she had come this far this quickly to see this man: he had the charisma of the revolutionary, the capacity to embrace and rebuke without apology, which is rooted in the understanding that life is a cycle of regeneration, and that regeneration is a cycle of pain, and that the great leaders are those who can inspire people to face the coming pain with strength and grace and a vision of life beyond it.

That night Rebecca Salan did not appear in St. William's dream. He dreamed instead of Felicia. In the reverie, she lay across the bed and spread her legs, and he saw her lower lips, which were sealed and folded in a dusky line, glistening like a keloid that had overgrown a wound, and he slid his tongue along it to console her, to ease the remnant of her deep, abiding pain.

The next morning, he arose to the sound of a rooster—the chief minister had ordered that the mechanism of the clock be removed—and found outside his door a package and a note.

Thank you for reminding me that I'm wanted. I almost slept with you. Yes, for a minute you could have stolen me, but I would have gone back to him. Accept this gift as a token of whatever, of two people, no, three people and a moment. It will be coming out this year. One love. Sorry that I couldn't make him sign it.

What a fascinating name, St. William thought as he tore the paper: *Natty Dread*. His thirty-second book was a translation and discussion of the lyrics in *sancoche*. In his memoir, published at his own expense on the eve of the millennium, St. William would describe it as "my most important work to date."

CONTRIBUTORS

Robert Scott Adams is a published poet and established jazz critic. A native of Rochester, N.Y., he attended Morehouse College. This is his first foray into the erotic fiction genre.

Curtis Bunn, a national award-winning sports columnist for the *Atlanta Journal-Constitution*, is the author of the novel *Baggage Check*, his debut work of fiction which remained on the *Essence* magazine bestseller list for five months. He is a graduate of Norfolk State University. His new work, *Bookclub*, a collection of five short stories, chronicles the lives and loves of members of five different bookclubs.

Colin Channer is the bestselling author of the novels *Waiting in Vain* and *Satisfy My Soul*. His novella, *I'm Still Waiting*, was published in the highly popular anthology *Got to Be Real*. *Waiting in Vain* was selected as a 1998 Critics Choice by *The Washington Post Book World* and excerpted in *Hot Spots: The Best Erotic Writing In Modern Fiction*. Channer is the founder and artistic director of the Calabash International Literary Festival, the only literary festival in the English-speaking Caribbean. A native of Kingston, Jamaica, he lives in Brooklyn with his family. Write to him at colinchanner@hotmail.com.

Brian Egleston is the author of three published novels, including his very popular *Granddaddy's Dirt*. An aspiring golfer, he lives with his lovely wife, Latise, in Georgia, where he spends most of his time writing, thinking of writing and longing to write.

Arthur Flowers is the author of two novels, *De Mojo Blues* and *Another Good Loving Blues*, and a nonfiction work, *Mojo Rising: Confessions of a 21st Century Conjureman*. He is a performance artist, Executive Director of New Renaissance Writers Guild–NYC, and fiction professor in the Syracuse University MFA program.

Tracy Grant's first novel, *Hellified*, won national acclaim. He earned his undergraduate degree at Georgetown University and did his graduate work there as well. After graduate school, he hit his stride as a freelance writer, publishing work in several magazines including *YSB*, *Today's Black Woman*, *Black Issues Book Review*, and *Mosaic Literary Magazine*. He is currently an adjunct English professor at the College of New Rochelle's School of New Resources. His second novel, *Chocolate Thai*, a political thriller, is forthcoming. He lives in New York City.

Kenji Jasper is a novelist, screenwriter and journalist from Washington, D.C. The author of two novels, *Dark* and *Dakota Grand*, his work has appeared in *Essence*, *Vibe*, *The Source*, and many other national publications. He currently lives in Brooklyn, New York.

Charles Johnson, a 1998 MacArthur Fellow, received the National Book Award for his novel *Middle Passage* in 1990. He has published three other novels, *Dreamer* (1998), *Oxherding Tale* (1982) and *Faith and the Good Thing* (1974), as well as two short story collections, *The Sorcerer's Apprentice* (1986) and *Soulcatcher* (2001). Among his many nonfiction books are: *King: The Photobiography of Martin Luther King, Jr.* (coauthored with Bob Adelman, 2000), *African in America: America's Journey through Slavery* (coauthored with Patricia Smith, 1998), *Being and Race: Black Writing Since 1970* (1988), *Black Men Speaking* (coedited with John McCluskey, Jr., 1997), and two books of drawings. His work has appeared in numerous publications in America and abroad. A literary critic, screenwriter, lecturer, and cartoonist, he has received the Lifetime Achievement in the Arts Award from the Corporate Council for the Arts as well as many other awards. Currently, he is the S. Wilson and

Grace M. Pollock Endowed Professor of English at the University of Washington in Seattle. You may visit his homepage at www.preview-port.com/Home/johnsonc.html.

Clarence Major is a prize-winning poet, novelist and essayist. A major figure in the Black Arts Movement, he won a National Council on the Arts award for his collection *Swallow the Lake* in 1970. He was a finalist for the National Book Award for another collection, *Configurations*, and has written several other fiction and nonfiction books considered milestones in African American literature, including *All-Night Visitors, No, Reflex and Bone Structure, Dark and the Feeling, Such Was the Season*, and *Surfaces and Masks*. His novel *My Amputations* won the Western State Book Award in 1985. He directs the Creative Writing Program at the University of California, Davis.

Brandon Massey is the author of *Thunderland*, his self-published debut novel which won a Gold Pen Award for Best Thriller from the Black Writers Alliance. The book will be reprinted by Kensington Books in December 2002. Massey is one of a growing number of African American authors who write horror-suspense fiction. He lives in Georgia.

Alexs D. Pate is the author of five novels, including *Amistad*, a *New York Times* bestseller, which was commissioned by Steven Spielberg's Dreamworks SKG. Pate's debut novel, *Losing Absalom*, was awarded Best First Novel by the Black Caucus of the American Library Association and a 1995 Minnesota Best Award for best fiction. *Finding Makeba*, his second book, was named by *Essence* magazine as a "top five family classic." His fourth novel, *Multicultiboho Sideshow,* won the 2000 Minnesota Book Award. He has published numerous essays and commentary in national publications. He is currently an Assistant Professor of Afro-American and African Studies at the University of Minnesota, where he teaches writing and black literature.

Eric E. Pete is the author of three novels, including *Real for Me* and *Someone's in the Kitchen*. A native of Seattle, Washington, he is a graduate of McNeese University. Currently living in the New Orleans area, he is working on his fourth novel. He can be contacted at heyeric@att.net.

Brian Peterson is the author of the novel *Move Over, Girl*. Born in Harrisburg, Pennsylvania, he finished his undergraduate degree and master's in Education at the University of Pennsylvania's School of Engineering. A resident of Philadelphia, he is currently finishing a new novel.

Gary Phillips is the creator of the Ivan Monk PI series and the mystery novels featuring Martha Chainey, ex-showgirl and Vegas cold cash courier. A native of South Central Los Angeles, he has also written several other novels, many short stories, and a wealth of articles and commentaries on pop culture for countless national newspapers and magazines.

Cole Riley gained notoriety as the author of five popular novels, including *Hot Snake Nights*, *The Devil to Pay* and *The Killing Kind*. Born in the Midwest, he became known as a master of gritty urban noir fiction in the late 1980s with the publication of his novel *Rough Trade*. His last work, *The Forbidden Art of Desire*, was selected by the Black Expressions book club as a part of the notable *Indigo After Dark* series. An extremely private person and lover of nightlife, he has been known to keep a low profile during waking hours. He is presently working on a new novel, *Harlem Confidential*.

Earl Sewell is the author of two novels, *The Good Got to Suffer with the Bad* and *Taken for Granted*. He studied fiction writing at Columbia College in Chicago. He presently lives in Palatine, Illinois, where he is completing his latest novel, *Grown Folks' Business*.

Jervey Tervalon is an acclaimed novelist, poet, screenwriter and dramatist. His well-received debut novel, *Understand This*, won the 1994 New Voices Award from the Quality Paperback Book Club.

Two other Tervalon novels, *Living for the City* and *Dead Above Ground*, captured the praise of critics, readers and fellow writers alike. A native of New Orleans, he earned his B.A. degree at the College of Creative Studies at the University of California, Santa Barbara and completed his MFA work in fiction writing at the University of California, Irvine. Today, he teaches writing at California State University in Los Angeles. He lives in Altadena, California with his wife and daughters. His most recent novel is *All the Trouble You Need*.

Kalamu Ya Salaam is a New Orleans–based writer, editor, filmmaker and teacher. He is the founder of the Nommo Literary Society, a black writers workshop, and co-founder of Runagate Multimedia publishing company. He also serves as leader of the WordBand, a poetry performance ensemble, and moderator of e-Drum, a listserv for black writers. His latest achievements are *360°: A Revolution of Black Poets* and *My Story, My Song*, a spoken word CD. He can be reached at kalamu@aol.com.

John A. Williams is the author of a dozen novels, among them *The Angry Ones, Night Song, The Man Who Cried I Am,* and *!Click Song*. His most recent novel is *Clifford's Blues*. In addition, he's published eight nonfiction books, three of which are studies on Martin Luther King, Jr., Richard Wright, and Richard Pryor. Williams has also edited or co-edited ten more works, published a volume of poetry, and written two plays and the libretto for the opera *Vanqui*, whose premiere was followed by seven additional performances. He is a former writer for *Holiday* and was a *Newsweek* correspondent in Europe, the Middle East, and Africa during the early sixties. He moved into academics as a Distinguished Professor of English in the CUNY system and later was the Paul Robeson Professor of English and Journalism at Rutgers University, a position from which he retired in 1995. He is a two-time recipient of the American Book Award, member of the National Literary Hall of Fame for Writers of African Descent, and winner of several other honors. He is presently completing three additional works.